FEAR THE DEER!

The doe took a single step back, studying me with curiosity but without apparent fear.

"Giraud," I said. "Look at this."

The doe's ear twitched toward him, but she didn't spring away from us, as I would have expected her to do. I thought I had never seen anything so beautiful. Her color, a warm honey-brown, darkened to black at her knees, her muzzle, and the tips of her ears. Her eyes, warm brown rimmed in kohl, with thick eyelashes and a sweet, trusting expression, seemed to me the very definition of gentleness.

She snorted softly, a sort of whuffling sound, and glanced behind me, and when I turned to see what she was looking at, I discovered that two other deer moved toward us from right behind me, while one came toward us from my far right.

"Hey, pretty girl," I said, and her ears pricked forward. The other deer moved in, stepping silently through the tall grass, moving slowly as if they didn't want to startle us.

I heard Giraud say, "Ha, you *have* to see this," to our dwarf companion as I rose and reached out to touch the doe.

Her lips curled back in a snarl and her mouth stretched back, and I saw, not the blunt bottom teeth of an herbivore, but well-developed, dagger-sharp upper and lower canines and a jaw far heavier and stronger than any plant-eater should have. I screamed. . . .

Novels of The Bard's Tale™

Castle of Deception
by Mercedes Lackey & Josepha Sherman

Fortress of Frost and Fire
by Mercedes Lackey & Ru Emerson

Prison of Souls
by Mercedes Lackey & Mark Shepherd

Escape from Roksamur
by Mark Shepherd

The Chaos Gate
by Josepha Sherman

Thunder of the Captains
by Holly Lisle & Aaron Allston

Wrath of the Princes
by Holly Lisle & Aarson Allston

Curse of the Black Heron
by Holly Lisle

Curse of the Black Heron

HOLLY LISLE

CURSE OF THE BLACK HERON

This is a work of fiction. All the characters and events portrayed in this book are fictional, and any resemblance to real people or incidents is purely coincidental.

A Baen Books Original

Baen Publishing Enterprises
P.O. Box 1403
Riverdale, NY 10471

ISBN: 0-671-87868-9

Cover art by Tom Kidd

First printing, March 1998

Distributed by Simon & Schuster
1230 Avenue of the Americas
New York, NY 10020

Typeset by Windhaven Press, Auburn, NH
Printed in the United States of America

Chapter One

I remember the beginning of the end of my world clearly, but not for the reasons anyone would usually associate with remembering such a day. Early morning dragged me from my bed, and the voice of the herald from the capital drew me out of Birdie's cool house into the town square of Blackwarren and into the already-sticky heat of the early summer day, where I stood beside my friend, Giraud dar Falcannes, and listened to the latest news from the city, shouted by a lovely young herald backed up by a contingent of cold-eyed enforcers.

"In this the Century of the Constellation Baragar the Hunter, in the year of Ten Firehawk and the season of Merroell, on the fifth day of the month of Tassetti, which We rename Varelle in our honor, We—Varelle dar Kothia Surdosti—declare that Salgestis Dargoman the Usurper has been cast down, and executed, and that We have lifted his head on a pike in Greffon's Great Square as proof and testament of Our intentions to all such usurpers." The herald sat astride her black horse, dressed all in royal red and empire blue, with a crest on her tabard that I'd never

seen and a weighted scroll in her hands that gleamed
at the edges with the sheen of real gold. She glared
down at all of us who stood listening to her decree,
daring us to dispute her.

I leaned over and whispered to Giraud, "Forgive
me if I'm wrong, but wasn't Salgestis the rightful king?
And isn't Varelle dar Kothia Surdosti the usurper?"

Giraud grinned at me. "Mmm. Well, she was until
she won," he whispered back, "but it would be awfully
impolitic of us to remember that now, wouldn't it?
And possibly hard on our necks, Isbetta. Never forget that the winners get to call the losers anything
they want."

The herald spelled out Varelle dar Kothia Surdosti's
decrees to us—that she would be empress, titled
Gloriana Majeste of all the lands of Terosalle; that her
capital city would be Greffon; that she would give par-
don and favor to all who acknowledged her as empress
and would execute those who did not, and with them
their every relation through ten generations; and so
on, and so on. The herald's reading made for an
impressive decree, but I must confess that discovering I had a new ruler in Greffon interested me less
than discovering I owned a new sheep would have. The
fact is, I was about to graduate to journeyman status
and be admitted to the Weavers' Guild, and my fos-
ter mother would, upon my graduation, owe me a
sheep as a gift—the first of what I hoped to turn into
an impressive weaver's flock. The sheep was both sym-
bol and material contributor to my future. Whereas
in Blackwarren the doings of the High Court were so
distant both in leagues and in their effects on our lives
that they didn't even make for interesting gossip.

I rolled my eyes. "This going to make any differ-
ence for you and His Lordship?"

"Oh, sure. The—" Giraud made a face "—the
Gloriana Majeste is bound to want an increase in taxes
to fill her empty war chests. And no doubt she'll want

Da to ride to her county seat in Kingston Bylake with my brothers to declare undying allegiance. Shouldn't be much trouble for him otherwise, though. If he hadn't been in high stink with King Salgestis, we wouldn't have been in stuck here in Blackwarren in the first place, lording it over the peat boggers and the blackflies."

"You don't think you'll have to ride to Kingston Bylake, too?"

"Nah. I'm third tit, Izza. With Storrin and Baylar ahead of me in succession, I don't even get invited to the dances in Straje."

"And we both know how you love to dance."

Giraud snickered. "I won't complain about my place in life. I'm as happy as I'm going to be, living in Blackwarren. And maybe with Varelle on the throne Da will win a place of favor and we'll be able to move closer to the capital and get a bit of culture from time to time."

I recall finding that possibility unlikely. "You think she'll grant your father new lands? But he didn't support her."

Giraud saw it as less of a problem, but then, he was always much more the optimist than I. Being lord's son instead of poor foster-daughter to a peat crofter will have that effect on your outlook on life. Giraud said, "He didn't support Salgestis, either. He wasn't crazy. From one day to the next you couldn't tell who would win their fight, or if both of them would lose and the damned Liedans would come sweeping down from the north by land and sea and annex us; and Blackwarren's so far from everything Da didn't need to make any passionate declarations of loyalty. Nobody even remembers we're up here, most times. He just kept his head low and kept it on his shoulders that way."

The herald had finished reading the new empress's decree, and sat rolling her scroll, preparatory to moving on to the next town . . . or considering our position relative to the rest of civilization, perhaps just heading home. I said, "That's it, then. The news of the world beyond comes and goes, and here in Blackwarren, nothing changes. Nothing at all."

Giraud rested his hand on my shoulder as we turned to head to my craft-master's shop. "That isn't true for you, Izza."

I had to smile. Giraud understood my reasons for anticipating my release from Birdie's care, and was friend enough to be excited with me. "You're right," I agreed. "Finally, change comes."

"How many more days?"

I closed my eyes and pretended to count, but actually the number of days I had left in my apprenticeship might as well have been carved straight through my flesh into bone, I knew it so well. "Nineteen," I said.

Giraud laughed. "One for every year you've lived. How perfect."

"I still have two years as journeyman weaver after that, before I can become a master and set up my own shop. It isn't as if I can leave Blackwarren right away."

"But no more Birdie, right?"

I nodded vehemently. That was, as far as I could see, the greatest advantage in achieving journeyman status. "Exactly right. No more Birdie. I've been asking around, and I've already found a place living with the Widow dar Nothellin. She'll give me bed and board in exchange for three pence a month, and one bolt of fine blue cloth winter and summer."

"That's less than Birdie's taking."

"Birdie takes everything I make, just because she can." The anger I felt at that fact was, for once, tempered with satisfaction. "But only for nineteen more days."

Giraud jumped onto the boardwalk that began where the cobblestone street became dirt and mud, and offered me his hand. I took it—I would have been rude to refuse, even though I was quite capable of swinging myself up onto the walk, and bounded upward. Giraud said, "I still don't know why the old bitch didn't send you off to Watchowl Bards' Keep to train as a bard. You've the voice, and *I* think a touch of the magic, too."

"You think so, do you?"

Giraud smiled, but his eyes were serious. "You've certainly enchanted me."

I tried to laugh, but the old bitterness came through too clearly and I stopped myself. I forced a lightness that I didn't feel and said, "But that's the way with apprenticeships. Our fosters choose what we shall be, and leave us the quandary of becoming good at what they choose." I pretended to shrug it off. "My parents wouldn't have fostered me with Birdie if they hadn't agreed with her that weaving would be the right path for me."

I was not, after all, alone in complaining about my foster-mother, or about the hardness of my life. Every other weaver-apprentice who studied with Marda dar Ellai complained, too. Of chores in the evening, of poor meals, of hard beds. I was alone in other ways, though. I alone came to Blackwarren not from a smaller town but from the greatest city of them all, Greffon. I alone recalled a life that was not bounded by the rising and falling of the sun, that was described neither by the movements of sheep and cattle through the pastures nor by the growing and harvesting of crops, nor by the cutting and drying of peat. I recalled the life I'd led as daughter of the king's own bard—I'd been a child with free run of court with friends up to and including the king's youngest daughter. I'd met Salgestis on occasion. I'd sung for him once—some trippery song about what a wonderful king he was. I recall that he'd been charmed, for I'd written the dreadful bit of doggerel myself, and had gone on to tell him that someday I would be a Bard like my father. Bard with a capital "B," not bard-little-b without the magic. And he'd clapped me on the shoulder and told me what a good bard I should be, too.

I was alone in other ways. Of all Blackwarren's fosterlings, only I never received a visit from my parents or an invitation to return home for the Long Holiday. I alone lived exclusively with my fostermother the year round, never so much as receiving a letter or an Ammas Day gift from my true parents. My fellow apprentices had endless theories about this, all of them ugly and hateful to one degree or another. Either I was an embarrassing bastard child, or my parents were mad and had been locked away, or I had done something in the past that was so terrible my parents had banished me from their lives, or I was an orphan from nowhere taken in by my fostermother and that I was, to boot, a dreadful liar who made up stories about Greffon and my life before in order to "give myself airs."

Giraud didn't believe any of the stories, and sympathized with my plight as a fellow outcast from a better life. He was old enough to remember when his father had been in favor at court, and to wish for the return of those days. For him, the Gloriana Majeste Varelle represented a possible door back.

Giraud had been considering my remark about my parents fostering me with Birdie. "I wonder," he said.

"As much as she hates me, I sometimes wonder, too—but I can't say that I see much point in thinking about it. I'd rather be a bard, but my life has gone another way." I peeked in the window of the dar Felpas bakery as the rich, delicious scent of goldberry pie tickled my nose. "Oh, I wish she'd shut the window when she bakes those. I always want one," I said.

Giraud ducked inside and bounded back out again with two large berry tarts. "For us, because we are almost free," he said.

I gave him a quick squeeze—not much of one, for not even the third son of a lord could be seen hugging a common weaver's apprentice, no matter how reputedly lofty her birth. I munched the pie as I walked along, closing my eyes as an especially rich bit of crust and berries melted on my tongue. "Don't you wish all of life was berry pies?" I asked.

"And warm, busy houses in big cities," he said, "with libraries everywhere, and colleges and fairs."

"And silk dresses and silver-stringed guitars and musicians on the street corners," I added.

"And I would be Lord Giraud in my own white-walled castle," he said.

"And I would be your chief bard, and wear gold chains around my waist and ride a black horse."

"And you would never have to look at another loom or shuttle," he said, grinning at me.

"And you would never have to open another history book."

Giraud chuckled and shook his head. "Maybe that wouldn't be such a good outcome after all. I like history considerably better than I like swords or politics."

"Lucky for you," I told him. I reached the door to Marda's shop and grinned up at him. "You'll be busy for months, rewriting all the records in your father's library so that they say 'the evil usurper Salgestis Dargoman,' rather than 'Our Illustrious Liege Salgestis III.'"

When he realized I was right and he began to contemplate the enormous task before him, Giraud's face fell. I laughed at him. Cruel of me, I know—but he was the only apprentice I knew who got to live at home and learn his work in his father's library, while sleeping in his own bed and having the comfort of knowing his father and brothers were nearby and that his master didn't dare beat him much, for fear of retaliation.

With such luck, he didn't deserve any sympathy over the amount of work he would have to do.

And that was how it started. We forgot about our new empress and went on with our lives. A week passed, in which I did the final work on my journeyman piece, a blanket that I wove in honor of my patron goddess Neithas, the goddess of both weavers and singers, as well as the goddess of knowledge, the goddess of handicrafts, and when all *wasn't* right with the world, the goddess of war. Very busy, she is, and encouraging to someone like me who has a hard time making myself finish anything. I was doing the blanket in subtle blues and greens around a central circle composed of interlocking gold rays and pale yellow diamonds, and all through the outer edge, I'd woven looms and chariots and cats . . . well, Neithas is the goddess of beasts, too. Besides, I like cats. The blanket was as complex as anything I'd ever tried, and both the overall design and the minor patterns that I worked into it required most of my time and all of my concentration. After all, the journeyman blanket was my chance to earn my way to adulthood and acceptance, and even if weaving was no path I would have chosen for myself, it was, nonetheless, an honorable path, and one blessed by my goddess.

Besides, I could sing while I worked, and that helped.

I barely saw Giraud the entire week I was finishing my blanket; as he'd predicted, his father and both his older brothers had to make the trip to Kingston Bylake to swear fealty, and he stayed behind to make sure Blackwarren's greathouse continued to run as it should. That job would have fallen to his mother, but the Lady dar Falcannes had died of the grippe in the winter past, and Lord dar Falcannes had not yet found her replacement. I knew from rumors among the other apprentices that he had taken a few young women to his bed, to test them for suitability, but no sheaves of wheat hung from the greathouse gates, so evidently he hadn't found one yet who was to his liking. Or perhaps he hadn't been to the liking of the women he'd entertained.

I'd met the man frequently. He had cold eyes and a cruel mouth and a way of never meeting my eyes when I talked to him, and I thought, personally, that only a very desperate woman would take him as her husband.

The day I finished my blanket, I sat for the better part of a candlemark just staring at it. I realized for the first time that I was good at what I did. Truly good. Neithas had blessed my hands and given me a talent with them that was, if not equal to the voice she'd given me, at least good enough to earn me a fine living even in a town bigger than Blackwarren.

I was proud enough of myself that I carried the blanket to Marda to show to her.

"So you're finished, then," Marda said. She gave the blanket a cursory glance.

I nodded, my heart sinking. I never asked Marda for her opinion of something that I'd done, because her opinion was always, "Is that the best you can do?" But I couldn't help thinking that this time, surely, she would see that the lovely patterns and fine cloth I'd created were a reflection of her own skill as a teacher, and she'd be proud of me. So, like an idiot, I asked her, "What do you think?"

Marda glanced from the blanket to my face, then back to the blanket for a longer, harder look. When she looked at me again, her eyes had become as cold as a winter wind across the peat bogs—as cold and as bone-chilling.

"We'll discuss it. But not now."

I left it with her at the shop and trudged home, completely unable to imagine what she had found to hate about my work. I ate a silent meal with Birdie, climbed up to my mat in the little loft about the single room of her cottage, and tried to sleep. My mind kept tossing me images of the blanket, and of Marda, and kept struggling to find some flaw that I'd overlooked in the work that would so disgust her that she would look at me the way she had.

No matter how long I lay there, or how much I tossed and turned trying to find a comfortable position on my mat, I couldn't sleep at all.

Which was just as well.

Finally in the full darkness of late night or possibly early morning, when the fire in the hearth below had guttered down to coals and ashes, as I lay staring up at the slats and thatching just above my head, I heard a soft scratching at the shutters below. It was so light it might have been a branch dragging against the wood in a light wind—except no trees grew anywhere near the window.

Next I heard Birdie moving to the door, something about her movements so surreptitious and stealthy that my gut knotted. Birdie's usual slow, clump-footed gait had been replaced by something light and quick and . . . dangerous.

I heard whispers at the door. "Should we go outside?"

"No. She's asleep. Been asleep for a while. Both of you might as well come in."

I could not imagine why anyone would care whether I was awake or asleep, but I didn't have time to ponder the oddness of the question. Others followed after it, each stranger than the one before.

"Did you arrange everything with the guild?" Birdie asked.

"Of course." In the soft reply I recognized the voice

of my craft-master, Marda. What could she be doing in Birdie's house at an hour which hinted that what she did, she wanted no one to know about?

"They've agreed not to wait until they pass judgment on the rest of the apprentices?"

"Why should they? With her, we have no worries of irate parents, and now we need not worry about interference from His Lordship, either. We'll receive their judgment just after first bell in the morning." Marda laughed. The sound was as ugly and cruel as anything I'd ever heard.

"I got news back from my messenger," a masculine voice said. I didn't recognize this voice at all.

Birdie's "Did you?" gave me chills.

"Lord dar Falcannes is dead along with both of his older sons."

"And your own pending lordship?"

"Guaranteed by none other than the empress herself," the stranger's voice assured her. "Her men will arrive in the morning and dispose of the last remnants of the dar Falcannes. When the heads of the household of dar Falcannes adorn pikes in the square, her duke will name me temporary governor, and I'll travel to Kingston Bylake to be knighted. *Sir* Aymar dar Ressti sounds so much better than just Aymar."

Now I knew who he was. I'd seen him from time to time, a clever, hawk-faced burgher who came into Marda's shop to buy bolts of cloth, and who had twice when I was alone suggested that if I came to his house and was "nice" to him, he would be sure I had pretty dresses and silver jewelry, and that I wouldn't have to worry about weaving for a living. He'd frightened me, but I had no one I could tell about his attentions. So I'd said nothing.

I'd been right to fear him. He'd found a way to have Giraud's father and brothers killed. He intended to see Giraud dead as well. I had to get out of the house to tell him—

"As soon as the guild rejects Isbetta's journeyman status," Aymar said, "I want her delivered to the Wolfshead Inn."

I froze, and my thoughts of charging off to get Giraud came to a halt. The Wolfshead Inn?

"I thought you wanted her for yourself first," Birdie said.

Aymar's chuckle was cold and evil. "I *intend* to have her for myself first. But I don't want her to be seen at my house. And the little bitch refused me—let her know from the beginning what price she'll pay for her refusal. Tassien will keep her in a room until I can get to her—after I've finished with her, he can put her to work."

The only work for women at Tassien's inn was whoring.

"The whore's guild doesn't object?" Marda asked.

"The whore's guild is willing to pretend she doesn't exist, as long as she takes only the trade the guild doesn't want," Aymar said. "Tassien offered to buy her outright from me, but I decided I'd rather have a percentage of the money he gets from her. In return, I'll pay you a gold crown every month in recognition of your status as her . . . her foster-mother." He chuckled. "For as long as she lasts, anyway; that will add up nicely for the two of you, won't it?"

"It will indeed," Birdie said.

Marda just laughed softly. "And to think I promised the Black Heron we'd kill her after we killed her father."

I jammed the side of my fist into my mouth to keep from screaming. My father was dead? And these were his killers? I'd always thought he'd returned to Greffon and the king.

For an instant, the darkness that welled up from the depths of my soul swallowed me. I didn't want to live. I didn't want to have to move. I thought, in just that brief, bitter instant, that I would lie in the loft waiting for whatever came to me; that I would give in; that I wouldn't fight, because I couldn't win. But self-preservation pushed back despair.

Birdie's voice raised slightly from its previous cautious low tones. "I told you there was money in orphans."

"Yes," Aymar said, "but even you wanted to whore her out as soon as we got her, and think of the income you would have lost from her weaving in the meantime. And she never would have lasted a month whoring at first. Now . . . well, now she might survive a year. And we've been paid thrice for her miserable life—the Black Heron's money, and the weaving, and now this."

They were silent for a while. I lay in the darkness, wondering how I could get out of the house and flee before they could catch me. Wondering how I could save Giraud. Wondering how I could get even with them for killing my father. . . .

"I'm still surprised," Birdie said, and her voice was thoughtful, "that the Black Heron didn't have his people kill us when we couldn't find those pages her father hid."

"He still hopes we'll find them. And I think we will. I'm telling you, the bastard hid them in dar Falcannes house," Aymar said. "I'll start looking for them tomorrow. And when we find them we'll copy them. We'll sell the Heron the originals for the hundred pounds of gold he promised. Then we'll figure out how to profit from the copies."

"How do you know you'll even recognize them when you see them?" Marda asked him. "Dar Falcannes has lived in that place for seven years since the bard left it, and he hasn't found them."

"Maybe. Or maybe he has and he's been using them all this time. Or maybe the bard hid them in a book in the library, or buried them in a jar in the garden. They were just parchment pages. They weren't

anything fancy—I suspect they were copies the bard
made from something else, since they looked new.
I couldn't read them—they were in that script the
bards use that only they know."

"I don't understand why you didn't steal the pages
when you had your hands on them."

They fell silent again. Finally Aymar said, "There's
an old saying—'Never steal from a live bard.' It's good
advice."

I thought, You shouldn't have stolen from a dead
one either, Aymar—you're going to pay for it. But I
certainly couldn't make him pay for it right then.

Both Marda and Aymar left at last, and I listened
while Birdie climbed the ladder to my loft. I had my
back to her, and I kept my breathing regular and slow,
and my eyes closed—I focused on feeling relaxed, on
being calm, on allowing my body to go limp. Meanwhile, I could feel her stare like a knife between my
shoulder blades, and I had to fight the impulse to
hold my breath. I wished her away, feeling as scared
as I ever had in my life. She was a murderer, and
she wanted to sell me to a whoremaster, and if I
didn't get away she would.

Chapter Two

Finally I heard her moving down the ladder again, and shuffling around. I heard the creak of her bed as she climbed into it, and the rustle of her blanket as she pulled it over her. Then I waited some more. I didn't dare do anything until she fell asleep. In the meantime, I had to be sure that I didn't give away the fact that I was awake, or that I knew what had happened and what was about to happen. So I continued to think calm thoughts to keep my body relaxed and limp and my breathing regular and slow and deep. Calm thoughts—green hills and the steady rhythm of shuttle through warp forming weft and the feel of a song in my lungs and my belly and my throat. Calm thoughts and a relaxed body, when all I wanted to do was run.

And at last I heard her breathing change, the soft burr of her snore; the only signal I would get.

I got up carefully and dressed, then packed my few belongings—my sleeping shirt, my other breeches, my other tunic, my other undergarments, the wooden flute my father gave me, my knife and whetstone, my personals. Everything I owned, when rolled tightly enough, fit into the pockets of my cloak. I wondered if I dared climb down the ladder to retrieve my boots. I had thought to just cut through the rope that bound the roofing slats to the crossbeams, then push my way through the thatching to get outside; but the more I thought about it, the more I realized I would have to travel in the mountains if I hoped to find some form of safety, and if I traveled in the mountains I had to have my boots. Which meant climbing down the ladder to retrieve them—and then, since time was my enemy as much as noise, lifting the bar that held the oaken door locked and slipping out of it into the street.

Then hurrying clear across the village without giving the impression that I was hurrying, to get Giraud up and out of Blackwarren before the empress's hunters came to kill him. Then running. East to the Stormfather Mountains, then through whatever passes the two of us could find, and north into Lieda. Running ahead of the soon-to-be-knighted Aymar dar Ressti and the empress's killers and the villagers who would come after us, eager for reward.

I took a deep breath and eased myself over the edge of the loft, braced myself on the ladder, and crept down. Twice as fast a I should have, a thousand times more slowly than I wanted to. The ladder didn't creak, and I stepped barefooted onto the wide-boarded floor of the cottage. I knew from experience that some of the boards squeaked; what I couldn't remember but desperately needed to was *which* of them. I hadn't been in the practice of sneaking out of the house; my only experience came from the rare hurried trip to the outhouse in full darkness, and in those situations, I'd had nothing to hide.

And that was my answer, of course. In the event that Birdie woke enough to notice me, I would say I had to go to the outhouse. Of course, when I failed to return, she'd come after me. I'd lose hours of the small lead I'd have anyway. So I kept quiet, tested each board with a cautious step before moving onto it, and balanced my weight as carefully as I could to avoid making any noise. Even so, something about my presence disturbed Birdie, for when I was more than halfway across the room, she rolled to one side and murmured in a half-awake voice, "Wha's tha'? Did 'ou say somethin'?"

Now I did hold my breath. And I prayed, *Neithas, if you love me, make her go back to sleep.*

Neithas heard me, for after a while that seemed like forever, Birdie's snoring resumed. I finished my trek across the single room, tugged my boots on—for if anyone saw me putting them on while sitting on the boardwalk outside our door, they would know instantly that I was sneaking about something—and lifted the door bar. I settled it on the floor in its customary place. I always left the house to go to Marda's shop long before Birdie woke and rose—she was accustomed to seeing it out of place. Only if she got up during the night for some reason and discovered the unbarred door would she realize something had gone wrong. If she didn't realize I'd left far too early, I could hope that she would assume I had gone to the shop, and that Marda would assume that Birdie was keeping me busy around the cottage.

The door opened quietly—Birdie had never been able to stand the noise of squeaking hinges, and so kept them well-greased. I pulled it shut behind me as I stepped out onto the boardwalk, then looked down the street in both directions. I saw no one, which was good for more than the obvious reason. In Blackwarren everyone rose when the sun rose and slept when the sun slept. Anyone out with me would be up to no good.

I jumped off the boardwalk and moved through the street, which was terribly dusty but at least not knee-deep with mud as it always became in the spring. I didn't mind getting dusty—I just didn't want my boot heels to clatter on the boards.

I hurried through the streets, keeping to back ways and always choosing dirt streets over cobblestone ones, because I could run faster and more quietly over dirt. I moved steadily uphill, between the huddled houses over Blackwarren that grew bigger and more attractive the further uphill I went. Blackwarren House stood at the top of the hill, unwalled and ungated because the greathouse held neither an army nor the wealth that would tempt invaders.

That worked in my favor, of course. It would have played havoc with my plans if I first had to work my way past gate guards and an army barracks and a houseful of servants. Lucky for Giraud his father was a poor, weak lord. Well, maybe not so lucky. If Lord dar Falcannes had been rich and powerful he might have still been alive, and his private army might have been intimidating enough that the Empress dar Kothia Surdosti would have thought twice about attacking his home and replacing him with some sneaking, murdering sycophant.

As it was, I went up the rose trellis outside Giraud's room and rapped on his window until, rubbing his eyes and yawning, he opened it.

"Izza! What in the world—"

"Get a change of clothes and your weapons and come with me," I said. "I don't have time to explain, other than to tell you that the empress's men will be here at first light to kill you."

Giraud never had a stupid day, and bleary-eyed and sleep-fogged though he was, he didn't have one then, either. Without argument or question, he ran from the window; only moments later, he returned. In that length of time, I'd had time to think.

"Which of your servants is most loyal to your family?" I asked him.

"Beidus. He served my father when they were both boys, and has been with us ever since."

"Get him quickly. Shortly after we leave, he needs to set fire to the house, then rouse the villagers to fight it; when all the village is stirred, he and the rest of your servants need to escape in the melee."

Giraud's eyes narrowed and he studied me for a moment while a cold and terrible blankness stole over his face, robbing it of expression. "Yes," he said. He vanished into the darkness of his room again, and this time took much longer to return.

"It's done," he said. "Those I trust will be wakened shortly, so that they'll have time to gather what few belongings they can. I've told Beidus to empty the stables and chase the horses into the hills, then set fire to the outbuildings first. I told him that Da had been murdered and the killers were coming for all of us next." He handed me one pack, and slipped a second one under his cloak and shrugged into it. Then he swung his leg over the window and only when his back was to me and I'd donned my own pack and we were both climbing down the trellis did he add, "That's what has happened, isn't it?"

"Yes," I said.

"And somehow you found out."

"I found out a lot," I told him.

We took only his two best horses. We would not travel far on horseback—we would be too conspicuous if we rode like lords instead of walking like commoners. But the horses would give us some distance from Blackwarren before anyone discovered our absence. We could cool the horses down and turn them loose before we got into the heart of the mountains—they'd find plenty of food in the uplands and we wouldn't have to worry about how we were going to feed them, rest them, water them, or get them over some of the worst of the mountain passes that led to Lieda.

We would have enough to worry about with just
ourselves.

We rode out of Blackwarren without a backward
glance. We cantered through the hills to the Gateway of the Mountains; we were all the way to the
first difficult traverse of the Gateway Pass before the
pink light of dawn began to creep between the black
spears of the trees that rose from the edge of the path
all around us.

We dismounted and surveyed our situation. The
path had been nearly level, with mountains rising to
either side of it. Now, however, it slid up onto the
hip of the right mountain and the left side of the path
fell away into steadily deepening ravine. Below and
ahead of us, we could hear water rushing.

"Time to get rid of the horses," Giraud said, "while
they can still turn around."

I sighed. I almost never got to ride anymore,
though when I'd been a young girl—before whatever
had brought my father to Blackwarren—I'd had my
own horse and I had ridden every day. I'd been
delighted to discover that I still remembered how.
When I swung down out of the saddle, I was less
delighted to find that, though memory had served me
well, my out-of-condition legs had not.

"Oh, Neithas, I'm sore," I muttered. The insides
of my thighs cramped, my calves ached, and though
this is surely indelicate, I'll admit that my rump
burned like a brush fire.

We stripped the saddles from the horses and threw
them down into the ravine, listening to them rattle
and thump and jingle until either trees stopped them
or distance muted their movement. We rubbed our
mounts down, walked them until they were cool, then
slapped them on their haunches and sent them back
the way they'd come.

Before us lay a sharply rising scree-covered ledge
that didn't look as if anyone had been over it in ages.

"I wonder why this is in such disrepair," I said. "The dwarves of Kekger Deshin travel the pass between their mines and Blackwarren several times a month during the summer."

"Slide must have just happened," Giraud said.

I looked at the mess, wishing that we could wait for brighter light before essaying out onto it. "I'm sure you're right." In the half-light of dawn, it seemed to me that prudence would almost demand that we wait just a bit longer. The ledge appeared to rise above the thick forest quickly, and the few trees that grew on the steep, rocky slopes above were stunted by their poor soil and twisted by wind—they would provide us with no cover. Once we had no trees on either side of us, the passage would become much more dangerous. Surely we needed better light before trying something like that.

To stall for time, I said, "I've never been through the dwarves' city. I haven't even spoken to any dwarves since I visited with the traders and officials who used to visit with my parents. Do you think they'll tell anyone we passed through their city?"

Giraud shook his head. "We deal . . . *dealt* . . . with them often. They don't care much about humans as long as we leave them alone. And as a rule they actively dislike human politics and human disagreements. I know this. My father and brothers and a handful of village volunteers went riding after a thief once—he'd been robbing the merchants blind every night—and the dwarves let the thief pass because he was alone and bothered no one. But when my father's party tried to pass, even when my father explained what they wanted with the man and why, the Kekger Deshinites blocked the roads with stone and refused them passage. The thief escaped."

"Good," I said, then glanced at him. "Not that the thief escaped, you know. Just that the dwarves will

possibly be kinder to us than they will be to those
who come after us."

Giraud said, "Let's get moving."

The light was a bit brighter. I nodded and followed
him onto the ledge. We worked our way up the path,
crouching over and brushing off scree with our hands
so that we could keep both feet firmly planted all the
time. Neither of us wanted to try kicking the debris
away only to lose balance and go bouncing down the
rocky wall of the ravine after it.

The path climbed more steeply, and I realized that
seven years of sitting on a stool and weaving had done
little to prepare me for a frantic climb through mountains with a pack of killers after me. We climbed for
the better part of a candlemark, I'd guess, during
which time we left the trees behind and at least part
of the air.

When we finally reached a level wide place, both
Giraud and I stood panting like dogs on a hot summer day.

"I have to . . . stop for a while," I told him.

He nodded. "Yes. This is . . . hard work."

I'd thought he would be more able to travel than
I, but I'd forgotten Giraud's habits. He spent his days
in a library with a tutor his father brought in from
Balter. He skipped every sword practice he could get
away with and avoided as much hand-fighting as he
could, too.

We sat with our backs against the stone wall behind
us, and I said, "If someone were to go through the
village and pick the two worst people to run away
through the mountains, they would pick us."

Giraud closed his eyes. "I know. I've been thinking that. We have no food with us, and no water, and
nothing to carry water; we don't have warm clothes
or sturdy mountain boots or ropes or picks or any
of the tools people use when they go through the
mountains; we have no map; we've never been on this

path; we have no idea where we're going or how long
it will take us to get there; we have no weapons nor
any tools with which to make them."

Until he listed the problems he saw, I was just
thinking that we were neither one of us in very good
shape to go mountain climbing. I hadn't thought past
that to the fact that we had nothing anyone would
need to survive in the mountains. "Thank you for
making me feel worse," I muttered.

He glanced at me. "You brought it up."

"I hadn't considered all the details."

"Oh."

We sat in silence a while longer. Finally he asked
me how I'd come to find out about his father's murder. I told him. He listened attentively, his face growing darker with every word.

"They were going to *sell* you?" he interrupted at
one point, and, "Your father is dead?" at another. But
other than that, he said nothing until I finished. In
fact, he said nothing for a while thereafter.

Finally he turned and put an arm around my shoulder and kissed me once on the cheek, firmly. "You
are my family, Isbetta dar Danria," he said, "and I
am yours. You risked your life to save mine and the
lives of my family's loyal servants, and I will die first
before anyone touches you against your will." He
stared into my eyes and I could see in them grief he
could not allow himself to release, and his fury at the
betrayal and destruction of his family. "We must swear
a pact, you and I," he continued, "that no matter what
happens, we will protect each other, and that someday
we will destroy those who tried to destroy us." He
held out his hand.

I thought of how ludicrous we looked to the gods,
sitting on that mountain pass with no guarantee that
we would survive the day, swearing the destruction
of our enemies—but I took his hand. "By Neithas my
patron, who tramples her enemies and feeds their

hearts to her owl, and by my blood and soul, I swear it," I said. My voice trembled.

"By Hadres my patron," Giraud said, "who remembers all things and who finds all things, and by my blood and soul, I swear it."

We sat looking at each other, hands still tightly clasped, until Giraud sighed and loosened his grip. "May we live to make it so."

A terrified whinny and a scream echoed up from the ravine below and behind us, distorted by distance and the rush of water. Both sounds seemed to me to come from a long way off, but as we walked, sometimes our own voices had bounced back to us, making it seem that we were some distance from ourselves. The whinny could have been from a wild horse down in the ravine attacked by some hunting beast, or from one that had fallen and broken a leg, or perhaps from one of the animals we'd set free that had become panicked or injured—any of half a hundred explanations would have explained it. The scream, however, had sounded human, which meant that however far off it was, it wasn't far enough.

"Do you think it's them?" I asked.

Giraud nodded.

"Maybe there was only one person coming after us, and he fell into the ravine," I said. I didn't believe it, but I said it anyway.

"Maybe we're that lucky. But sensible people wouldn't travel into these mountains alone. If that scream was because one of our hunters fell to his death, I'd almost guarantee that there will be others behind who will be more careful."

I looked around. The wide spot where we sat was the only place we'd yet found along the path carved across the face of the mountain that might let two or three pursuers on horseback turn. If there were more, only the last three would be able to turn around. The first travelers would have to continue on. And if we could force them to travel on to the next wide spot—all of them—while we hid somewhere, we could, perhaps, double back and set a trap for them . . . or . . .

I didn't know what we could do, but I knew we needed to do something quickly.

Wary of the echoes that might whisper my words to Giraud into the ears of the hunters behind us, I leaned close to him and said, "We need to figure out a way to go on far enough that their tracker will be sure we intend to stay on this path, then either climb up the rock face above us or down over the side below us and find someplace to hide until they pass us."

"So that we can go back the way we came?" he asked, raising his eyebrows. "But that's stupid. We want to get away from Blackwarren."

"I know. But if we just keep running along this path, sooner or later they'll catch us. If it isn't in the next hour or day, it will be when we arrive at the other side. Maybe when we go back we can set a trap for them. Maybe. Or something." I stared into his dark eyes, feeling uncertain and scared, and said, "I don't know what we should do, Giraud, but my gut says we have to do something. Soon. Now."

He nodded and rose. My gut feelings were a bit of a joke between us—along with my father's musical ability, I had inherited his instinct for coming trouble, but where I recalled his instinct being almost magically accurate, my own was erratic. Sometimes embarrassingly erratic. At that moment, it didn't matter to me how wrong I'd occasionally been in the past. I *knew* we had to get off the path.

"Fine," Giraud said after he'd studied my face for a moment. "Let's move on. We'll be sure to leave a clear trail at least until we're completely out of sight of this shelf. Then we'll go either up or down, depending on what we find."

I stood and readjusted my cloak. I felt the

emptiness of the pack he'd brought for me on my shoulders, and the weight in my pockets that wasn't food and wished I'd taken something to eat from Birdie's larder before I ran, or that I'd had the presence of mind to tell Giraud to get us something . . . but perhaps if I'd taken that time, we wouldn't have lived to escape. And better alive and hungry than dead with a full belly.

We moved along the path, this time constantly looking both up and down for places where we might safely get off of it. Giraud spotted something promising, stopped, and pointed. "Look up," he whispered.

I looked up, and saw more of the same damnable rock covered with the same red and white and green lichens I'd seen all day. But Giraud said, "There's another ledge up there, I think. It's just a place where a line of red lichen becomes green."

Then I saw it. In fact, looking carefully, I could see that the lichens didn't match up, that a faint, straight line divided a span as broad as a tall man's outstretched arms.

"Let's go up," he whispered.

And as sure as I'd been that we needed to get off the path, I suddenly and as certainly knew that we didn't dare go up.

I looked down. I could see no sign of haven there at all, but instead I shook my head, put a finger to my lips, and carefully moved off the path and down.

Giraud's mouth dropped open, and he waved his arms wildly, gesturing for me to return, but I just shook my head and kept on moving downward. I moved a hand around the smallest of knobs, shoved a foot cautiously into a tiny crack, shifted balance cautiously from left to right, then from right to left; I scrabbled and slipped and clawed, and all the while, as I crept down the cliff face, the feeling of the void beneath my feet weighed on me as heavily as a kicking child clinging and fighting me, and I felt the sheer expanse of nothingness behind me and the certainty of my own death if I fell.

And at the same time, I had the oddest certainty that I was *right*. That gut feeling, much maligned—and often for good reason—assured me that I was heading in precisely, exactly, the right direction. Hand to tiny rock knob, boot toe wedged into little crack, shift my weight from hip to hip, slide down and to the left, tapping with one toe for a foothold, making sure I was steady with both hands and the other foot, and then, with both feet steady, moving one hand away from its safe grip, I made progress.

Moving down, and down, and down. And always at my back I felt the void between me and the floor of the ravine. I could feel myself toppling backward through space; I could feel myself hitting the rocks before my body tumbled into the rushing water. I could feel—but I kept going anyway, while the *rightness* of my present course drew me onward and downward, and grew ever more compelling. I'd had such feelings many times before, but never in my life had I been so *certain*. . . .

Now I could hear voices bouncing off the ravine walls at me.

"They're not too far ahead of us."
                    ahead of us
"How do you know?"
                    do you know
"Here. See? They sat here for a while, resting—"
                    resting
"And then they moved on. They were less careful about clearing the scree from the path. You can make out the clear edges of footprints here and here."
                    here and here
"Then we go after them now?"
"Of course. If we rest, they'll gain the lead they lost when they rested."
                    when they rested

rested

"Why do you suppose they went this way?"

went this way

I listened closely, for I was as interested in the question as the answer, but neither men nor mountains replied, and I was left to wonder what our pursuers meant. Went *this* way? As opposed to southward, deeper into Terosalle and trouble? Or as opposed to taking another road through the mountains, a better one that would have been safer?

I heard Giraud slip and swear. Gravel skittered past my ear, slapped my right hand, and smacked into the top of my head, and I flattened myself against the rock face, praying that he wouldn't lose his grip and fall, taking both of us down into the ravine. I heard him scrabbling and digging, and then all sounds from above me stopped, except for the heavy rasp of his breathing. He'd found something to hang on to.

The shower of stones finally ended, and I began moving downward again. My arms and back and thighs and calves all burned, and my hands and feet hurt. The place in the back of my mind that didn't believe the feeling in my gut screamed, "You're never going to have the strength to make it back up. Never. You're going to die down here." But the instinct that drew me downward was far stronger than that rational fear. I *knew*, though I did not know how I knew, I'd find safety.

Then I fell.

Chapter Three

One instant I was sliding my right foot down to tap around for my next foothold, while I clung with a firm grip on both handholds and kept most of my weight balanced on my left foot. The next instant, the left foothold crumbled out from under me, my swinging right foot encountered nothing but air, and I lost my grip and dropped. I had only enough time to realize I was doomed, and then I slammed into a stone shelf, twisted my right ankle as I landed on it, and pitched forward into darkness.

I kept sliding, face-first, downward—not quickly but steadily—until I came to rest in deeper darkness. My ankle throbbed and burned, a worse and distinctive pain against the background of overall pain that gnawed at my muscles and bones and skin. My eyes adjusted slowly. I closed them for a moment to help, then opened them again.

The darkness resolved into areas of lighter and darker vagueness. I twisted around to look behind me. I'd fallen into a narrow crevasse in the rock face behind which lay a surprisingly large cave. The angled pile of rock scree and debris down which I'd slid terminated in a fairly level rock floor that was easily two times bigger inside than Birdie's house had been, and half again as high.

I tried to stand so that I could walk to the entrance, but my ankle wouldn't carry my weight. So I crawled back up the shallow slope and leaned out the opening just in time to see Giraud move past on my right, evidently oblivious to the opening. He was climbing too fast, and not very carefully, and I realized he thought I'd fallen into the ravine and he was trying to get down there to find me.

"Pssst. Giraud," I whispered. I hoped I wouldn't startle him so much that he lost his grip on the cliff.

He stiffened and his head jerked in my direction. "Izza?" His eyes grew round as eggs and his mouth dropped open. "By Hadres, you're safe."

"Hurt my ankle, but that's all. Hurry up and get in here."

He started working his way toward me, still moving too fast . . . but the voices of our pursuers now seemed to come much more from above us than behind us. The time for caution had passed. He scrambled toward me, fingers and toes digging, face red, his breathing harsh and labored. They could probably hear him moving, I realized, and could probably hear him breathing, too. If they followed the source of the sound downward, we would be discovered.

He lost a handhold and flailed out—I braced myself and leaned far out and grabbed his waving hand, and pulled. For the next few instants, the two of us struggled desperately to get him out of sight from the ledge above. I pulled, he swung and jumped and scrabbled, and then the two of us were rolling down the scree into darkness, gasping and shaking, to lie together in a little heap at the bottom.

"STOP!"

We froze.

The gentle *clop-clopping* of hooves, which had grown clearer and clearer, ceased. I tried to quiet my breathing; Giraud, still gasping from his exertions, pulled up his tunic to cover his nose and mouth. That muffled the sound enough that I didn't think it would give us away.

A tiny rockfall skittered past our window to the outside world. They had stopped directly above us. Did that mean they knew where we'd gone?

"You see? The tracks go no further." The voice was triumphant.

"Then the scream we heard . . . was that one of them falling into the ravine?"

"Perhaps. Perhaps not." Silence followed that thoughtful reply. We waited. Then, "Aha. Look up. You see that line of lichen?"

Giraud and I stared at each other. If we'd gone that way . . .

"I see it," a second voice replied in unison with a third that said, "Yes, right there!"

Third voice said, "We can't stop here or turn around, though. We'll have to go on, leave the horses at the next wide place, and come back."

First voice, scornfully, said, "Whoever told you that you had a brain? And let them climb down and get away while we do that? Let them run back the way we came, as they doubtless planned? No. I think not. Dischi, you're first in line. You ride on and our horses will follow you to the next landing. Macs and I will dismount here and go after them. You turn around as soon as you can and come back for us. We'll be waiting with them."

And when Macs and whoever was with him climbed up and didn't find us, what would happen? They'd climb down and find us. And when they found us, we would either go with them or they would kill us. We had no weapons, no fighting skills, and no place to run.

I heard the horses clopping away, and then the sounds of our hunters climbing. They called to each other as they went up the face of the rock, and from time to time a stream of debris would rattle down into the ravine as they knocked it loose. Aside from those few noises, though, we waited in silence. I wished I could think of some way out of our trouble, and from the expression on Giraud's face, he shared my wish. We didn't even dare move further back into the cave—sounds carried preternaturally well at this spot in the path, and we didn't want to give away our location.

We might still hope, after all, that they wouldn't be able to find us.

We waited.

"I'm almost there."

"I can't find a handhold beyond this one."

"Hold on. Hold on, will you."

"I can't find . . ."

"*By sacred Anyu's dugs . . .*"

"What?"

"You won't believe this!"

"Throw me your damned rope so I can get up there, and I'll decide whether I believe it or not."

Another silence this time, followed by grunts and muttered swearing.

And then, "There, you see—"

—and two horrible screams.

A man hurtled downward past the opening to our cave, followed immediately by a second. My blood chilled in my veins and my heart nearly stopped.

We both scooted up to the "door" on hands and knees and looked out. Far below, we could make out the two crumpled bodies of what had been our enemies.

For the longest time, neither of us said anything. Finally Giraud said, "We almost went up there."

I nodded. I couldn't speak; I was having a hard

enough time breathing around the lump my heart made in my throat.

A cold, low, slightly lisping voice behind the two of us said, "As well you did not. Neither promise nor prophecy guarantees even *temporary* safety to visitors at my *front* door."

I turned. Slowly. Very slowly, in case whoever stood behind us felt inclined to view any movement as a threat. My eyes had to readjust to the darkness. First I saw only the size of the one behind us. Its head reached halfway to the ceiling, making it nearly as tall as Birdie's house.

Then, as my eyesight improved, I could see its head, long as a horse's but skeletally lean, and make out the pallor of its skin and the burning insanity that gleamed from the row of dark sockets that housed its many eyes. It moved forward soundlessly, until it towered over the two of us.

"And there are no guarantees of your safety, either. Unless you are . . . well . . . we'll determine that."

It crouched down onto all fours, and its hands came out of the sleeves of its robe, and they weren't hands at all, but claws like those on the little stream crabs the boys in the village caught and sold. "We . . . will . . . determine . . . that," it said again.

It leaned toward the two of us, and instinctively we shrank back. Its face wasn't merely lean but utterly fleshless, with long jaws hinged far back and a black, darting tongue that it flicked in and out, in and out. And from eight deep caverns, its hideous eyes glared out at us, unmoving unblinking crystal-faceted gems that in the dim light reflected all the colors of the rainbow, but stained those colors with a horrible oily darkness of their own.

"So . . ." it said, and chuckled softly. "What are you doing sneaking into my home through my back door?"

I cleared my throat. "We were hiding from the men who were chasing us."

"Why? Are you thieves? Scoundrels? Vagabonds?"

Giraud said, "I am the son of Anjourd dar Falcannes, lord of Blackwarren. I'm no thief. And she's the daughter of Bard Haral dar Danria . . ."

"I have no use for the 'sons of' or the 'daughters of','" the monster said. "No use. What . . . *are* . . . you?"

First I thought "human," but "human" had done the hunters no good. "I'm an apprentice weaver," I said. The "apprentice" part stung. "He's an apprentice historian."

"So you are . . . are students. Unfinished. Like . . . like books half-written."

That seemed an odd description, but Giraud and I both nodded.

"Sing for me . . ." the monster said. "The song I sing." It cocked its head to one side and, in a shockingly pure voice, did a few phrases of a song in a language I didn't know, with a tune that danced across the range of a good singer's voice.

I have a good memory for music—a gift left over from my early childhood as a bard's daughter. I repeated the song back to the creature, as clearly as I could, trying to match its sweetness and purity of tone, though I certainly failed there. I was almost sure I'd gotten the words right, though, and I was certain I'd matched the melody.

It studied me for only an instant, then said to Giraud, "Now you."

It sang the song again—the same words, but this time in a lower range.

Giraud nodded, then sang it back. He mimicked the monster, too.

The monster hissed and rocked backward on its heels staring from one of us to the other, then back. It rose from its crouch, moving gracefully, and its claw-hands vanished back into the folds of its robe. It stared at us still, its head turning slightly left, then right, then left, then right.

"Two will come," it said, in the voice of one reciting poetry,

> "Two will come,
>   Unfinished stories.
> Books half-written,
> Carrying nothing
> Containing everything,
> They flee death,
> Bring life,
> Promise the future.
>
>
> Wait by the back door;
> To them give the key."

It watched us a little longer, as if by waiting we would figure out the meaning of that odd half-song, half-riddle ourselves.

Finally Giraud asked, "What does it mean?"

It cocked its head. "I don't know what it means. It's a riddle, and I have the key, but I don't have the answer. I must . . . I must *assume* . . . that your lives are the answer. Or at least your living of them. And if you are to be an answer I don't like, then I will be better off to kill you now, for all that I've waited here for you long beyond the time I thought I would."

That didn't sound at all promising. But I had no idea what to say. *Don't kill us* sounded weak and cowardly, while *We won't do anything to cause trouble* was a promise that, quite frankly, I didn't think I was qualified to make. I didn't know enough about the situation I faced to make any promises at all. And lying to a monster such as this, my gut told me, would be a very bad idea. So I said nothing.

Giraud evidently couldn't think of anything useful

to say, either. He watched the bony nightmare too, doing nothing more than blinking and breathing. We were mute and scared and at the same time intrigued. After all, for what reason in the universe could such a monster be waiting in a cave on the side of a mountain for us to visit?

After a long silence, it said, "So you can hold your tongues, too." It turned with a fluidity the angular, bony form of its body made especially improbable. "That's fortunate. Come, then."

Giraud stood. I tried, but the instant I put weight on my ankle, the dull red throbbing pain in it became a white-hot agony, and I started a scream that I immediately cut short. Tears started in the corners of my eyes, and I balanced on one foot, now terrified. Giraud moved to my side and let me lean against him so that I could hop, but the monster had already turned and was watching me.

"You're injured," it said.

"Not badly. Nothing that won't heal—"

"—with time," it said. "Nothing that won't heal *with time*. But for all that we had the time from the day the song was born until the sun burned to ashes for you to get here, now that you're here I'm afraid we're in a bit of a hurry."

It walked back to me, reached for me with those dreadful claws, and Giraud threw himself in front of it, trying to block its access to me. The monster brushed him aside as if he were no more significant than a gnat, and picked me up with a gentleness that shocked me.

"Don't be ridiculous," it said to Giraud, and with me caged in its bony arms, it slid through a doorway of rock that opened before it, glided into a faintly lighted passageway that led upward, and after numerous twists and turns, through passageways that branched, folded, and wove around and up and down, came at last to a bright, high-ceilinged cavern lit by the reds and golds and deep, rich purples of a brilliant, beautiful sunset.

"Ah-h-h-h," it said. "The finest place in the mountain to see the closing of the day." It put me down on a bench, and said, "Tell me where it hurts."

I pointed. As I was showing it, Giraud burst into the room, panting like a beast, with sweat dripping down his face. He glared at the monster.

"You almost lost me in there."

The monster glanced from me to him, shrugged slightly, and returned its attention to my ankle. "Had I lost you," it said, "you would not have been the ones, and I would have killed her, then come back looking for you."

My breath caught when it said that. It spoke so calmly of destroying us, as if doing so would be a matter of no concern to it. And then it touched my ankle, and the skin began to glow, and for just an instant I could see the bone beneath it. And the pain went away.

"There," it told me. "Now you'll be able to walk on it. Be careful not to hurt it again. The next time, you won't find anyone who will fix it."

It straightened and looked at Giraud. "Sit beside her. Wait for me. I'll return."

Giraud sat and waited. Neither of us talked—I said nothing because I feared it might be listening to us, and I was afraid that I might say something that would make it decide to kill me. I didn't ask Giraud his reasons for keeping quiet, of course. We sat on the carved stone bench, holding hands, staring out through a beautiful carved archway at the blazing sky and the creeping edge of twilight that slid down the sky behind it, and we waited.

"You're hungry," the monster said, reappearing behind us so suddenly and soundlessly that we both jumped. "I have food for you—to eat now, and when you get ready to leave, enough to get you where you must go."

It handed us a heavy wooden bowl full of little brown crunchy morsels all mixed in with seeds and dried fruits and shreds of dried jerky.

I glanced from the meat to it, and it said, "Wild goat," as if it knew that I wondered where it got its meat. I had no wish to discover after the fact that I'd eaten a bit of someone who'd just been passing through.

It left the food with me, vanished back into its hole in the wall, and reappeared, this time with two tall goblets. They held water, I discovered, and sweeter, more welcome water I have never tasted. I drank slowly, savoring each drop. And when I finished, I dug into the bowl and tried some of everything. I liked the nuts well enough, and the dried fruits were very tasty, and the jerky had that strong flavor I've come to associate with goat. The brown, crunchy tidbits, though, tasted like nothing I'd ever had before—slightly salty, meaty, incredibly rich, with just the faintest hint of unfamiliar spiciness. Those I tossed down by the handful.

I glanced over at Giraud as I ate, and wondered if I looked as much the starved wild beast as he did. Not that I cared. After a day without food, I would have shoved my face into the bowl and eaten without using my hands had that been my only way of getting to it.

Giraud and I devoured every bit of the meal—I felt near to exploding by the time I finished. Then the monster settled itself on the stone bench, lit the lamp it carried, and set it on the floor between us. The flickering flame cast pale light upward, illuminating our faces from below and casting distorting shadows that made Giraud look like a stranger and transformed the monster into something almost demonic.

"You do not need to know my name," it said without preamble, "but you need to know why I've waited for you. Listen closely and say nothing until I've finished, for I will not answer questions, and I will not repeat what I tell you.

"I am one of the nantatsu," it said, and those words froze my heart as solid as river ice in the darkest days of winter. Like every child, I'd been told stories of the nantatsu—of their magic and their evil; of the way they haunted the mountain passes and hunted among travelers for their next meals; of the rumors that they tortured and sacrificed and devoured their victims. They were known as the White Spirits of the Mountains, and every story I'd heard insisted that they were virtually inescapable, nearly unkillable, and utterly without mercy.

The monster glanced from my face to Giraud's, chuckled, and said, "Always, travelers know of the nantatsu. You will be unique among travelers, however, in that, if you do as I tell you, you will survive our meeting. This time."

Giraud took my hand and held it.

"I have been in this cave for a long time—longer than you can imagine. It is my home, the place where I was born, but it is *not* the place where I will die," the nantatsu said. "I am older than I choose to be, but because of a spell cast on me by a long-ago bard, I have been unable to travel to the dying grounds to prepare my egg or bring forth my successor. I have been trapped here for long ages, awaiting your arrival.

"When I caught the bard, I refused to give him his life, but before I could kill him, he cast on me this songspell."

It began to sing. I immediately recognized the first part—

"Two will come,
Unfinished stories.
Books half-written . . ."

It sang clear to the last line of the song it had quoted to us when it caught us in its cave-room before:

"To them give the key."

It didn't stop there, though. It began another verse of its song.

"Bag of bones,
Box of wood,
String and voice,
Words and breath—
And as within
So without
And as together
So apart.
Guardian be
By my will
Until they come
Until they come—
Worldsinger and
The voice of time.
And when the song
Is sung, is sung . . .
You will be free."

"Killing that misbegotten snack didn't break the spell, and trying to destroy the objects he'd left behind in my care proved impossible, and the Worldsinger has not yet come through my door, though I tell you I have tried everyone who has. To some who arrived before you I've given his cursed pack, and let them try to leave—but the pack will not leave with any save the right one, and will not let me leave until the right one comes.

"I've puzzled this out for years on top of years," it continued. "I know what you have to do. You're to take the spell I've marked in the book, and you're to go to the Pillar of the Sun at the summit of Hearthold Mountain, where you're to sing it." It growled. "I've tried my best to decipher the meaning of the song, but I cannot. I don't know the bards writing, and I don't know human magic. No doubt it's a spell I won't like much, but that doesn't matter. When you sing it and I'm set free, I'll travel to the breeding grounds to breed and die, and I don't care what happens after that."

I said nothing. Giraud said nothing.

The nantatsu snarled. "All these years, bards and wizards have come looking to reclaim their magic book. They feel it out with their spells, and they follow it to me, yet none of them has freed me." It stared at me, then at Giraud. Its eyes sparked fiercely in the dim light of its lamp.

"Tomorrow at sunrise, I will give you the pack and try to take you to the road to Hearthold Mountain, so that you can sing the damned bard's cursed song. If the pack will let you leave—if you are the two 'unfinished stories' that I've been waiting for—I will accompany you as far as the base of the mountain, so that I can be sure that you don't get lost or forget the task you are to be about. When you climb up to the peak of the mountain to sing, I will wait for you below. If you succeed, I will be freed, and I will go to the dying ground. If you fail, or if you do anything to betray me, you will find me waiting for you when you come down."

The monster picked up its lamp and rose.

"You will stay in here tonight. Don't try to leave, of course."

It turned and moved quickly away, slipping through the stone door that opened before it and slid noiselessly shut behind it.

I squeezed Giraud's hand.

"Well," he said softly.

"What do you think it is?"

"The spell?"

"Yes."

He shrugged. "I was trying to think of stories from the history I know—tales of bards with spells who went into the mountains and were devoured by nantatsu, or stories of wondrous magical spells lost and never recovered." He shook his head. "I can't think of anything that would seem to apply to our situation—but if the Watchowl bards still consider the spell something that they must retrieve, perhaps they haven't let word of its existence get out."

I'd done something similar, trying to remember, as I listened to the monster's story, the conversations my father had carried on late into the night with his important visitors from all over Terosalle. Like Giraud, I came up empty.

But if I couldn't remember any useful stories or rumors, I could do something practical toward improving the chances of my survival. I took my other clothes out of the cloak pocket I'd carried them in and stuffed them into the empty pack. I didn't have anything else to put in it. If I had to sleep on a stone slab, I wanted to do it with a decent pillow. I could use my cloak as a blanket. The stone bench would be a cold, hard bed, but after years in Birdie's loft, I wasn't used to much better.

When I had my pillow made and my blanket readied, I gave Giraud a quick kiss on the cheek, then moved to the other bench and stretched out on it.

"You're going to sleep?" he asked.

"We're to be awakened at sunrise, and I thought I ought to get a good rest first."

"Well, yes . . ." He didn't look convinced. Giraud was no doubt hatching some thrilling plan for sliding down the side of the mountain without making a sound, thus escaping the clutches of the nantatsu. He would have all sorts of historical precedents for such heroics, and would be certain that we could get to safety before the nantatsu realized anything was amiss.

I decided I needed to forestall the suggestion of heroics that would surely be coming my way. I said, "I'm not going to try to escape from such a monster in its own lair."

"But you don't think we're the ones this magical spell that the monster spoke of has been waiting on, do you?" he asked.

I raised an eyebrow. "No. I figure we're doomed no matter what happens, but I would rather live for tomorrow's chances than die for sure tonight." I shrugged. "If we're going to die, nothing I can do will change that. But if we're going to live, then I need to get a good night's sleep, because tomorrow may be as difficult as today was."

Giraud sat on his own bench watching me for a moment. I thought he was going to try to talk me into running, no matter what I'd said, but he didn't. "You're disgustingly practical sometimes." He shrugged, though, and gave me a wry half-smile. "I won't leave without you," he said. Then he pulled off his own cloak and divested it of spare clothing. He made himself a bed like mine, and settled in to sleep the sleep of the hopeful.

Chapter Four

The feeling that something watched me woke me. The nantatsu stood near the doorway into the stone room, arms crossed and hidden within the deep folds of its sleeves, alternately studying Giraud and me. In a soft voice, it said, "Your scent fills my home, little morsel. Pray you are the ones who can break the bard's spell, and pray you can do it quickly, for my appetite grows with every instant that we linger here."

How wonderful, I thought, to wake and find myself considered in the role of breakfast snack. I did not wait for the nantatsu to suggest that I get up. Initiative was best, I thought. Instead, I jumped up and shook Giraud until he awoke. The momentary bewilderment in his eyes, before he remembered the terrible day that had brought the two of us to that place and that predicament, could have broken my heart. I wished I could give him back his father and his brothers, his home, his safe, quiet future as a historian—I wished I could give myself back the feeling that I knew what was going to happen next in my life, or that I had some control over it.

Well, I couldn't, and what's more, I didn't have the time to worry about it right then, either. I said, "Get up—fast. It's time to go."

He yawned and stretched, and half-way through his stretch, saw the nantatsu. He bounded to his feet, tucked his extra clothes into his pack, and said, "Well, I'm ready."

The monster watched us, head tipped to one side and jaws clicking out an unnerving, staccato beat. It sad nothing for the longest time, and then it giggled. My skin crawled. "Are you truly ready?" it asked.

And how were we to answer that?

I took a deep breath and stood straighter and said, "Yes. We are."

It handed each of us something wrapped in oil-cloth and tied clumsily with thick string.

"Your rations," it said, and turned its back on the two of us. "Now follow me."

The monster hurried along its stony passage, and Giraud and I scrambled after it, not daring to let it get too far ahead, even though it seemed bent on losing us in the twisting labyrinth of its home.

It moved down into the darkness, away from tiny, cunningly concealed windows carved out of the rock face, to a place where no natural light touched. In that place, the corridors twisted steadily downward, and I felt, as I ran behind the nantatsu, the weight of the mountain growing over my shoulders and head, as if I were carrying them with me. The corridor walls glowed a sickly green—I could feel the touch of magic in the light, but it was magic of an ugly, twisted sort.

The ugliness got worse quickly, scraping against all my senses. I noticed a slight tickle of scent at the back of my throat. Something light but unnerving. It became denser as we descended, though, and at last became almost unbearable. Sweetness, cloying sweetness. And the stink of rotting meat. My eyes watered and I gagged, but I kept hurrying after the nantatsu.

I held one edge of my cloak over my face and breathed through it, and was grateful that I'd taken the time and care to weave the material tightly.

I knew that I headed into something terrible, and with all my heart I wished I could retreat back up the way I'd come. But the monster seemed to be hoping for some sign that Giraud and I were not the people it needed to set it free, because if we gave that sign, it would devour us. It was hungry, we were its natural prey, and it restrained itself from killing us only with difficulty.

"Here," the nantatsu said at last. "Come in." It giggled again, that same mad sound that set my teeth on edge and made me want to flee. "Oh, *do* come in."

Only the faintest of lights illuminated the center of this room. The edges lay in darkness, and the darkness, like the smell, had its own frightful weight. The stink here lay so thick in the air it seemed to be the mother of the blackness that shrouded us; tears ran down my cheeks and I breathed through my cloak in little, shallow gasps and prayed that my nose would go numb. Beside me Giraud made muffled gagging noises through the folds of his cloak. We stepped together into the darkness at the edge of the sickly light, holding hands tightly. I drew courage from his presence. It would have been a terrible place to be alone.

The center of the room held a narrow pillar only a little shorter than me, and on the pillar lay a worn leather pack so old that I could see from where I was that the leather was rotting. The pack looked like the sort peddlers carry, or traveling priests, or some bards.

"There," the nantatsu said. "There's the bard's prize. Go get it."

I took a step forward, and Giraud moved with me, but a sudden crawly sensation at the back of my neck stopped me. Giraud started to take another step forward, but I tightened my grip on his hand until he said, "Ow," and tried to yank it free. He stopped and elbowed me in the ribs and muttered, "That hurt."

"Go ahead," the monster said. "Take it."

"No," I told it. "Something's wrong."

"Something's *always* wrong," it said. "Just as something's always right. The trick is to figure out which is which, isn't it?"

Neither Giraud nor I answered.

"Your prize is waiting."

I sensed Giraud turning to look at me in the darkness. I couldn't see his face. I couldn't see much of anything but that faint glow of light, and the pack atop the pillar, and the light that just barely reflected off of the nantatsu, enough to make it visible to me. It stood to my right, waiting, head cocked to one side, jaws again clicking.

"You've done something to it, or to the path to it," I said, suddenly certain this was the case.

Silence greeted that assertion, a lingering, uncomfortable silence in which I thought I could hear the monster imagining ways to cook me before it ate me. Then the nantatsu sighed. "Very well," it said. "You prove again that you are not my meat."

The light in the room's center grew brighter, intensifying from the ugly greenish light to one brighter and yellower and somehow healthier. And now I could see what I had not seen before—that thirty or more doors led into the room from every direction; and that the floor in front of each of them had been carved into a deep pit; and that long, exquisitely carved and polished spikes of stone rose out of the floor of that circular pit. No safe path led to the pillar. I could see, too, that others before me had been led into this room, and that many of them had tried to reach the pack and had failed. The fleshless skulls of some of my predecessors stared up at me with grinning jaws and empty eye-sockets; other more recent victims of the nantatsu still wore a few remnants of decaying flesh over the framework of their bones.

The monster giggled. "I've had my dawnmeal and duskmeal many times over in this place," it said. "I'd hoped the two of you would join me here for a quick bite, as well." Then it shrugged philosophically and snapped its fingers; the pack lifted itself off of the pillar and floated to the monster. "To daylight," the nantasu said, "before I grow weary of the novelty of letting you live. Perhaps if I killed and ate you, I would find some sort of pleasure in living forever or eventually the bard's spell would be broken anyway." It hissed. "No, no, that wouldn't work," it mumbled to itself. "I'll be forever in here unless the spell breaks; I become mortal when they go and take the bard's pack with them. If I kill them I will never die, but I will never mate, and if I never mate I will never have my young." It backed into the passageway while it mumbled to itself and began moving back upward through the tunnels and corridors again.

"It's crazy," Giraud said.

I nodded vigorously.

"We have to go with it though."

I nodded again.

He hurried after it as quickly as he could. I followed.

What were we supposed to do about the mad monster? Could we do anything? It had every advantage over us—at least every advantage I could see. So we followed it as it demanded we do, and we tried to be unobtrusive.

I wondered if all the nantatsu were mad, or if only this one was. Perhaps this one had lost its mind from having been alone so long, trapped in its lair. The stories of the nantatsu always said they were terrible creatures, but never mentioned that they were insane. I had time to wonder while I followed the monster up the passageway. I hoped, of course, that I would never make close enough acquaintance with another such horror that I could compare.

At last we reached a dead end.

"This is where we stop," the monster said.

The tunnel, lit with the same green light as all the rest of the windowless tunnels, simply stopped, as if someone had wearied of digging it. I glanced at Giraud. Had the nantatsu taken us all this way just so it could kill us here? But it said, "Now I must do the magic that will take us out of my home—if you are who you say you are."

Neither of us had said we were anything special. Still, faced with my imminent death, I found myself praying that we were, because either we were the heroes foretold by a dead bard's last prophecy, or we were doomed. I didn't like our odds.

The nantatsu wasn't paying attention to either of us right then, however. It stood behind us, blocking any hope of escape, and it tucked its long chin against its chest and began to mutter. As it mumbled words I couldn't understand, it began to glow, and quickly transformed from a solid, very real monster to a transparent, milky white specter. As it changed, so did its robes. When they became translucent, they began to whip around it like the tattered edges of a storm cloud, or like fog come to life. I gasped, and Giraud said, "The White Spirit."

The monster screamed—an ear-battering ululating wail that went on and on and on, as if the nantatsu didn't breathe like humans did, but used air only to fuel its mad screaming. As it screamed, my entire body began to tingle, and the air thickened and grew terribly cold, and I felt myself beginning to freeze solid. My eyesight blurred, and I grew lightheaded.

I woke face-down on cold, damp rock, aware first of the aching pain in every muscle of my body, and next of the thunderous roar of falling water nearby, and finally of the fact that something was trying to wake me. That something shook me and chittered at me, and suddenly pinched me. I came bolt upright with a shriek of pain, and jumped back as I looked into the grinning, attenuated death's-head face of the nantatsu.

"I thought I would have my meal for sure," it told me. "But, no. I don't want to eat you . . . yet. I'm not yet fully unbound. If you fail me, you'll be my meal."

I looked around for Giraud. He lay behind me, still not moving, though I could see him breathing.

"What did you do to us?" I asked the nantatsu.

It chuckled. "You cannot walk through the world-walls as I can. You are weak, or untrained, or perhaps just stupid. A wizard or a bard would not have fainted."

Oh. It was my fault. It figured.

I started to try to wake up Giraud, but the nantatsu grabbed my shoulder with its claw the instant I turned away, and snarled, "You shall not leave."

"I'm not leaving. I'm going to get Giraud up so that we can do whatever you want us to do."

"Oh." Its claw released my shoulder. I could tell I was going to have a bruise there in a day or two. I didn't complain, though. I just went to Giraud, dropped to my knees at his side, and started shaking him. "Giraud. Giraud. Get up. You've got to get up."

He rolled over, stared up at me, and frowned. "I dreamed you already woke me—" and then his voice trailed off as he realized we were no longer in the nantatsu's house, but in a valley at the base of a huge, single mountain peak that stabbed up through the trees around us and pierced the black blanket of angry clouds that butted up against its higher reaches.

"That's Hearthold Mountain?" he said.

I followed his glance to the flashes of lightning that

sparkled along the upper reaches and turned the roiling underbellies of the clouds momentarily gray before darkness returned. "Evidently. I haven't yet discussed it with our . . . companion."

He frowned and rose. "So now we all travel up there, do we?"

The nantatsu joined us. "No. As I told you, I will wait here. You will follow the path upward—you will not find it terribly difficult, for all that it is long and steep. You will have resting places along the way, and as long as you avoid meeting anyone who might be there, you should reach the top alive."

Giraud said, "Anyone . . . ? Like other nantatsu?"

"There are no nantatsu on Hearthold Mountain," the monster said. "Yet."

Sounded like a good place to be, as far as I was concerned. "So who are we likely to meet?"

"The Karger Magad dwarves."

"Dwarves are often allies of humans," I said. "They won't hurt us, in any case."

"I've touched you," the nantatsu said, and lowered its voice. "My touch and my magic will be as clear to any Karger Magad as if I had carved my name on your flesh. And no matter what the Hearthold Mountain dwarves might think of you, I guarantee you they do not harbor any warm feelings for me. Too many of them have found a resting place among my piles of bones, while their tough flesh served to abate my hunger for a little while."

So. The potential allies we might have found on the mountain, and the potential safe harbor we might have hoped for, would be denied us because we bore the monster's mark. We could not hope for any help or any kindness, nor for any supplies, either going up the mountain or coming down. Worse, if we were discovered, we could expect active resistance. More danger. More enemies.

I didn't feel I *needed* any more enemies in my life.

And then the monster said, "Come here. You must know what you are to be about," and beckoned the two of us nearer with a hooked claw.

Reluctantly, I went to it, and Giraud went with me.

"This is the destiny created for the two of you long before you were born," the nantatsu said. It opened the ancient pack and from it pulled forth a book that looked quite unusual to me. Its pages, creamy yellow and unevenly hand-cut from sheets of parchment, were bound in octavo by waxed twists of gut string knotted through the back. The pages were protected by thin wooden covers hinged along the left and kept in place by three wooden dowels driven through the binding. It appeared to be a sturdy book, but it also looked awfully heavy.

"One of the First Age books," Giraud said.

The monster studied him, and said, "Indeed, little scholar. Its type is quite recent in relation to the history of my people; quite ancient, no doubt, in relation to the history of yours. From what I could gather from the bard who . . . gave . . . it to me, it is a commonplace book, and was owned by a succession of bards before the one I ate."

The monster turned the pages carefully, and I could see that its claws were poorly designed for the task. When it arrived at the last entry, it pointed to the scrawling black letters written by a heavy, graceless hand and said, "This is the spell and the song that my dinner was trying to take to Hearthold Mountain. Before his demise, the bard told me that Hearthold Mountain resonates with *karai*, which he said was the basic and essential magic of the earth itself." The nantatsu chuckled. "His words, not mine. He also said the world's *karai* energy has been thrown out of tune by some sort of interference with the living rock, and the resulting magic is subtly warped. As a result, events in our world are turning ever darker and more evil."

"That would explain a lot," Giraud said.

I glanced at him. "If it were true, it might. But why would it be true?"

The nantatsu said, "Perhaps it isn't. But whether it's true or not doesn't concern you. Your only concern is to reach the Pillar of the Sun alive so you can sing this song."

Giraud said, "But maybe what the bard was telling you was important."

The nantatsu glanced at him. "Not to me, it wasn't. He went on at some length, discussing *karai* and synchronicity and the evil in the world; trying to tie them to my actions and me to evil. A lot of blather, really. *Evil* would be if people quit going overland via my path. The rest of what he talked about was what snacks do when they aren't being eaten, and who cares about that?"

We do, I thought. But being a relatively bright girl, and fond of my skin, I kept quiet.

"He thought he'd found a cure for this evil, of course. I don't doubt at all that's what the song is."

It handed the book to Giraud, who stuck it in his pack. "So go on. Up the mountain, both of you. Sing the song and free me, and you'll never see me again."

Giraud said, "Let's go."

"Don't fail," the nantatsu said as we hurried toward the path that led up the side of the mountain. "Because if you do, you will see me again. But not for long."

So we had an old book with a song in it that we were supposed to sing; we were under strict orders not to cross paths with any dwarves on fear of death either from them or from the nantatsu should we survive them; we didn't know where we were to go other than up; or what effect the song we were supposed to sing was intended to have; and on top of that, it started to rain. Light rain at first, but the further we climbed, the harder it got.

And we did climb. The smooth slope of the path became slick, and changed at some point to steps. We were too wet and tired to talk to each other. And I, at least, could think of nothing to say. I had a pleasant enough voice, but I knew only a little more of bardic magic than the average bogger, and that only from half-remembered conversations with my father when I was very young. How was I to do magic? How was Giraud? He was no more a bard than I.

I wish I could say that I felt somehow special— that the nantatsu's strange prophecy and murmurings of magic and bards and spells made me believe that I had a task in the world that set me apart—but it wasn't like that. I was cold, and I was wet, and I was scared. Under such circumstances, you don't feel touched by the gods. You don't feel courageous and invincible. You just feel the hard rock under your feet and the ache in your thighs and the rumbling in your gut, and you wish you were home in a warm bed, with someone to take care of you.

The steps we climbed grew steeper and narrower, and the rain began sluicing down them as if they were a riverbed readying itself to flood. The dwarves had carved gutters on both sides of them, and grooved channels into them to prevent such dangerous flooding. But the dwarves hadn't planned for the rain that suddenly dropped out of the sky like entire lakes upended.

And later still, I realized when I stopped to catch my breath that we had lost the clear, easy path the nantatsu had set us upon. We were still traveling upward, and we still had endless switchbacked steps, but these steps were worn and crudely cut. No rain channels, no neat gutters to either side.

Giraud came back down to me and shouted over the rain, "These aren't the same steps!"

"I know. I just realized that!"

"Do you want to go back?"

I thought about losing ground, only to have to turn around and climb again. I didn't want to climb anymore. The adventure of the day before had left me hurting and weary, and the endless climb in the rain had added to the pain and the exhaustion, and was giving me chills and an aching head besides.

"No. Up is up. All of them will take us to the top sooner or later. I want to keep going."

"Me too. But what if we can't get to where we need to be from here?"

"I don't care," I said. "I don't want to backtrack."

He gave me a quick hug. "Then what do you want to do?"

"Find shelter," I told him.

So half-blinded by the rain, scared bootless by the lightning that rattled the upper reaches of the mountain, buffeted by shrieking wind, we began to climb again.

We didn't climb far before we found the cave. I never would have guessed it was a cave; I would have mistaken it for a waterfall, the way the water poured off of it. But I'd been going forward and I took what would have been the logical next step up and forward and there was no step there, and I lost my balance, staggered forward even further, arms braced to catch myself on the rock wall ahead and to my left . . . and I kept right on falling, through a thin sheet of pouring water and into darkness and dryness.

My first instinct was to get Giraud. I lunged back out and screamed for him, and somehow he heard me over the wind and the thunder. He came back and we tumbled together into the wonderful, tiny cave. Considering that my situation at that moment resulted from a previous foray into a cave, I'm surprised I didn't listen to my second instinct, which was to rush back out into the cold and the wet, with the lightning and the wind.

The rain drowned my second instinct, though, so I stayed with the first one. Giraud and I sat together, our teeth chattering, trying to warm ourselves and each other.

"Have you . . . ever . . . been so wet?" he asked me.

"Not . . . not ever," I said. I felt the cold all the way into my bones, as if I were frozen clear through and my stupid heart simply didn't know enough to stop beating. I rubbed my hands over my arms as quickly as I could move them, but with wet clothes, wet skin, and cold hands, the warmth I managed to create for myself was little and less. "Do you think it will ever stop raining out there, or is it always like this?"

Giraud said, "It couldn't possibly rain like this all the time, or whoever carved all those steps never could have carved them."

"It rains this way more than you might imagine, though," a third voice said behind both of us, and as we both yelped and started to jump to our feet to flee, added, "Oh, don't move. I'd hate to have to kill you before I even found out who you were."

Chapter Five

We both put our hands up, palms out to show we held no weapons, and we turned. Slowly. I looked way up, expecting to see another of the accursed nantatsu, expecting that this time I was going to be a midday snack for something big and ugly. I discovered . . . nothing.

I lowered my gaze slowly.

And lowered it further.

And further.

And at the level of my waist—and I am not the tallest woman alive by any means, nor was I the tallest girl—I discovered the top of the head of a short, squat, exceedingly ugly dwarf who held a crossbow aimed upward between the two of us, pointing his arrow first at Giraud and then at me. My initial impression of him was that he was even uglier than the nantatsu, which seemed to me even as I thought it to be odd. After all, I couldn't think of a single story where a dwarf ate a human, and that should have made him seem more attractive than the nantatsu right away. Still, he was the ugliest dwarf I'd ever seen. His nose sat off-center on his face, looking like a melon that had fallen off a farmer's wagon to the cobblestones and split. His upper lip, swelled to enormous proportions, protruded from his face almost as far as his dreadful nose. His eyes were merest slits peering out of swollen purple-and-green bruises, though a pair of rimless spectacles perched on the bridge of his nose, looking delicate and utterly out of place, added a comical touch of the civilized.

I stared at him a moment longer, and then I began to laugh.

Giraud glanced at me like one stricken, and then he stared back at the dwarf, and then, terribly, a snicker escaped him, too.

The old folks say the gods watch out for children and fools, and we were, at that moment, both. The dwarf glared at us, then he lowered his crossbow, and started to chuckle. "I look terrible," he said. "But you should see yourselves. I've seen corpses pulled out of a river that looked better than you."

We looked at each other, Giraud and I, and saw ourselves as we must have looked to the stranger. Our skin had turned blue-gray from the cold and, in the poor light of the cave mouth, seemed to glow with a distinctly corpselike, waxy sheen. Further, our hair hung in our eyes and clung to our faces in snaky ropes, and our clothes stuck to us and dripped in puddles on the floor.

Giraud said, "Our last two days have been . . . difficult." I heard the catch in his voice when he said it, and so did the dwarf.

"I understand difficult," he said. He bowed stiffly from the waist, in the manner of dwarves, and said, "My name is Maydellan Ha. I am keeper and owner of this small, miserable cave, at least until such time as I enlarge it and make it comfortable, or conversely leave it to seek my fortune elsewhere. In the meantime, welcome, both of you, to such hospitality as I can offer. Since you invited yourselves in, anyway."

For someone who was supposed to be ready to kill us on sight because of the magic mark we bore, he seemed rather friendly. Gruff, but all the same, I thought I could deal with gruff much more readily than murderous.

"We fell in," I said, hoping to smooth over our abrupt arrival in his home. "We couldn't see where we were going."

He nodded. "And where were you going? I haven't seen humans here in . . . well, let's be honest. I haven't ever seen humans here."

"Where were we *going?*" I repeated.

"Where *were* we going?" Giraud asked.

"Up," I said, and nodded as if that answered the question.

"Up." Maydellan Ha raised one bushy eyebrow and said, "I suppose sooner or later you would have to get where you were going, then, if you were just going . . . up? But . . . by Tharkas, in this weather? Without rain gear or weapons, you were climbing Hearthold— and you fell through my door, too, and I'm not close to any of the main upwalks." He shook his head. "Hospitality calls for a measure of honesty in return. If you don't mind me saying so." He snorted. "Or even if you do."

Giraud and I looked at each other. I thought if we left out the part about the nantatsu we'd probably be all right, but then what reason could we have for climbing to the top right then, instead of waiting for a day when a thunderstorm didn't wreath the peak?

"It's like this—" I said at the same time that Giraud said, "It's a long story."

I deferred to him. Who better than a historian to tell a long story? Except after he told the part about Birdie and Marda trying to sell me to the whoremaster, and after he told about the death of his family at the hands of the new empress's men, and after he told about our daring escape into the cave in the cliff, he told about the nantatsu, too, and the bard's book, and what we had to do to survive. He made the story longer than I would have, and included things I would have left out, but I will admit he told it better.

Maydellan Ha was a fine listener. He built us a fire while Giraud talked, and settled himself closest to the door so that he partly blocked the wind that blew in on us. He murmured appreciatively at the exciting parts, shook his head at the sad parts, and sat gape-mouthed at the mention of our run-in with the nantatsu. And he didn't shoot us then, either, which made him my favorite sort of listener. When Giraud stopped telling the story, Ha turned to me. "Incredible. Do you have anything to add?"

"Only that the nantatsu said if we crossed paths with any of the dwarves here, they would kill us because they would see its mark on us."

"Its mark." Ha shoved his spectacles up his nose in what looked like a habitual gesture, but when his hand touched the swollen flesh, he yelped. "*Damn* Thatterburgan Vo!" he muttered. "And consign him to the lowest circle of hell's icefield, head-first." He sat with his eyes closed for a moment, rocking back and forth, breathing deeply. I could tell he was trying to gain control of the pain, or perhaps of himself. "That burns like a white-hot brand in the eye," he added. Then he opened his eyes and sighed. "You don't have any mark on you that I can see, nor any mark that I can feel. I'm not the most magically sensitive dwarf in the world, but you don't glow in the dark or trail a dreadful cloud after the two of you. You look to me about as dangerous as any other drowned rats."

Giraud laughed a little.

I was starting to feel better—my clothes were beginning to dry out, and along with them my hair and my skin; the warmth of the fire began soaking through to my bones; and I could only think of one pressing need that I had. Well, two. And the second I thought the dwarf would have the facilities for.

I was right. When I got back, and then Giraud left and returned, I said, "Would you mind if we ate? I'm starving, and I don't know what sort of supplies the nantatsu gave us . . ."

He waved me to silence with a tiny gesture. "Eat. I'll join you. And perhaps add a bite to your fare while I'm about it. I have a little larder. My own situation is not . . . good. Not at all good. But I can certainly spare some food."

He rose, ducked into a little tunnel off the "room" where we sat, and returned with bread and cheese and long strips of smoked jerky that was tougher than shoe soles but wonderful on the tongue. Giraud and I pulled out the nantatsu's packets and unwrapped them. They were both filled with more of the same sort of thing we'd eaten the night before.

While Giraud and I ate, trying not to gorge ourselves or deplete his larder, Ha said, "I'm interested in this trip of yours to the top of Hearthold and beyond. I have a real need to be elsewhere for a while . . ." His voice trailed off into silence and he stared up at the low arch of the tunnel overhead. " . . . Yes. Elsewhere. And I think, considering I've seen no weapons on either of you save the knives you eat with, that you might appreciate some protection from the . . . ah . . . the obstacles you might find on your path."

"The person who beat you up likely to come after you again?" Giraud asked.

"I wish it were that simple." Ha glanced at him, eyebrow arched. "The fellow I fought with is in much worse shape than I am. Much worse. There was, when I left the alehall, some question of whether he would survive his last fall. Which is especially unfortunate since he's Gamber Tok, Fimbal Tok's son, and Fimbal Tok has spent most of Gamber's life buying him out of the trouble he got himself into. He'll send trouble after me if Gamber doesn't survive."

I felt uneasy. This ugly, generous young fellow could turn out to be a killer? I hoped there would be some logical explanation—perhaps the Tok son had attacked Ha over the love of a woman . . . or perhaps it had been mistaken identity . . . or a fight over honor. So I asked him, "What happened?"

"We got drunk, and we bet we could knock each other down," Maydellan Ha said. And there went my hopes of a story of unrequited love, or even of honor. Men and their drinking and gambling—it would be that, wouldn't it? I wrinkled my nose; Ha noticed. "Not something a lady would do, eh? Well, we weren't ladies, and we were quite drunk, and we got onto the stage and started punching each other. I had a friend of mine hold my glasses—my eyes have never been as strong as my fists." He grinned.

"Or your mind, either, I bet," I muttered.

"My ears work fine, though," he said. "I grant you, it wasn't the cleverest thing to do, to bet Tok's son that I could knock him down before he could knock me down, and it got worse when I found out he had little bags of lead clutched in his fists. That's how I got these." He pointed to the wounds on his face.

"But I'm a good fighter, and if you have time for it to come down to skill, the good fighter will win, even if the cheater has more weight in his hands."

"So you beat him up so badly that he might die," I said. I felt sick to my stomach.

Ha looked startled. "Of course not. I hit him until he fell down, and said I'd won the bet. He got up, one of his friends, a fellow named Thatterburgan Vo, tossed him his knife, Tok charged me, I jumped out of his way, and that ass Tok fell off the stage. When he fell, he stabbed himself in the belly with his knife and hit his head on the corner of a table when he landed. The healer thinks he might have broken the

bones in his neck, too, but neither of those injuries
may even get the chance to matter because he has
a crack in his skull and he hasn't woken up since he
fell."

So it hadn't been Maydellan Ha's fault after all.
He'd been fighting a cheater who tried to kill him
when he won—and the terrible injuries had all been
accidental.

I couldn't see much he could do about that, or why
he should be in any trouble with anyone. I said as
much.

"I agreed to fight him," he said. "He's the one who
demanded the wager and the fight—I have a reputation, and he thought I didn't deserve it. But his
father feels that I should have refused the fight. So
he's made it known that he'll be sure I pay for not
having done so."

Giraud leaned forward, looking bewildered. "Even
though Gamber cheated? Even though he tried to kill
you after he lost?"

"This is a family that has never taken responsibility
for anything," Ha said. "Tok the Younger gloried in
the trouble he could cause everyone else because he
knew he could get away with it. Tok the Elder is a
mean bastard with too much money, who could never
see that shielding his son from the consequences of
his own actions might not be as good for him as
allowing him to take his lumps when they came.
Together the two of them need to be dropped down
a deep well, but that isn't going to happen." He
sighed and put another few scraps of wood on his
little fire.

I watched the smoke curl up through a crack in
the top of the tunnel and thought about people I'd
known who'd been like Tok the Younger. In the limited world in Blackwarren, I could only recall two—
tiny Blackwarren didn't have enough people to have
any particular type in large supply, and spoiled

children of wealthy and powerful men were scarce. But my memories of my court days with Salgestis and the children of court hangers-on and high officials were rife with examples of the sort of people who traded on their immunity from punishment. Truth be told, I much preferred the company of the children of other bards and those outside the circle of the court to the majority of the offspring of the high-born and high-climbing; like me, they'd had a bit of civilization thumped into their backsides and knew their privileges *were* privileges, not rights.

Giraud said, "Then what are you going to do?"

"Well, I was going to live here for a while. It's a long way from my real home, hard to find, and inconvenient to reach." He chuckled. "Which doesn't seem to be sufficient to keep complete strangers from falling through my doorway."

"It probably won't be much of a hindrance for Tok the Elder if he's determined to get to you," Giraud said.

"I've been coming to the same conclusion. And as for comfort, I think I'd be more comfortable someplace dry and warm and green and sunny—in other words, someplace far from here."

I could see the dwarf as our companion. He was someone who knew how to fight without weapons and who surely had some skill with weapons as well. He looked ferocious enough to frighten off at least some of the people—and non-people—who were hunting for us and who wanted to hurt us. He would be another set of eyes and ears and hands. He would surely have his own weapons—which made him somewhat better off than either Giraud or I were. And he had a pragmatic air about him that meshed well with my own views of the world.

Frankly, I liked him. I said, "So come with us. We could use a friend."

Ha laughed. "I'd say so. If the nantatsu doesn't get you, the Blackwarreners will."

"The Blackwarreners won't find us. You know your way through the mountains."

"I do. But I don't want to go through the mountains. Your nantatsu wasn't the only one, I guarantee you, and you aren't likely to find another one with a curse on it that keeps it from devouring you. Besides, I have someplace I'd like to go."

"You do?" I asked. He'd said that with a wistfulness that startled me. I suppose I'd never considered that a dwarf might be wistful about anything.

"I've always wanted to become a doctor—a nonmagical healer." He shrugged. "I have no talent for magic at all, but I've always had some skill with herbs and poultices, and I think I have the stomach for the work. I have little love for mining, even if it is what my father and his father before him did. Tradition is just another way of enslaving yourself to someone else's ideas, after all."

"And you have to go someplace to become a doctor?"

"I've heard there's a good school south of here, in Galarialle. I've always thought someday I'd find a way to leave here and go there—just to see, you know, if I could convince them to take me as a student."

"But we don't dare go back into Terosalle," Giraud said.

"You don't—not as yourselves. But you can be someone else easily enough. And quite honestly, neither of you is any major threat to anyone." He looked at Giraud. "The empress's men will give up their hunt for you in a few days and tell the empress you died in the mountains." He turned to me. "And you're not important to anyone. The whoremaster will lose a few coins, and your craftmaster and your fostermother will harbor a grudge against you for spoiling their plan . . . but while you might have once been the daughter of a High-Court bard, you're nothing but a runaway apprentice now."

Giraud and I looked at each other. I think both of us had seen ourselves as the subjects of unending hunts and our clever escapes as something that would cause enormous consternation. And the idea that people wouldn't care—that our absence would not set up a hue and cry from one end of Terosalle to the other, while in a way comforting, in another way stung quite a bit. I know I sat there feeling wounded, realizing that even to the three people from whom I'd escaped, my life meant nothing of any real importance.

"So what are you going to do?" Maydellan Ha asked.

And that was the problem. We didn't know what we were going to do. I got out the pack the nantatsu had given us, and opened it, and from it pulled the book. It felt heavier than it looked; I pitied Giraud, who'd been stuck carrying it up the side of the mountain. "I suppose we'll look through this and figure it out."

I started thumbing through the pages of the commonplace book. The first dozen or so entries were written in a crabbed, completely illegible hand.

The handwriting of the next half-dozen was round and smooth and flowing, and I still couldn't read it. I could figure out a word or two, but the spellings and some of the letter-forms were different than anything I had ever seen. It had been a long time since I'd done much reading, though. Maybe, I thought, I'd partly forgotten how.

The next handful of entries, in a third hand, remained utterly unintelligible to me, and I realized that no matter how familiar the writing looked, I couldn't read it. In frustration, I handed the book to Giraud. "I thought I knew how to read," I told him, humiliated by the admission, "but I've forgotten."

He glanced at the page to which the book was opened, then frowned. Then his expression cleared, however, and he began to chuckle. "You haven't forgotten how to read, Isbetta. This is bardic shortscript. A lot of the bardic documents are written in it. They can write it faster than regular script, and it hasn't changed over the past few hundred years, even though regular writing has. Here . . ." He looked down at the page he was studying and ran a finger along the first line, then the second. " . . . This one says, 'A Spell for Becoming Inconspicuous, to the tune of the chorus for "Fat Lady's Stroll" or other Three-Beat Dance:

> 'Here I'll be
> Now you'll see
> No one important
> No one who
> Makes you think
> You ought to stay
> Here I'll be
> Don't see me
> I'm not important
> You can just
> Turn back, just
> Walk on away.' "

He smiled a little. "The bard who's writing this says it came in very handy one night when the patrons at a tavern got too rowdy. He substituted it for the regular chorus of 'Fat Lady's Stroll' and walked out before they realized he was gone."

I laughed. "It doesn't seem like it could do anything. It's ugly verse—no imagery, no grace, just that lumping three-beat canter." I started singing it, imagining as I did the bard and his tavern full of unruly customers . . . and both Giraud and Maydellan Ha turned away from me. They started talking to each other, completely ignoring me. I thought they would laugh, but neither of them even smiled. I said, "Well, I thought it was funny. I'm sorry you didn't."

Giraud started reading another of the verses to Ha, and I got angry. "If you didn't like the song, that's no need to be rude."

They still didn't pay me any attention. Furious now, I punched Giraud in the arm. "Jackass," I said.

I wasn't prepared for his reaction. He jerked around and jumped and yelped, pulling back from me. Ha suddenly stared at me, too, and his mouth dropped open. "Where were you?" he asked.

I realized then they were making fun of me. "Very funny." I crossed my arms over my chest and glared. "Pretending you didn't know I was here—I get it now. You aren't as funny as you think you are."

Giraud didn't crack a smile. Neither did the dwarf. Instead, they both sat staring at me like I'd grown two heads and wings.

"You aren't going to pretend you forgot I was here," I said.

Giraud said, "Who's pretending? How did you get here without me seeing you, and where did you go?"

I looked from him to Ha. "You're playing a game with me."

The dwarf shook his head slowly.

"You honestly didn't know I was here."

Both of them said no.

"That stupid spell actually works?"

"It works when you use it," Giraud said after a pause. "I told you I thought you could be a bard."

"A bard-to-be in our midst!" Maydellan Ha grinned. "Ho, young bardling," he said in a silly voice, "enchant some young women for me, so that they'll love me."

"Some," I said, smiling slightly. "Not one, but some. Aren't you the greedy one?" I made light of the moment as Ha was doing, not because I thought what had happened was funny, but because I was uneasy with the little piece of a miracle I'd wrought. I wasn't sure how I'd done it, or why the stupid spell had worked; I'd always thought intent was a huge part of the process of bardic magic. What was more, from everything my father had told me, I had always believed a bard needed his lute, or his harp or his darumbie in order to create resonances. Wasn't that what Da had said? That a bard's voice and his instrument created resonances? And if that were the case, then why had the stupid spell done anything? What other than my voice created those resonances?

Giraud had begun to eagerly flip through the pages, studying the writings he found.

"Listen to this, Izza—a spell for the compelling of truth, and one for calling rain . . . well, I guess we don't need that one. Pity there isn't one for sending away the rain . . . and . . . oh, this is marvelous. Some of the bards' regular writings get out from time to time, you know—their histories and their records of travels and such—but I don't know that anyone has ever found one of their spell records. And there are diary entries in here, too. This is fascinating."

Maydellan Ha said, "The bards guard the secrets of their magic carefully. I'm surprised this book got out."

"It didn't get out, exactly," I said. "The bard who was carrying it got eaten."

Giraud interrupted. "Your father's name was Haral, wasn't it?"

"Haral dar Danria."

Giraud frowned and read. "Have you ever heard the name Tanil?"

"No."

"How about Black Heron?"

I nodded, remembering Birdie and Aymar and Marda talking about how they'd tricked the Black Heron. I hadn't mentioned the name to Giraud before, but . . . "Yes," I said. "I've heard of the Black

Heron. Birdie said she sent word to him that she'd killed me. Evidently he wanted me dead."

"He wanted a lot more than that." Giraud glanced at Maydellan Ha. "You want to hear this?"

"Certainly."

Giraud began to read.

Chapter Six

7 Brightsmonth. The Black Heron sent the message to the court of Salgestis today—Giraud read—informing the king that the Watchowl Keep bards uncovered a plot against his life centered in Blackwarren. He told the king the bardmaster requested the presence of Haral dar Danria in the investigation. I'll accompany Bard Haral when he travels to Blackwarren, where we have allies. Haral will trust me—we were friends in school. Heron's allies will take him off my hands when we arrive, and Heron will replace Haral as the king's chief bard.

He should be in place by the time I reach Hearthold Mountain for the second phase of our work; I'll make sure the news of Haral's tragic death reaches the king's ears promptly.

18 Brightsmonth. Haral dar Danria arrived at the Keep today, with his young daughter in tow. Asked why she hadn't been left with her aunt back at the court. Haral said he'd done a farseeing spell, and the child's presence was the determining factor in the success or failure of his mission. As if he had a mission, but he can't know that. We've shielded against farseeing. He cannot possibly suspect.

Don't relish the idea of killing the girl, but the Heron says when the time comes, I must.

20 Brightsmonth. Two days of hard riding brought us to Blackwarren. We're to meet with the local bard, who knows nothing, then with the local lord. I've arranged us rooms with a merchant who is willing to help me make Haral and his daughter disappear, and who says he'll be able to eliminate any curiosity about their whereabouts. That's the good news. The bad news is that Haral is far too suspicious, and far too clever. I've taken to hiding this spellbook. I can't let him discover what it contains.

23 Brightsmonth. Haral has managed to question most of the people in this sorry excuse for a town. Of course he's found no evidence of a plot of regicide. Further, I know he suspects me of something. I catch him watching me, and when I do, he smiles. No matter. Tonight he dies.

Giraud paused and glanced over at me. "This next entry was written by your father, just under that last statement."

My apologies, Tanil, for not dying so easily. But I've discovered that there truly is a plot to destroy the king. I'm sure he'll find your notes and spells most interesting. I'll see you at court— you and your Black Heron.

Haral dar Danria

"Then it goes back to Tanil's handwriting again."

23 Brightsmonth—evening. He's taken my notes and his daughter and fled Blackwarren. If I cannot catch him before he reaches the king, I have lost everything. Aymar is loaning me his men, and they'll be ready to leave within minutes.

24 Brightsmonth. He's dead. The girl wasn't with him, nor the papers. Now the search begins.

26 Brightsmonth. He stashed his daughter with a poor peat-bogger in Blackwarren, and gave the child the papers he stole from me, along with a his notes and several spells of his own, and few personal effects. Don't know what he thought hiding the girl would accomplish. We have everything now.

The women is an ignorant peasant, and greedy. I've paid her to keep the girl and lie about where she got her if anyone asks. The Heron wouldn't like this if he knew, but the child is utterly unremarkable, and I see no need to kill her. Can do what's best for Terosalle without resorting to murdering children. Unlike her father, she had no part in this.

Maydellan Ha said, "They're always doing what's best for their country." He shook his head and studied me. "How are you taking all of this?"

I wasn't sure, to be honest. I found myself listening to this tale of a plot to murder my father and to overthrow a king and wondered why the conspirators thought they needed to do that. What had my father done to them? I wanted to hurt Tanil—but he was already dead—and find the mysterious Black Heron, but how could I ever hope to do that? Still, I wasn't filled with despair, as both Giraud and Ha might have thought. Instead, I had to wonder. My mother had left my father when I was quite young. But surely she'd had some connection to him still. She must have taken some interest in my welfare. Why hadn't she come looking for me?

Thinking about it further, that seemed plain enough. If she'd heard anything, she'd probably been told I was dead. Except how could she have been? Did she know the Black Heron? More importantly, was she still alive? Could I find her? I'd lost much, but sitting there listening to the dead Tanil's tale of treachery, I found my reaction to be mostly one of hope.

"Keep reading," I said. "I want to know what else is in there."

Giraud shrugged. "There isn't much. There's another entry that says he's on his way to the Hearthold Mountain to 'sing the crystal.' I don't know what that means."

"I do," Ha interrupted. "But go on."

Giraud flipped the page. "Then there's an entry about being captured by the nantatsu, and holding it off for a while, and thinking he can bargain his way out, and about a spell he's prepared just in case his plan doesn't work."

"Which it didn't," I said.

"Right. And a final remark. *He who gains the last look into the future cannot help but win the game.* Then there are some loose pages. They look like the pages that I noticed had been cut out earlier. One is titled 'Black Heron's Curse.' The other is 'Changewind Song.' They're palimpsests. I can't tell what was written underneath either of them, but they're both in a different hand than the rest of this."

I looked at the book. I felt strangely disappointed. "Is that all?" I asked. There should have been, my gut told me, something more.

"Yes." Giraud lifted the book by its wooden covers and gave it a good shake. "See?"

A piece of pale paper slipped out from between two pages and floated to the cave floor like a leaf in autumn. Giraud frowned and reached for it, but my hand got there first.

"That wasn't in there," he said, but of course it had been. He simply hadn't seen it.

I unfolded the paper and discovered that I still remembered how to read after all.

> *My beloved Ceebie,*
> *If you are reading this then I am dead and your world's future is uncertain. I've sought out and studied those omens that I could find, and know that any hope of salvation it might have lies in your hands.*
> *Dearest daughter, you must travel to Heart hold Mountain and sing the Changewind Song at the Pillar of the Sun. When you do this, the Black Heron's darkness will lift and your world will be set right.*
> *Always remember that I loved you.*
>
> *Tatta*

Ceebie and Tatta. I remembered calling him that. Remembered sitting in a huge chair beside him and talking to him, asking him a thousand questions, and having him pretend to steal away my nose and tell me, "Ceebie, if questions were gold we'd be rich as kings." I remembered riding on a horse beside him, in the company of a laughing, pale-haired young man, on our way to an adventure.

Suddenly I realized the pale-haired young man had probably been Tanil, and the adventure had been the trip to Blackwarren and Tanil's betrayal and subsequent murder of my father. All that had been so long ago, and I had forgotten so much. So very much. My Tatta. A lump rose in my throat, and my cheeks burned. Blinking back hot tears, tasting their salt, I

handed the note to Giraud and said, "From my
father." The words came out in a croak.

He read the note, then took my hand and squeezed
it. "I'm sorry, Izza. Really sorry."

"Me, too."

The dwarf was reading the note by that time. He
sighed. "I can take you to the Pillar of the Sun first
thing in the morning. Don't expect any sun—the
weather at the top of the mountain is hellish. But the
pillar is still there, and you can sing at it."

I nodded, saying nothing.

"I'll work out the song for you," Giraud said. "It's
short, but there are a lot of technical remarks below
it that you'll need to keep in mind." He rummaged
through the wood-bound book until he came to the
pages he'd called palimpsests. He took out one and
said, "Here. 'Changewind Song.' The bard who wrote
out the spell is specific—it's to be sung by a solo
bard."

"I'm not a bard. I'm a weaver. *Apprentice* weaver."

"Solo singer," Giraud said, talking over my queru-
lous mutterings. "The singer is to have a clear mind
. . . or an empty mind. I'm not entirely sure of the
meaning of the phrase. It's a technical term. *Manta-
claria*." He paused, looked from me to Ha, and when
neither of us said anything, shrugged and said, "We'll
do the best we can and hope we get it right. You can
have accompanists, though—the writer recommends
bagpipes for their . . . hmmm . . . looks like 'thought-
clearing nature' to me, but again, he's using words
and constructions I don't know all that well. He uses
a lot of bardic terms. 'Rote-airy' and 'belling' and
'sostrenadio' and 'teppio.' Those aren't words that
show up in the history texts, so I don't know what
a lot of this means."

"Well, bagpipes," the dwarf said, "I don't know if
they clear your thoughts so much as they trample
them flat and jump up and down on them, but maybe

that was the effect he was looking for. I can't begin to guess at the rest."

Giraud forced a smile. "We'll hope that these things are merely augmentary and not essential."

I leaned toward Ha and said, "You don't play pipes by any chance, do you?"

"I sing no music, play no instruments, and consider the bagpipes an abomination created by madmen to further their madness." All of that he said with a scowl, but he softened the scowl with a wink. "I like music, though. Ballads, mostly. And love songs—like 'I to Dalliance Never Fall.' You have a pretty voice. Do you know that one?" His grin was conspiratorial. "Could you sing it for me? I've never had a pretty girl sing a love song for me."

He was trying to cheer me up. I wanted to be cheered. So I nodded. "I remember it." Everyone knows that one, of course. It's like asking a singer if she knows 'Sweet Robin of Spring.' If she isn't dead, she knows it. But since I lost my parents, no one but Giraud had asked me to sing, and I found myself overcome with such shyness that I almost forgot the words.

I sang:

"I to dalliance never fall,
    And never to another flee,
    You hold my love in your strong hand,
    And so hold all the best of me.
        And as you hold me I hold you;
        I look for promise in your eyes,
        So swear to me you will be true,
        And love me till the day you die."

They were both listening, both smiling as I sang. I'd planned to sing only the first verse and the chorus, but, honestly, I loved the way my voice echoed and rang in the tunnels of the mountain, and if the two of them were so pleased by my singing and so willing to listen, I thought I'd at least do the next two verses.

> "I who wander far and near
>   And, weary, travel hard and long
>   Yearn for your love when I am here
>   And wait to hear your answering song."

"My answering song," Giraud sang in his pleasant baritone.

"My answering song," Maydellan Ha sang in a rich, if raspy, bass.

> "And as you hold me I hold you;
>   I look for promise in your eyes,
>   So swear to me you will be true,
>   And love me till the day you die.
>   If into sorrow's clinging hand
>   Or to misfortune's grip we fall,
>   Beside you I will take my stand
>   If you just love me above all."

"Love you above all," Giraud and Ha sang.

> "And as you hold me I hold you;
>   I look for promise in your eyes,
>   So swear to me you will be true,
>   And love me till the day you die."

I held the last notes, closing my eyes and listening to the shivery echoes of my own voice that rang through the tunnels and bounced back to me. I opened them to find Giraud on one knee, facing me, and beside him Maydellan Ha with his hands pressed to his heart and his head lifted.

"I swear I will be true and love you till the day I die," Giraud said, and half a beat behind him,

Maydellan Ha repeated his exact words in his exact tone of voice.

They were both staring at me, the expressions on their faces identical—both lovestruck and somehow fierce.

Only for the briefest of instants did I think that they might have been trying to play a joke on me. That thought died as quickly as it occurred. Their eyes held no faintest hint of humor, their mouths no slightest curve of smile. They both believed that they loved me.

Somehow, with nothing but the words of a stupid old love song and the sound of my voice, I had enchanted them.

Chapter Seven

I rested poorly that night, kept tossing in wild, nightmare-riddled sleep by fear of the nantatsu that waited somewhere below for us to finish our task, and by worse fear of the accidental magic I had unleashed, and by worry for my friend Giraud and my new associate Ha, whose feelings I had accidentally altered. I knew from my father's discussions of magic that simple bardic spells usually worked only a short time before they wore off. I hoped that this one, performed accidentally and without intent, would be gone by morning.

At least, I thought, I know I can do magic. For what that's worth.

But when the sky outside Ha's tunnel went from black to gray and the first light of morning made the miserable pouring rain a visible source of gloom instead of just an audible one, nothing had improved. Ha greeted me with a wistful smile and breakfast, Giraud kissed my hand and offered to do anything I needed.

I asked him if he would please not be in love with me, and his eyes filled with tears, and he told me that he couldn't do that. I wanted to thump him on the head and tell him to get over it, but of course I couldn't. The way he felt wasn't his fault.

So we ate breakfast and I had Giraud write the words of the 'Changewind Song' into the book in a form I could read. I practiced them in my head, and because I didn't know the tune the dead bard had suggested, I came up with one that I could put to the words. Da said the specific tune didn't matter to a spell as much as the intent behind it and the fact that you could sing it clearly, without squeaking on any of the notes.

I *didn't* try singing the spell out loud in Ha's tunnel. The bard had been specific—the spell had to be sung from the Pillar of the Sun, which was near the top of Hearthold Mountain. Nowhere else would it do what it was supposed to do.

And so we came to the dilemma that worried me most of all. What exactly *was* it supposed to do? The writer of the spell, whoever he had been, noted that it was to bring peace and joy and harmony to everyone it touched. He said he'd created it to repair the wrongs in the world.

To me, that seemed vague, and the words of the song struck me as equally vague. The bard undoubtedly thought they were clear enough, but a refrain of, "Whirl wind and clear want, banish sorrow and need. Silver fountains of laughter where once there flowed tears," while a pretty sentiment, didn't give me much idea of what I was supposed to look for when I sang the stupid song.

The bright point of my morning, and it was a small one, came when I found out that we didn't have to climb any further up the outside of the mountain. Maydellan Ha said his tunnel connected to another, and that tunnel led, with some winding and twisting, up the inside of the mountain to the summit near the Pillar of the Sun. He said that aside from the singing of the "Changewind Song," I need not deal with the wind or the slashing rain or the thunder and lightning that still pounded the mountainside. He brushed a kiss on the back of my hand and bowed when he said it, and I cringed.

Ha packed those of his belongings that he wished to keep. "I won't be coming back here," he said. "So I want to be sure I don't leave behind something I might need."

When he told us he was ready, he carried little more than we did. Each of us took as much of the food from his larder as we could; for the first time, the pack Giraud had given me weighed something, and it was a good, reassuring sort of weight. Other than food, Ha carried a bedroll, a shortsword, clothes and a single, small book.

He perched his spectacles on his battered nose, took his lantern in hand, and led off.

We followed him for half a day, and we were footsore and weary when we finally reached our destination.

"All you have to do now is sing it," Ha said, pointing out of a carved cave mouth into fog, "and then we can get on our way to wherever we choose to go. Anywhere, my beloved."

I nodded. I stared out. Clouds swirled across a flat-floored bowl, alternately obscuring and revealing a single crystal pillar that soared upward higher than ten tall men standing one atop the other. Six-sided and colorless, the pillar's sides were unblemished by any touch of decoration. I wondered if someone had found a way to drag it all the way up the mountain, or if someone, digging into the summit in search of gold or precious stones, had discovered it and dug the bowl out around it.

Ha answered the question before I could ask. "As far as any of us can tell, it goes all the way from here to the center of the earth. No one has been able to find a place where it isn't, though after a while my people gave up trying."

"Why?"

"It protects itself. It just sits there doing nothing, but if you try to tap out a chunk of it with a chisel, you die. At least that's the story, and I don't know of anyone in my lifetime who's tried to challenge it."

I looked at the crystal pillar. I would like to say that I felt something magical about it, or that it stirred in recognition as I approached, or that I could somehow sense its importance or recognize its purpose. The fact, though, is that it looked like a big, plain piece of clear rock, and it felt like one, and it had about as much to say to me as any other chunk of rock I've ever found.

I tried to cheer myself. I said, "At least it isn't raining anymore," but that was too small a comfort for the situation I faced. I was scared. Scared to walk out there by myself, scared to sing the song alone, scared of what would happen. Everything would have been easier had I not accidentally cast a spell over Giraud and Ha that lingered even then; if I'd never known I could cast songspells, I wouldn't have been afraid of doing it. Those who say ignorance is bliss are right more often than most of us are willing to admit.

Scared, scared. So I handed Giraud my wooden flute and said, "Play along with me."

"I don't know the tune you'll sing," he said, not unreasonably, but I didn't care at all about reason.

"Match pitch with me and follow along. What you sound like doesn't matter—I just want you to be out there with me. I'm scared to do this alone."

And I dragged Maydellan Ha into the dreary, drizzling, shifting mist, too, and shoved the bard's commonplace book into his hands, and told him, "Here, drum on the cover of this book to keep time."

And the spell that made them both love me to the point of ridiculous infatuation still held, for neither of them argued. I prepared myself to sing. I thought perhaps I ought to touch the pillar while I did it, but the stone, cold and wet and unwelcoming, changed my mind quickly enough. I stood at the base of it, though, facing east, which is the direction of new beginnings. Giraud stood a third of the way around the pillar, to my right, Maydellan Ha a third of the way around to my left. As I looked at them I could see parts of each of them refracted in the crystal, warped and partly hazed by imperfections and occlusions within the heart of the stone.

The fog that skirled and writhed around us muffled echoes, but the steep walls of the basin amplified sound. The result was eerie. When I spoke to Giraud, telling him to start with a few notes from "Merry Make" to give me my pitch, my voice sounded flat but very loud. I hummed the opening bars of the old song and felt the vibrations of that soft humming clear to the soles of my feet.

I closed my eyes. With them closed, I could see the words that Giraud had written out for me. I knew the song—knew all of it, and knew how I would sing it. And I knew, as well, that I *shouldn't*. That gut feeling again.

The omens that had brought me to the hold of Hearthold Mountain, the coincidences and the bits of old magic, all felt like the hand of my goddess telling me that she wanted me to be where I was. Neithas had to have a hand in what I was doing, or else I would never have survived to be there doing it. My father's note told me that I was to sing the song if ever the world were to become as it should be. I knew that I was special, or else the dead bard's spell would not have allowed me to take the book from the nantatsu. I *had* to do what I was doing, too, because if I didn't the nantatsu would find me and kill me. So many signs, so many omens that said, "Sing, girl."

And counter to every argument my mind could muster, my gut said, "This is wrong. You'll live to regret this."

And my unruly brain, the part of me that has caused me *so* much trouble in my life, said, "I certainly am, because living to regret it is better than dying today."

Giraud did the introduction to "Merry Make" again, looking impatiently at me as he did, and Maydellan Ha drummed on the book with his fingertips. The reedy, thin wail of the recorder joined the whispery, leathery sound of the drumming. The music fit the gray, cold midafternoon—thin and ephemeral, it was the sort of music to which ghosts would dance; it was somehow both joyful and ominous.

I closed my eyes and began to sing.

> "Sing the wind down,
> Sing the sun gold.
> Sing the sky blue,
> The day hot, the air cold,
> Sing the people to joy,
> Sing abundance and life,
> Banish toil, banish pain,
> Banish care, banish strife
>
> >   Whirl wind and clear want,
> >   Banish sorrow and need.
> >   Silver fountains of laughter
> >   Where once there flowed tears.
> >   Change wind and change day
> >   Change sea and change sky
> >   World sings now with laughter
> >   And never with fears."

The refrain ended on an open note, so I went back

to the first verse and sang it again. My voice rang, and the wooden recorder played a bright, quick-tempoed counterpoint, and the makeshift drum pattered merrily.

As I sang, I realized that the fog was lifting, and then the sun suddenly burst through and I discovered why the Pillar of the Sun bore its name. It seemed to catch fire; it glowed and sparkled and scattered its captured light back out in rainbows that lit the bowl in which we stood and made all of us look like spirits who had just stepped through from a better world.

I kept singing because the spellsong called to me, and as I sang, I thought of a world without work, without pain, without any sorrow, without any need, and I thought of how wonderful that world would be. Then I thought of Birdie, and Marda, and Aymar and Tassien, and the empress who'd had Giraud's family killed, and the nantatsu who had killed so many people, and the villagers of Blackwarren who had hunted Giraud and me.

I could not wish them joy. I wished them the opposite, and heard the tone of my voice change as I sang. But I kept singing. No matter, no matter, I thought, because my heart filled with the joy of the song, with the glory of the sunlight, with the magic I made while I stood there. I wished all the world happiness except for the people who were evil, and to them I wished that the evil that they'd sown would race back to them threefold and devour them.

No matter what I wished. The song I sang spelled out only goodness. Only joy. No sorrow, no fears, no pain, no regrets.

A whirlwind dropped into the basin where we stood. It screamed down out of the cloudless sky and swirled around the bowl in which the three of us stood and played.

Call down the wind, I heard myself sing, and

realized this was the maelstrom I had summoned—
this whirlwind; magical Changewind; howling twisting glittering banshee that shouted me down as I sang.
I felt my control of the spell I'd woven, such as it
ever might have been, weakening. The whirlwind that
I'd summoned didn't listen to the sound of my voice,
didn't ride on the notes of my song. It moved in
toward us, beautiful beyond description but somehow
threatening. I sang louder, Giraud blew harder, Ha
drummed faster. None of us could hear what the
other one did. I began to understand why the cre-
ator of this spell had wanted bagpipes to back him
up—nothing softer or more delicate than the mur-
dered-cat howling of bagpipes could cut through the
raging chorus of the wind's many voices.

Louder I sang, and louder yet. I leaned against the
pillar and screamed the words of the song at it . . .
and the racing winds kept back from the three of us,
though only by the width of a finger. This was magic,
and I knew nothing of magic, nothing of control or
finesse, and I could think of nothing but brute force
to keep the spell from devouring us.

The racing winds knotted tighter and faster, and
the light from the Pillar of the Sun streamed into the
newborn tornado and illuminated it, and the twister
began to glitter as if it carried the jewels of all the
fiefdoms and kingdoms and princedoms of the world
in its raging heart. I felt the pull of the spiraling
winds, but resisted being sucked out and up. Giraud
and Ha both moved against the pillar. All of us stared
at each other, and I could see my fear mirrored in
their eyes. We did not dare stop, though sweat beaded
on Giraud's brow, and Ha's tanned face had turned
as white as bleached linen, and my throat felt raw
as a flayed carcass. If we stopped the spell might stop
. . . or it might simply devour us before it went on
its way.

Any joy I had felt at the beginning of the song was

gone, transformed into exhaustion and fear. Beneath
my hands, the Pillar of the Sun darkened, seeming
to match my mood. The wind grew louder, the shimmering spiral around us grew taller, and I could only
think that if it didn't do whatever it was going to do
soon, I would collapse.

As I thought that, the single giant whirlwind
spawned, shattering into a thousand lesser whirlwinds
that spun out from the center like shards of a shattered gemstone exploding across the land. And everything they touched, they changed. The barren stone
of the basin seemed to melt beneath the hungry
mouths of those glittering, howling wind-devils; its
steep walls transformed into gentle curves and those
curves sprouted thick emerald grass and carpets of
flowers. A brook began babbling somewhere nearby.
The Changewinds raced away from Giraud and Ha
and the pillar and me.

In the sudden silence that followed, I became
gradually aware that I was still singing. I realized, too,
that I had no idea how many times I'd repeated the
same verse and the same chorus. My throat burned
and my mouth felt dry as emery paper, my back ached
and my legs throbbed.

> "Change wind and change day
> Change sea and change sky
> World sings now with laughter
> And never with fears."

I sang those last words on a descending note, and
that last time, closed the chorus so that it didn't invite
me to leap to the verse again. Giraud dropped the
recorder from fingers that looked as stiff as wood. Ha
groaned and sat with a thump on the soft grass.

I shook my head, and tried to speak, and my voice
came out as a croak. "Look at the sun," I whispered.
It was about to set. I wondered how long we had

stood there. How long had the Changewind blown around us? How long had the magic held us in its thrall?

The Pillar of the Sun glowed blue and deep and beautiful as spring hyacinths, reflecting not just the sun in the west but the sky in the east that already wore its robes of royal purple. The scene reached into me and shocked me with its perfect beauty, but suddenly I wanted nothing more than to be away from Hearthold Mountain and the Pillar of the Sun. I wanted to be on my way somewhere, anywhere.

Maydellan Ha crouched over a map he'd scratched in the dirt with a stick. "If we head due south and keep to our course, sooner or later we'll cross Stone-break Pass. From there we can head west to Anatta, and from Anatta go south to the Burrinee River." He sketched in a couple of tiny squares along the snaky line of the river. "Here and here are dockhouses where we can buy passage downstream. The river will take all of us to the Bards' Keep."

"I thought you wanted to go to Galarialle," I said. "To study to be a doctor."

Ha looked surprised. "I can't leave you, my love. And you are obviously meant to be a bard," he said, and swung his arm in an arc that encompassed the rolling hills that had once been jagged, sere mountains; the waterfalls and tiny lakes and fields upon fields of wildflowers; the edges of beautiful forests where nothing had grown before. "Look at what you've done." He smiled at me with that gushy, lovestruck smile I'd hoped I would never see again.

And I thought, Right. Look at what I've done.

Neither he nor Giraud showed any signs of shaking off the love spell I'd accidentally cast on them. Neither of them seemed in the least bit jealous of each other, for which I was infinitely grateful—but they both remained devoted to me. If I had any idea how to do it, I would have tried to break the spell, but I wasn't a bard. I knew only enough about bardic magic to know that if I tinkered with the spell I'd created, I might make it worse as easily as I might make it better. As the situation stood, neither of them suffered anything for being in love with me. When we reached Watchowl Keep, I'd have a real bard unspell them—if the love spell didn't wear off first.

Meantime, we had more important worries.

"Do you think we ought to be traveling in the dark?" Giraud asked Ha.

The dwarf shrugged. "You're the one with a nantatsu who threatened to come after you if the spell didn't work to its satisfaction. If you think all of this was what it hoped for, then we don't have much to worry us. If it was expecting something else, though, we should try to put some distance between us and the places where it's likely to start looking."

Giraud looked to me. "Beautiful Isbetta, we're going to have to travel tonight. I wish we could rest, but I don't want anything to happen to you—"

I'd had enough of that nonsense. I said, "Giraud, shut up. You don't love me. We're friends. Remember that? Friends. You carry Adalane dar Penalda's favor, and you're in love with her."

Confusion flickered across his face, and for a moment I thought I was getting through to him. Then he said, "Adalane . . . I'm going to have to give that back to Adalane."

"Not *now*."

He leaned close to me and pressed his cheek to mine. He murmured in my ear, "You fixed everything, beloved. We can go back to Blackwarren now. I can give her back her token—"

"You *brought* it?" I yelped. I remembered the circumstances under which we'd escaped Blackwarren, and wondered at the impulse that would make him hunt around in the darkness of his room for a small sapphire ring tied with a silk scarf rather than using that time to get us some food.

"Of course I brought it. I love . . . *loved* her. And I promised her my undying affection. . . ." He looked at me, and he looked very much like a fawn caught between hunters and the cliff.

"You did," I agreed. "You promised her your undying affection."

"But I love you."

"You don't."

"We have to go back to Blackwarren. Honor demands that I make this right . . . that I make her understand."

"We can't go back to Blackwarren." I looked to Maydellan Ha for support, but he frowned at me—the slightest of frowns—and said, "I'm afraid I must agree with Giraud. He cannot leave this girl Adalane thinking that he loves her when he loves you instead. That would be . . . cruel."

I stared from one to the other.

"We *can't* go back to Blackwarren."

"You might stay here," Giraud said. "After I've returned Adalane's favor, we'll come back for you."

Ha smiled. "Of course. You can sleep in my tunnel. I'm sure it will be much nicer now. More suitable for you, my beloved."

I looked from him to Giraud, and back to him. I gritted my teeth and said, "I'll go to Blackwarren with you, thanks."

We walked through darkness, heading back to the northwest, guiding ourselves by the Faithful Star since nothing else remained as it was. The thunder of distant waterfalls serenaded us as we forded uncounted rushing streams; the songs of night birds accompanied us as we moved through meadows waist-high with richly scented night-blooming flowers. The stars above us seemed brighter than I had ever seen them.

They cast shadows that left us not entirely in darkness, but what we saw could never have helped us find our way.

My spell had reshaped the earth. No mountains remained around us; instead, we crossed rolling hills that spread away from us in all directions.

Maydellan Ha said, "We should have passed Kai."

"Kai?"

"The mining city for the mountains around Hearthold. The city your nantatsu was no doubt eager to avoid. We've been heading in the right direction— it should have been off to our right."

I looked to my right and saw nothing but the darkness, and the blacker outlines of the hills against the starry sky. Nothing that seemed to be a city. "Would we see lights?"

"Kai never slept." Ha frowned. "Perhaps we should, though. Perhaps we should camp here, and when we wake check to see if Kai still exists."

We hadn't done anything that would kill people, I thought. Certainly nothing that would destroy cities, or hurt anyone.

While we set up our meager camp, I kept telling myself that, and telling myself, that we would find, come morning, that we'd been walking in the wrong direction, and that the city of Kai was still where it was supposed to be . . . changed, of course, since the mountains were gone, and any mining the dwarves did would perforce have to be of a different sort. But still there.

Giraud said little. Ha said less. And I . . . well, even though I was exhausted from our walking, and our spellcasting, and from the fear that hadn't left me since I discovered Birdie intended to sell me to a whoremaster, I said nothing at all, and when the time came to sleep, slept poorly, and what sleep I got was infested with dreams of whirlwinds that touched and changed, leaving nothing recognizable in their wake.

Chapter Eight

A cold, wet something shoved against my cheek
I opened my eyes to bright daylight and waist-high
field grasses and wildflowers and something silhou-
etted just above my face. Large, mobile ears, long
slender neck, big, blunt nose . . .

A doe.

I sat up and the doe took a single step back, studying me with curiosity but without apparent fear. She
didn't look unusual, other than that I was seeing her
from such a short distance. She seemed healthy
enough—plump and glossy, with bright eyes—and I
knew for a fact that her nose was both cold and wet.

"Giraud," I said. Croaked, rather. My voice still
hadn't recovered. "Look at this."

Giraud groaned. I couldn't see him; the tall grasses
hid him from me as effectively as we'd hoped they
would hid us from anyone who might be hunting for
us. But I could hear him just off to my right, rustling and turning over.

The doe's ear twitched toward him, but she didn't
spring away from us, as I would have expected her to
do. She didn't flick her tail in the air, or shudder, or

roll her eyes with fear. All of these responses I would have expected, but instead she simply glanced calmly toward Giraud when he sat up, then returned her attention to me.

I thought I had never seen anything so beautiful. Her color, a warm honey-brown, darkened to black at her knees, her muzzle, and the tips of her ears. Her belly and throat were a pale, creamy almost-white. Her eyes, warm brown rimmed in kohl, with thick eyelashes and a sweet, trusting expression, seemed to me the very definition of gentleness.

She snorted softly, a sort of whuffling sound, and glanced behind me, and when I turned to see what she was looking at, I discovered that two other deer moved toward us from right behind me, while one came toward us from my far right.

"Hey, pretty girl," I said, and her ears pricked forward. The other deer moved in, stepping silently through the tall grass, moving slowly as if they didn't want to startle us.

I heard Giraud say, "Ha, you *have* to see this," as I rose and reached out to touch the doe.

Her lips curled back in a snarl and her mouth stretched back, and I saw, not the blunt bottom teeth of an herbivore, but well-developed, dagger-sharp upper and lower canines and a jaw far heavier and stronger than any plant-eater should have. I screamed at her and fumbled for my dagger, and as I did, the other deer all attacked.

I pulled my dagger and jumped to my feet, and the doe that had been nuzzling at me raised up on her hind legs and slashed out with her forefeet. Fire ripped through my left shoulder and blood welled from the cut. Giraud and Ha made it to their feet, fending off the deer that attacked them.

My mind refused to accept what I was seeing. I fought, flinging my cloak over the face of the doe; then hacking at her throat when the folds of cloth blinded her. She slashed me and tried to bite me, but my cloak ruined her aim and eventually tangled around her front legs. When she tumbled forward, I grabbed her head and fought it upward, and slashed through her throat with my knife. Behind me, Giraud brought the animal he'd caught to the ground. Ha, armed with his sword and a fighter's reflexes, had dispatched the other two. We stood in the center of the downed deer, all three of us soaked in blood and breathing hard.

I found myself wanting to weep. This horror that had happened to the deer wasn't right—it wasn't right at all. I hadn't done anything that might turn deer into meat-eaters. I'd always liked them, I'd always thought of them as gentle, peaceful creatures. That they had attacked us, that they had tried to kill us—that they would have eaten us if they had been successful—these facts left me miserable and hopeless. I felt betrayed. Lost. And very, very frightened.

Maydellan Ha said, "If they had been any more experienced at being the hunters instead of the hunted, they would have killed all three of us before we knew they were even dangerous."

I looked at the dead animals and shivered. "What happened to them?"

Ha raised an eyebrow and studied me. "Something about your spell went amiss, I expect." He wiped his bloody hands on his pants, then cleaned the blade of his sword on the grass. "I hope the spell only went awry in its effect on the deer."

We packed our few belongings in silence and followed Ha's lead toward the place where he felt certain Kai should be.

We came across a lovely road after a while; it was paved all in wide, flat, carefully-shaped stones and bordered on both sides by morningmary and summer jonquil and giant freesia and lavender, and the scent that brushed against us as we walked was surely the scent of the Summerland.

My ears were keenest. I picked out the sounds of ela-lute and danceharp before either of the others.

"Music," I said, and began to run forward.

"Wait." Ha grabbed my sleeve and pulled me back. "We'll get off the road and go on that way. Among my people, this isn't the time for music."

"It's *music*," I said, unable to see where anything could be wrong with those cheerful sounds.

"They were *deer*," he reminded me. "What's sweet on the outside isn't always so on the inside."

And how could I argue with that? I had a hard time, though, imagining how the joyful music I heard could presage anything but goodness.

We moved off the lovely paved road and into a grove to our right that looked like a park. Its old chestnut trees spread outward and upward, their graceful boughs sweeping near the ground, reaching just far enough to touch the next tree in each direction. No dead leaves lay on the ground; instead, short green grass that looked like it had been cut to a regular height covered the ground like an enormous Liedan carpet.

Ha said, "The dwarves had no places of this sort. No nut groves, no parks, no glades for dancing and playing music—we had alehalls and tunneled homes and mines and guilds and shops within the mountains."

Giraud said, "The dwarves I met didn't seem like the sort who would do much playing."

"We played, all right. Wrestling and quarterstaff fights and knife throwing and rope-walking—common entertainments for men. Not dancing around in a circle to harp music."

We moved forward, always keeping the road to our left. The music became louder and eventually we found its source. Two dwarvish women sat on elaborately carved stools, their skirts swept up and their faces twisted in some bizarre parody of pleasure. One played the ela-lute, the fingers of her left hand flying across the broad fretboard while her right hand plucked, its movements a blur. The other attacked the harp with a frenzy that would have stood the three of us in good stead when we fought of the deadly deer.

All around them, the dwarves danced, though watching, I could not think of what they did as truly dancing. None laughed or chatted or called out to each other as dancers did in the faire dances I'd attended. They spun and leapt and stamped in utter silence, sometimes crashing into each other as if they hadn't seen each other, sometimes falling to the ground. At the periphery of the rough circle in which they cavorted, two men ran into each other, and without missing the steps of their dances, drew shortswords and began to fight; their swords flashed and their feet stamped, and for an instant I thought the fighting was in jest, or perhaps some sort of mock ritual, until blood spurted from the off arm of the nearer man. He kept fighting, silently grinning, still dancing, while the blood soaked through his shirt and poured down his arm. He got in a vicious cut to the belly of the other. Gray coils of intestine spurted from the wound, but *still* both fighters continued their dance—the one with the gut wound held one hand over his belly and swung his sword with the other.

"Are they mad?" Ha whispered. He crouched beside me behind a low hedge, watching the same fight I watched. "A gut wound like that should have shocked the man to his knees. How can he keep fighting that way . . . unless he's drugged . . . or insane . . . or . . ." He fell silent as the gut-wounded fighter lunged forward and ran the other man clean through the left chest. The point of the blade pierced the back of his shirt, and as the attacker pulled his blade free, the other man fell dead to the ground.

The surviving fighter, guts still held into his abdomen by a single hand and blood pouring through his fingers, began to stamp and leap with the other dancers again, though he didn't last long. After only two turns around the circle, he staggered to the periphery near us and collapsed. I could tell from looking at him that he was dead. He stared up at the sky, pale eyes unblinking, with foam flecking his beard and sweat still beaded on his bleached-white forehead.

None of the other dancers looked at him. None seemed to notice that he'd fallen, any more than they noticed the other bodies that lay around the edge of their dance circle.

Beside me, Ha clenched a fist and held it to his forehead while he closed his eyes. "Avert," he whispered. "Avert."

He caught me looking at him and flushed dark red. "It won't help," he said. "This has nothing to do with spirits. But it won't hurt, either."

I nodded. I knew the sign for warding off evil. And I had to agree with him: watching those poor dancers dropping dead as they danced, I could only think to press my fist to my forehead and pray to Neithas. Something had gone wrong with the bard's songspell—terribly, impossibly wrong. And I had no idea what it might have been, or what I might do to fix it.

"Do you know any of them?" I asked.

"I know all of them." His mouth had set in a thin line. "Living and dead."

I swallowed. "Are any of them . . . family?"

"No." He didn't look at me. "My family is back in Rakkatar, for which I am grateful. Maybe this spell hasn't gone all the way to Rakkatar." He blinked faster, and I saw him swallow before he turned his face completely away from me. "One of them, however," he said, still looking away, "was my dearest friend."

"Which—?"

He pressed a finger to my lips. "One who is beyond

any help I might offer." I saw tears slide down his broad cheeks. He tapped Giraud on the shoulder and said, "Carefully get that sword. We might need it."

Giraud lay on his belly and slid forward, under the hedge, close to the body nearest us. He reached out, always watching the remaining dancers, who paid him no attention, and slipped the shortsword away from the dead dwarf.

He crawled back and started to hand the sword to Ha. "It's for you," the dwarf said.

"I could get another," he said. "They aren't paying attention to anyone at all, and the other dead are close to the hedge.

"Yes. One other, then, so that Isbetta also will be armed with something other than a knife. Keep out of sight, though."

When Giraud retrieved a second sword, all of us crept back into the depths of the chestnut grove. As soon as we were safely out of earshot—for even though the dwarves didn't seem to notice anything around them, we didn't wish to test this and discover we were wrong—Giraud said, "If we go back to the Pillar of the Sun and you sing again, Izza, can you undo all of this?"

"I'd had the same thought," Maydellan Ha said.

I looked from Giraud to Ha. Both of them watched me expectantly.

"I'm not a bard," I said. "I don't know the first detail about crafting spellsongs. All I could do right now is make the situation worse—tangle another wrong spell on top of this one that would make the task of untangling what I've already done impossible for the best of bards."

"But your father was a bard, and you have the talent to be one—"

I cut Giraud off. "I have the voice and possibly the will, and maybe with training I can be a bard. But I don't have the knowledge. I've already proven that no one but a bard should sing these spellsongs. No matter what the will of the gods might have been, no matter that I did the best I could, I wasn't capable of doing what I needed to do. And look at what happened."

"Yes." Ha nodded slowly. "Look at what happened. I find it hard to imagine worse, yet I'm sure that is only because I lack imagination, and not because worse is truly impossible."

Giraud scrubbed at the blade he'd taken with clumps of grass, trying to get the blood off. "Then what should we do?"

I didn't know why he was looking at me for answers. If I knew what to do, I would have done it. "Only a bard could tell us that."

"Well, there's a bard in Blackwarren," Giraud said. "Kethu dar Edder kept his study and his shop next to the mill."

I frowned. "He wasn't a bard. He was a minstrel."

Giraud shook his head. "He was a bard. The guild sent him to Blackwarren a long time ago, and he settled in and started selling instruments. He kept the fact that he was a bard secret. He made reference to it one time when he and I were talking, and stopped himself in midsentence. I pressed him, and finally he admitted the truth but swore me to secrecy. Until right now, I've never said another word about it."

I thought of dar Edder sitting in his doorway, carving the pegs for a lute or stringing a sambrel or playing a light dance tune on a flute. I thought of him fading into the shadows, selling the instruments he made and occasionally standing at a crossroads at Summer Faire, singing for his dinner. Entertaining at parties by singing ordinary ballads in his ordinary voice. Surely he wasn't a bard.

But I thought, too, that he knew all the important people in Blackwarren and was welcome in their homes. He was a harmless, cheerful, sociable, entertaining man, a delightful storyteller—an adequate musician of no particular skill, though a fine luthier. Perhaps he was more than he'd seemed.

"So we'll seek out this Edder," Ha said. "We'll see if he can set the spell right."

We'd planned to return to Blackwarren for Giraud's sake. Now we went there for all our sakes. And my gut insisted this was the right thing to do.

We headed almost due east, staying off the road that seemed to follow the track that had once been the road through the mountains. We thought if we kept our bearings and walked at a steady pace, we could expect to reach Blackwarren by midday.

Of course the straight path proved to be not the quickest way to travel. We crossed half a dozen streams and skirted several lakes, fought off another small herd of deer and watched a pack of rabbits bring down an unwary fox, got lost in a second, huge chestnut grove, and evidently wandered too far to the east, for finally we met up with Little North Road, and from that determined that we were directly south of Blackwarren. So we kept to the tall grass to the right of the Little North Road, hiding any time we heard anyone passing, and backtracked. It was close to nightfall by the time we pushed our way through the last of the bracken and dragged our weary legs over the top of one final hill, and saw Blackwarren nestled in the valley at the edge of a shining lake just ahead of us.

"No bog anymore," Ha said. He shook his head. "Wonder what happened to the people out cutting peat in the center of it when the spell hit."

"Should we chance going in while there's still light?" I asked. "Or do you think we would be better to wait until dark?"

"I say dark," Giraud said. "We don't know what to expect if we're recognized, but if no one can see us, we won't have to find out."

"I agree," Ha said. "Wait for dark. We can slip in, locate this bard's house, and discover what we have to do to end this curse. We're going to need time and privacy, and if we go into town now, we won't get either."

From the hilltop, I could see movement in the streets. Far too much movement, as if everyone who lived there had come outside at the same time. I didn't hear music, but the sound of many voices shouting reached me clearly enough. Lines of torches snaking, with erratic stops and starts through the streets, added to the frightening aura of discord that radiated from the entire village. I knew the Change-winds had touched Blackwarren. The lake where the peat bog had been proved that. The neat pavestone road that led through the village added to the proof. If those two details weren't enough, my third proof was that the houses, which had been mostly wattle-and-daub with thatched roofs, were now exclusively built of cut stone or fieldstone, and the roofs were of the sort of heavy, curved red tile that I'd seen before as a child, in the far-south city of Greffon. In Blackwarren, not even Lord dar Falcannes's great-house had had such a roof.

That was, I suppose, a silly detail to notice, considering the circumstances. But to me, Blackwarren no longer looked like the poor village it had been. Now, though still tiny, it appeared to be as rich as the greatest cities of Terosalle. Rich, but somehow sick.

We waited well off the road, hidden in deep grass and with our backs to a hollow in the hillside, so that we could only be attacked from three directions. Nothing came at us, though, and at last night blotted out the details of Blackwarren, leaving only the stuttering lines of torches.

Finally, even the torches died out, and the village descended into darkness.

We headed down, located the main street, and with

it found the first corpse. Mouth covered with foam, eyes wide, she lay on her back. Her blouse had been ripped open, her skirt dragged up around her waist. I felt my gorge rise. Her name had been Darcelle, and she'd been an apprentice weaver who sat next to me sometimes and chatted about her hamlet deep in the hills—four houses, five families, a flock of goats. She had planned to settle in Blackwarren, which had seemed huge and sophisticated to her. I had liked her a lot.

She had been my friend. She was dead.

I had killed her.

We moved on. The shapes of the streets remained the same, but all of them were paved. The tall wooden boardwalks were gone, replaced by raised stone sidewalks. The houses all displayed elegant doors and glass windows instead of shutters and scraped oilskin window covers tacked to wooden frames. I had a hard time keeping track of where I was—little clues remained to guide me, but they were subtle.

"Fishmonger Street," Giraud said, and we turned down it.

After Darcelle, I wouldn't look at the bodies. I knew everyone who lived in Blackwarren—perhaps two hundred fifty people in all. We counted ten of them lying in the few roads along which we crept. I suspected that more would die if I couldn't find some way to repair the damage I'd caused. I knew, too, that the dead I saw were not the only dead. Wherever the Changewinds had traveled, people were at that moment caught up in dancing madness or defending themselves from marauding packs of carnivorous deer or fighting off whatever form of death had found Darcelle, or things worse. Unimagined, but worse.

I cursed the nantatsu that had killed the bard, and I cursed myself for cowardice and stupidity. If I'd been smarter or cleverer, I would have found a way to escape the nantatsu, or I would have realized that I couldn't cast the spell properly because I knew nothing of bardic magic, and I would have run. The nantatsu might have caught me and killed me, but what was one life when weighed against so many?

With those dark thoughts in my mind, I followed Giraud and Ha through Blackwarren's back streets, to the house of the bard Kethu dar Edder. Unlike every other house in the village, his home and shop remained a construction of wattle and daub with a thatched roof. His door remained a poor plank affair, his windows had shutters flung open and scraped oilskin stretched over the frames within. No lights burned within the house, but we discovered in the worst of all possible ways that he was home.

Someone had nailed him to his door.

Spikes driven through the joints of his shoulders and hips kept him in place, and one additional spike through his belly guaranteed that if someone had taken him down, he would not have lived. I could only think that there were no good ways to die, but that his had been worse than most.

"Let's get him off of there and bury him," I heard myself saying.

"We don't have time to bury him, but at least we can carry him into his bed."

Impossibly, Edder lifted his head and stared at us. "It didn't touch you?" he asked.

Oh, Neithas, he's still alive, I thought.

"It was a spell," he said. "It took me by surprise, but I fought it off as best I could. . . . I never had much power or any great talent with the magic. . . . I made the best song I could and played as well as I could, but I couldn't save anyone but myself." He drew a ragged breath, then groaned. "The magic touched all the rest of them . . . but you've seen that, of course. Nothing is the same, and nothing that is good will survive long." He managed a bone-dry laugh. "But I found what I was looking for."

Ha and Giraud moved forward to pull out the spikes.

Edder said, "Don't. When you pull them, I'm dead, and I have important news to give you. You have to carry the news to Remeys. The 'Song of Belangia' has been sung . . . you tell him that, you understand? The 'Song of Belangia.'"

I touched the old man. "What was the 'Song of Belangia'?"

He gave me a hard look. "I know your voice, but I can't see you—too dark, and my eyes have gone bad. And I'm dying. Who are you?"

"Isbetta dar Danria."

"The bard's girl."

He knew me? Knew who I was? Knew my father?

I asked him. He said, "I knew him. Your father was killed because someone else wanted the Song to be sung, and betrayed him because he was powerful enough to reverse it, and protect both king and kingdom, and was in the position to do so."

"I knew part of that," I told him. "I just found out about the Black Heron, and Tanil. And the fact that they wanted to work a spell. But who was the Black Heron? What did he want."

"The question is, who *is* the Black Heron," the old man said. "I've been here all these years to keep something important away from him, whoever he may be. I've waited here to get word that the Watchowl bards had found him, and that he was dead, and that I could go home. They never did."

"Why?" Ha asked. "Did you have another spell like the 'Song of Belangia' that you were hiding?"

"No." Edder hung his head. "Something else."

Giraud said, "I want to know about the songspell. How do we counteract it?"

Edder hung there, his chest rising and falling like a bellows, and he didn't answer; I could hear the air rattling in his lungs and the back of his throat. "This hurts," he said after a while. And after a longer while, he seemed to draw strength from the air, for he raised his head and said, "The song was the work of a bard gone bad . . . a spellsong written by Belangia the Hawkbard. His colleagues found the song before he could sing it, and hid the book away. They should have burned it. Should have . . . and didn't, because they thought it made a good object lesson . . . and so, I suppose, it has." His voice weakened.

Giraud ran inside and returned with a tin full of water, which he held to the old man's lips. Edder sipped until he'd had enough, then hung there gasping a while longer, and finally nodded again.

"My thanks," he said. "The man the bards know only as the Black Heron hired another bard to steal the book. Tanil, probably—I don't know that anyone knew for certain which bard who went missing in those dark days did so to betray us, and not because he'd been betrayed himself. Your father sent word shortly after he arrived here that he'd found the book, and had stolen the applicable pages, and was on his way back. But he never arrived. Neither, apparently, did Tanil, for our spies still tell of search that remains in progress across Terosalle for the book—financed, rumor has it, by the same Black Heron."

I swallowed. I knew where the original book had ended up. And the stolen pages. And the fate of the thief who had stolen it. The world would have been a better place if the book had come to the same end as the bard.

Edder sighed and hung his head. "You'll go. You'll tell the Watchowl bards the 'Song of Belangia' has been sung, won't you? They will know what to do."

"We'll tell them," I said.

The dying bard shook his head. "Something else. I can't forget this. You, girl . . . you take the black lute . . . it's hidden beneath the floorboards under

my bed. . . . I only just had time to hide it before
they came for me. The lute is . . . special. Protect
it until you get it to Watchowl and give it to . . . I
don't know who you'll give it to. The lute will know."
His head dropped forward again, and he drew another
ragged breath. When he looked up, his eyes focused
for the first time. He stared at Ha. "You. Dwarf. I
claim kinbond by deed and oath to the Clan of Sher,
and by kinbond I claim right of grace."

I saw Ha stiffen. "What was your deed," he asked
softly, "and what was your oath, to claim kinbond?"

I was thinking about that cryptic remark, "The lute
will know." I only half-listened to the old man and
Ha. Their words had, to me, the sound of ritual. I
didn't know what they meant, but I sensed that what
passed between them signified more than it seemed.

"My deed was the clearing of the Hills of Chirs
Chase of the legions of the walking dead. I stood
beside Fikkgund Sher and swore I would not turn
back until the hills were clean. Nor did I. And when
we were done, I swore the Oath of First Brothers."

Ha bowed so deeply his head nearly touched the
ground. "Honorable deeds; the story is known to me.
You are brother to the Sher, and so are my brother.
Have you aught to send your kin?"

The words were old words, oddly spoken—stiff and
high and formal; within those old words, power
moved. Power to command loyalty, to extract promises, to demand favors. It was not the power of magic,
but the power of honor, and I felt its force moving
between Edder and Ha as surely as I'd felt the power
that raised the Changewinds moving through me.

"I do not bind you in that way," Edder whispered.
"If you see them, tell them I died bravely, and that
I brought the Clan of Sher no shame. That's all."

"I swear I shall do it. How shall I give you grace?"

The bard hung on the door, only his chest moving as he drew in one labored breath, and then

another, and then another. "I'm ready now. Don't waste time putting me in my bed or worrying about the proprieties. The proprieties died with the spell-song. Just do it and get the lute and go."

Maydellan Ha's back went rigid, his face set into a stiff, thin-lipped mask. Not even the darkness could hide the struggle raging inside of him. "Go in and get the lute, Isbetta. Giraud . . . help her find it. Quickly."

I nodded and pushed the door open. Gently, for the old man hung on it, and I didn't want to cause him any more pain. I slipped past him and Giraud followed me in. Neither of us said anything—we both knew what would happen when we were out of sight. We found Edder's narrow bed and moved it, and felt around until we located a loose floorboard. That and boards to either side lifted; Giraud pulled them up and held them out of the way while I reached in and felt around until I discovered a soft, padded leather case. I lifted it out. It was the right size and shape to hold a lute, but I had no wish to flee Blackwarren only to discover the bard hadn't put the instrument back in its case.

I loosened the ties and slipped a hand inside. A lute nestled in there—its wood felt warm to my hand, and it vibrated almost as if it were alive. "I wish we had some light," I whispered. "I need to be sure it's the right one."

"I'll stir the coals in his hearth with a tinder stick," Giraud said. "Maybe I'll be able to get enough of a flame that we'll be able to see it."

Outside I heard a thud against the door. No cry, no clank of metal, nothing but that one soft thud. But I knew it was over. Edder had received his grace. I swallowed hard and shivered at the thought of another death on my hands.

A moment later, Giraud, holding a stick with a tiny flame on the tip, knelt by my side. "Let's see it."

I pulled the flaps on the case back. Black wood gleamed back at us, so finely fitted and rubbed and so perfectly shaped that it seemed not a creation of the hands of a man but the flawless work of a god.

"I've never seen anything like it," Giraud whispered.

"Nor have I. If its sound is the equal of its construction, it will be the finest instrument I've ever seen."

I quickly covered it up and tied the ties. I slipped the strap of the case over my shoulder, and Giraud and I hurried back into the night.

Chapter Nine

We stole three horses, but only after we'd checked their teeth and their hooves to be sure that the Changewinds had not turned them into monsters that would creep up on us while we slept and devour us. If the madness that enveloped Blackwarren continued, I thought it likely that whoever had owned them would never realize they were gone, probably wouldn't *survive* to realize they were gone.

According to Ha, who had traveled there once before, Watchowl Keep lay almost directly south of us, a day's ride away if we dared to ride straight. But the Watchowl Forest lay between us and our destination, and Ha said its inhabitants had been terrifying before the Changewinds passed through. None of us wanted to think of what they might have become afterward.

So we decided we would not chance travel directly through the forest. We would ride south as far as Straje. From there, we could either go east until we reached Anatta and the Burrinee River, where we would probably have to steal a boat, or we could ride west along the Black Rock Reaches, then south on

Forest Road until we got to the path through the forest that led to Galarialle and, beyond it, to the Watchowl Keep. Neither direction would be safe, and the one that lay entirely overland had the disadvantage of being longer. We thought we would probably go to Anatta, but we didn't want to decide until we found out whether any vestige of normalcy survived in Straje.

Giraud said, "I think if we keep traveling west, we'll come to the end of the spelled area soon. Then we can travel though safe lands until we reach the keep."

"That's true," I agreed. "If we go east at Straje, we'll be heading closer to Hearthold Mountain."

"You're assuming that somewhere to the west a place exists that hasn't been touched by the spell," Ha said.

I shrugged. "Of course. No spell could be powerful enough to cover the whole world."

Ha brought his horse just ahead of mine and looked at me over his shoulder. "Under normal circumstances, I'd say no. But you sang at the Pillar of the Sun, and I think the pillar was your instrument. I think it resonated for you the way an instrument resonates for a regular bard—"

I cut him off. "How did you know about that?"

"About bards and their magic?" He shrugged. "I've traveled. I have friends—even a bard or two. I've watched and I've listened, and I've pieced together observations and bits of conversation and other petty details about bardic magic. My knowledge is certainly incomplete, but just because I can't do magic doesn't mean I can't figure out some of how it works. In any case, this is what I observed. Hearthold Mountain sang with you. Perhaps it did so for a reason no more mysterious than the pitch of your voice vibrated precisely right. Maybe not; you might be the One True Messiah of the bards, or some such rot, and when we get to the keep we'll discover that they've been foretelling your arrival for the last thousand years. More likely, the truth lies somewhere in between." He reined his mount in and edged closer to me. "All I know is what I observed, to whit: without accompaniment, you sang a spell from that book, and your friend and I failed to notice you until you nearly beat us over the heads. Then you sang a song I requested, again without accompaniment, and I fell in love with you. As did your friend, who was sworn to love another, in the manner of all young idiots." He sighed. "Perhaps young Giraud is a starry-eyed romantic, but I, beloved, am not. And while I am still passionately in love with you," he smiled a wistful smile in my direction, "I have gained control of my reason. And I am far too much a realist to think that this ridiculous passion comes from within me."

I considered that for a moment. "So you think the crystal pillar accompanied me. What effect would that have?"

"The Pillar of the Sun goes deep into the earth. Perhaps it goes all the way through to the other side. Perhaps, as some of our storytellers suggest, it is the true heart of the world, and when you sang, it sang with you. If that's the case, then when you sang the 'Song of Belangia,' maybe all the world fell under your spell."

I got queasy thinking about that. What if with a single song I had destroyed my world? Not just a small area of it, which had been nightmarish to contemplate, not even an entire country, or a whole continent . . . what if I had destroyed my entire world?

I rode in silence for a while, imagining the entire world as terrifying as Blackwarren. The ebon night through which I rode, in which the stars glittered cruelly, could represent not just my village and my country, but every place I might ever run to. And unlike the night, this would be a darkness from which there would be no hiding, and no escape—perpetual night, from which daylight could never escape.

Giraud interrupted my gloomy ruminations. "So you're saying we shouldn't go west. That there's no sense looking for the place where the Changewinds stopped."

Ha shook his head. "No. I'm saying if we go west, it should be because the route looks safer. Places untouched by the magic might not exist, and we shouldn't waste any time trying to find them. If we come across them on our way, well and good. We can take comfort from that. We shouldn't build our plans around something that might not exist."

Giraud grumbled something that I didn't quite catch. In a louder voice, he said, "You're right, I'm sure. But look here. What if the Watchowl Keep has fallen under the spell of the Changewinds, too? What if the bards have danced themselves to death or gone mad in some other way, as so many others have? What if Watchowl Keep has been destroyed?"

Ha shrugged. "Then our problem will be worse than it already is, won't it?"

The dead glared at us from the streets of Straje. Dozens of them hung by their necks from balconies that jutted over the street, staring down out of empty eye sockets. Crows, as well as smaller birds, perched on their shoulders. Vultures studied us as we rode along the outskirts of the town, their eyes keenly interested. They hoped, perhaps, that we would furnish later meals for them. I realized we might, and began to hate the birds.

We heard screaming and mad laughter from somewhere near the center of the town. Once I caught a glimpse of women armed with spears and swords chasing a naked man through the streets. I thought of my friend Darcelle. The terror went both ways, I realized—lone men were no safer than lone women.

I could find no comfort in that thought; evil was no less evil if both men and women participated in it.

We approached the last few houses in Straje, keeping our attention evenly divided between what lay in front of us and what lay behind. Behind us, the screaming grew louder and more terrible. Ahead of us lay quiet and stillness.

Then two bright-eyed children stepped out from behind a house to watch our approach; they smiled fearlessly, and something about their calm, in the midst of all the madness, sent little skittering spider-chills down the back of my neck.

"Wouldn't you like to take us with you?" the boy called out as we approached. "We want to go away from here."

The girl said, "I'm afraid. Please help me."

They were the first children I'd seen in all of this. As soon as I realized I hadn't seen any children anywhere, I wondered what had happened to the others. The pictures my mind painted made me shudder.

"We ought to take them," Giraud said. "Their parents will be glad enough to have them back safely once this is over . . . if they're even still alive. And if they aren't, we'll be able to find someone who will take them in."

"Don't go close," I said.

"They're only *children*." Giraud looked at me as if I'd become as mad as the people we feared.

"The deer were only *deer*, too," I said, paraphrasing Ha. Intuition did not whisper at me; it screamed.

"Quite so." Ha nodded. "Stay well back. If they're still alive when we return, we'll help them then."

"That," Giraud said, "will be far too late to do these two any good."

Which was the truth. If they needed help, they needed it right away, and not in a couple of days. So I asked them, "What are you doing?"

"Running away. And hiding," the boy said. "Mama and Dada ate the baby, and we don't want to be next."

I winced. Well, if I hadn't wanted to know, I shouldn't have asked.

Giraud glared at me. "And you think I should just leave them there?"

Ha groaned. "No. Of course not. We *can't* leave them here now, can we?" He jerked his horse's reins and the animal grunted, but took him toward the two of them. Giraud followed, and even I wheeled around so that I could offer to ride one of them pillion. I was furthest back, so I saw the movement before either Giraud or Ha did. A simultaneous shifting from the left, behind a woodpile, and from the hedgerow to the right—colors that I realized I'd seen before, but that, now that they were in motion instead of stationary, my mind declared deadly.

"Get back!" I screamed, spurring my horse. "It's a trap!"

At the sound of my voice, other children poured out of their hiding places—a dozen from behind the woodpile, as many or more from around both sides of the hedgerow, and even more out of the door to the house, which I suddenly realized had never been entirely closed.

Giraud and Ha yelled and wheeled their mounts around, and we galloped down the road, the predatory children falling behind us. Evil, evil—everything that was not evil was dead, I thought. No matter how lovely my world had become, with its transformed houses and beautiful fields of wildflowers and gently rolling hills and crystal streams and waterfalls, it was as full of corruption as a rotting corpse.

Giraud's comment, that perhaps we would find even the bards' keep changed by the spell, made me shiver.

We reached the intersection and looked down the road to the east—the one that led to the river. Both

Giraud and I saw a tall, black-garbed, bone-white figure in the distance, which stood surveying the countryside, then crouched over a dark pile of something unidentifiable that lay in the road.

Nantatsu, I thought, and as the word crossed my mind, Giraud spoke it aloud.

Ha stared at the form we pointed out. "In truth? I'd never seen one."

"And you don't want to see one now, either," I said.

As simply as that, our decision made itself. We rode west, settling into a rocking-horse canter that covered the ground without too seriously tiring our mounts.

We passed houses burned to the ground, more corpses, occasionally small bands of people. Most of them were bent on misdeeds of their own and gave us no more attention than a sideways glance as we rode past. One group of bloody, scarred, wild-eyed men and women dropped out of trees to either side of us as we rode along a part of the road where forest grew up to the pavement on both sides. They charged us with swords, but they were on foot. Ha killed the leader with his pike, and both Giraud and I slashed at the others with our swords; our height, and the fact that they attacked us instead of our horses, allowed us to escape unhurt.

My left shoulder, the one the deer laid open with its hoof, began to give me trouble. I'd been unable to do anything more for the wound than bind it from time to time with fresh strips of cloth ripped from my second-best tunic. It had stopped bleeding quickly, and I thought it would heal without causing me grief. I thought wrong.

My shoulder started to burn like fire as I rode; the pain that had been a forgettable dull throb while I was walking now felt like someone jamming a knife blade into my shoulder joint. Every hoof that hit the ground jarred the wound and increased the pain a little more.

Finally, I couldn't take it anymore.

"Ha, we have to stop."

"We're making good time," he said, and then he saw my face. It must have looked like a philosopher's description of the Coldhell, because he said, "Giraud, make sure this place is safe." And he pulled up and sat studying me.

"What's wrong with you?" he asked me.

"Shoulder," I told him.

"Shoulder?"

"Where the deer got me."

I saw surprise in his eyes. "The deer? I didn't know it had done you any harm."

I nodded. "I've been taking care of it. Clean strips ripped from my other shirt when we stopped, washing it as often as we find clean water—I haven't been able to do much, but I've done what I could."

"Oh, Grum." He glowered.

I didn't know who or what Grum was, but it evidently was something bad.

"Let me see what you've been doing."

Giraud came back. "Nothing around right now, though we don't dare stay for long."

"Right. She's been riding with a hurt shoulder, and didn't bother to tell us," Ha said. "How bad do you suppose it's gotten since yesterday morning?"

"Couldn't be too bad," Giraud said.

I'd had the same thought.

But Ha just snorted. "Couldn't, eh?" He peeled the bandages away, and I whimpered as the crusted blood ripped off. "Oh, have mercy, Grum you motherlover," he muttered. "Too much more of your heroics, girl, and you wouldn't have had a shoulder to worry about, or an arm either."

"What?" I frowned at him. I preferred the soothing administrations of a healer when I was unwell, and kind reassurances that I would be fine, not the gruff warnings of an irate dwarf. I said as much.

"Is that so?" His eyebrows slid up, and his mouth, somewhat less swollen and bruised than it had been, twisted into a cold little smile. "Soothing words and vague reassurances don't cure infection."

"But a good spell would."

"A good spell *might*." He shook his head, disgusted. "Would you use the heel of your boot to drive a nail?"

"Of course not."

"You might." He glowered. "If you didn't have anything better, you might use your heel to drive a nail, because it might be able to do the job, and if the job needed doing, and all you had was your boot, you'd take whatever tool you had. Magic is a bootheel. Physical sickness is a nail. You *can* use magic to cure illnesses, but what's the first law of spellcasting, eh?"

"Part of the whole acts on the whole?"

"Farting, fire-eating Grum!" His eyes grew narrow. "That's the *second*. Anyone with even a trace of magical ability ought to at least know the laws of operation of magic."

"You said you have no magical ability."

"And *I* know them anyway, because if you don't understand the world you live in, you aren't living in it, are you? You're just wandering through with a stupid expression on your face, getting surprised when events don't go the way you wish they would, even though any reasonable person could see that they were going to turn out the way they have because *that's . . . the . . . way . . . life . . . works*. I *know* how life works." He took a deep breath and waited for a moment. His face, which had gotten quite red while he was shouting at me, returned to a more normal color. "The first rule of magic is: Like begets like. Remember that. Like begets like."

"Like begets like," I repeated. I didn't want him shouting at me again. My head was starting to feel light and my temples were pounding, and I felt hot and cold at the same time.

"Another way of saying the first law is that effects resemble causes. And a logical extrapolation of the first law of magic is that if something is caused by magic, magic will effect a reasonable cure. However . . ." his heavy eyebrows drew down and his voice began to get louder again, "if something isn't caused by magic, then magic will not offer the most effective cure. Or solution. You don't hammer nails with the heel of your boot."

"Right," I said. I'd begun to notice that Maydellan Ha when he was angry reminded me more than a little of Poor Gojas, who had been god-touched when he had a terrible fever, and whoever afterward walked around Blackwarren shouting at the skies and demanding that everyone worship him because he was the second coming of Thural. Ha even had the same expression on his face. I wondered, briefly, if he would stand up and start tearing off his cloths, as Poor Gojas sometimes did. I hoped he wouldn't. "I need some more willow bark," I said, hoping to distract him his tirade.

"Willow bark?"

"For the pain in my head and my shoulder. I've been gathering it whenever we stopped and chewing on it as we rode—"

"That's exactly what I mean," Ha said. He started digging through his pack, snarling. "You *don't* need willow bark. That just hides your symptoms until you're so sick everyone else can see it, too. Idiot." He pulled out a small vial of yellow powder. When he opened it, the stink of rotten eggs assailed my nose. He took water from a vial and poured it onto a square of coarse cloth and without warning began scrubbing at the cut in my shoulder. I yelled. The wound, which had been closed and scabbing over, opened, and blood and pus covered his rag.

"Idiot," he muttered again. "You'll have a scar from this, and if you had said something sooner you

wouldn't have, but at least I got it early enough that
the wound won't kill you." He was still scrubbing. I
tried to pull away from him, but he was incredibly
strong. And determined.

"You're hurting me," I said through clenched teeth.

"If you hadn't been stupid, you wouldn't have this
mess now." He poured some of the egg-stinking powder into the wound. Pain whited out the sky, and I
howled as if he'd run my shoulder through with a
sword. He patted at the cut with his rag, forcing the
powder into all the places it hadn't reached on its
own. The pain, incredibly, got worse. "Effects
resemble causes. If you have an injury of non-magical
origin, you need a non-magical cure to obtain the best
results. Healers know this. They just keep going back
to magic when situations are gravest, and they're going
in the wrong direction. Everything they know tells
them this, but they do it anyway."

I nodded my head, trying to look like I agreed with
everything he said. I would have agreed with anything
if it made him quit digging into my shoulder.

When he did quit, he wrapped the wound in soft
white cloth and told me we had to redress the wound
at nightfall, when the potency of his stinking powder would have worn off.

I could barely contain my excitement.

Once he was done, he mixed white powder in a
thimbleful of his water and made me drink it. The
taste was bitter beyond words, but somehow familiar. "What was that?" I asked him when my face had
unscrewed itself enough to allow speech.

"Willow bark powder," he told me. No expression
crossed his face.

I nearly exploded. "Willow bark powder! I thought
willow bark was the evil remedy that that would kill
me!"

"Not at all." His voice, so even and calm, was meant
to chastise me for my display of temper. Never mind

that he'd been the one with the temper moments before. "No harm in treating the pain if you're also getting treatment for the wound-sickness. Just don't expect it to do more than make you hurt less."

As the day wore on, I was grateful enough for the willow bark powder, bitter though it was, and for Ha's ministrations to my shoulder. I moved stiffly, but I could almost believe that stinking burning stuff he'd poured onto my skin was helping. I no longer felt both hot and cold. I still ached, but the jarring of my mount's hoofbeats no longer seemed like an attack. Lucky for me, because just outside the village of Konatar Bridge, where we stole replacement horses, Giraud, who had become increasingly distant and quiet, broke one long silence to say, "I may have imagined this, but I thought I heard hoofbeats behind us."

We stopped, and from the line of trees where the road curved out of sight, we heard what might have been the echo of our own mounts' hoofbeats echo into silence. Three extra beats, maybe four, and then the day became still. The road curved ever further southward and Watchowl Forest on our left hid what lay behind us as well as what lay ahead.

We looked at each other. "Might have been nothing," I said.

"Might have been," Ha agreed, face impassive. "But we dare not act as if it was."

"One of us ought to double back?"

Ha shook his head. "Poor strategy to split our forces when we don't know what's back there, or what's yet to come."

I thought of the book I carried, and the black lute. I thought of magic that I didn't understand, and couldn't control, and I thought of death that might or might not be riding behind us, and lives I'd cost, and lives I might yet save.

As we urged our horses forward, south and west toward Dar Betis, I said, "I could sing the song I sang in the tunnel. The one that made you not notice me. I could wait behind and see what follows us, then ride ahead and tell you."

"And you could die trying it, too," Giraud said. "If we stay ahead of the rider and stay together, we'll have the best chance of reaching the keep alive."

"The road had been empty of travelers. If someone else is riding a horse, maybe he's someone like us. Someone not touched by the Changewinds."

Ha snorted. "Then why does he hide himself back of us? Why doesn't he show himself?"

"Maybe he's as afraid of us as we are of him. No one else seems sane. Maybe he's afraid we're mad." I wanted so much to believe someone remained untouched by the nightmare I'd created. I wanted to think we might reach a place where the Changewinds hadn't blown. Someone else normal would be like a gift, or a promise. There might be an end to this horror.

Ha shrugged. "Then that's damned sensible of him, and we ought to leave him back there with his fears. Fear will keep him alive a lot longer than hope."

I wondered if the dwarf had always been such a miserable pessimist.

"Fear might have saved Adalane," Giraud said softly.

I glanced over at him. "She might still be alive."

"She isn't," he said.

"You don't know that."

"Yes, I do. I saw her and her mother and sisters hung in front of their house when we were leaving town."

I stared at him. "You didn't say anything."

"What was I supposed to say? They were dead. I couldn't help them. I couldn't do anything but slow us down and we couldn't take a chance of being slowed down, could we? We have to get to the keep."

I tried to remember anything that might have been Adalane hanging from a balcony in Blackwarren, but I'd made a point of not looking at the bodies. I didn't want to know, as we left, who was only possibly dead and who was dead for sure.

"I'm sorry," I said. I felt as inadequate as anyone ever feels when faced with offering a dear friend sympathy at the death of someone he loved. I wished I could do something to make everything better. Knowing that if not for my actions, Giraud's beloved would still be alive, I wished I could make myself disappear.

Well, I thought, I *could* make myself disappear. Maybe. If the spell still worked for me when I was away from the mountain. But what would my instrument be? Certainly not the lute—the worst of idiots wouldn't try to play a lute while riding a cantering horse.

Did I remember the spellsong? Well enough, as I thought about it. It had been written to be sung to the "Fat Lady's Stroll." Why? I hummed the tune of "Fat Lady's Stroll," and fell easily into the rhythm of my horse's canter.

Of course. Three-beat tune.

My skin prickled with the idea that came to me. I knew of bards who sang to the rolling beat of a hand-drum. Could the drumming of my horse's hooves be my instrument?

I hummed, trying to feel anything happening as I did it—DUM-bah-da, DUM-bah-da—and tried to remember the words the bard had created to get himself out of his fix. They don't have to be exactly right, I thought. Not exactly. They only have to be close enough to do what I need them to do.

DUM-bah-da, DUM-bah-da . . .

It took me a moment and some effort, but finally

I had the words in my head, close enough to be satisfying. I started singing softly, rocking to the drumming of my horse's hooves, riding the beat clear through my body. I'd find out who rode behind us, if anyone did. I'd make myself useful.

> "Here I'll be
> Now you'll see
> No one important
> No one who
> Says to you,
> You ought to stay

> "Here I'll be
> Don't see me
> I'm not important
> I can just
> Turn back, just
> Ride on away."

We hadn't been talking before, so I couldn't tell if Ha or Giraud had forgotten about me. Maybe my spell was doing nothing—I was probably an idiot to think I could use a horse as a musical instrument. I kept singing, though. Sang through my version of the song again, and then again.

I started to drop back a bit. Neither of them looked sideways. Neither of them noticed me at all. I reined in a little tighter, but not enough to encourage my mount to shift from a canter to a trot, which was a four-beat rhythm that—if my spell were working, of course—could shatter it all to bits.

Still cantering, still singing, I turned the horse and headed back the way I'd come.

Chapter Ten

I can't say that I had a plan. I only wanted to find out if someone was following us, and if someone was, then who and why. So I rode back, singing softly in time to the beat of my horse's hooves, not sure how far the spell would carry, or when Ha and Giraud would notice I was gone, and not sure how far ahead the spell would reach, either, or whether it would work on the person or people who followed us.

I thought I'd hide right at the edge of the woods as soon as I heard hoofbeats. I didn't get the chance.

Someone was following us, but that someone had decided to hide in the trees beside the roadway when he heard my horse approaching. Evidently as I got closer, the songspell took effect, because he was just riding out of the trees as I came around the bend. His appearance so startled me that for an instant I lost the beat of my song. I got it back, but for just that instant I thought he realized I was there.

He was an old man, but not in the manner that I was accustomed to thinking of old people. His hair was white, certainly, and his face deeply creased, but he did not have the stoop that I associated with the very old, or the slowness of movement, or the general air of frailty. His eyes, hooded like a falcon's and deepset beneath thick, straight brows, were quick and fierce and observant. His hands, spotted by time and sunlight, remained thick and knotted with muscle. He'd filed his nails to points in the manner of the southern dancing warriors. He rode easily, with his back straight and his shoulders relaxed.

I tried to figure out what he was. I had never seen clothing as fine as his, nor as odd. He dressed all in black and emerald green silk—his shirt, cut with billowing sleeves and worn under a plain green tunic, was black embroidered with black in a pattern so thick and detailed and many-layered that to me that the old man appeared to be sprouting black dragons. His sword hung in an emerald green scabbard that was polished so deeply and to such perfection that it could have been carved from a single gemstone.

His horse was as black as his shirt and pants; the horse's trappings green silk, the saddle dyed green leather with onyx trimmings. I wondered if he always wore black and green, or if he had other saddles to match his other outfits.

I rode along beside him, watching him, trying to figure him out. He gave me no notice, never glanced in my direction, kept himself just behind the curve that separated us from Giraud and Ha. He was altogether the most intriguing human being I had ever seen, and I wondered why he followed us.

"I'm following you because you and your friends are the only sane people I've found other than myself, and you seem to have a destination and a plan. Since I found myself without either, I decided to borrow yours," he said. He still didn't look at me. The shock of his reply to a question I'd only asked in my mind shook me so badly I lost both song and rhythm, and nearly lost my balance as well.

My mount shifted from her smooth canter to a

bone-shaking trot, and I let myself be bounced around for a long, painful moment before I got control of both of us again. I urged her forward, and caught up with the old man.

"Your little spell almost worked, by the way," he told me. "In spite of the wards I've set round myself to prevent such surprises, you almost had me. I'd be more than a little curious to discover how you accomplished that."

"How long have you known I was here?"

"Since you came around the corner and lost your place in your song."

"Then why didn't you say something . . . or do something . . . ?" I felt like an idiot. I'd been riding along gawking at him, thinking I could do so without him knowing, and I was embarrassed beyond words to discover that he'd known all along.

"Why didn't *I* say something? Because, quite frankly, I wanted to know your intentions." For the first time he looked over at me, and I saw that his eyes were as intensely, unrelievedly black as his shirt, his saddle, his horse . . . He smiled. If nothing else about his face was reassuring, still he had, I thought, the gentlest smile I'd ever seen. "I wanted to know whether you would try to kill me if you thought I didn't know you were there, or if you would do what you did—ride along trying to figure out what I wanted."

"And now that you know?"

He looked forward again. "Now I will see if you and I can convince your two friends to let me travel with you. This road, after all, is no place for one old man—even an old man as capable of taking care of himself as I happen to be."

He looked like a fierce old man, but upright and honest and honorable—and by Neithas, I liked him. I didn't trust him—I wouldn't have trusted my own father if I met him on the road right then—but I liked him. I said, "Well, I can't guarantee that they'll want to travel with you, you know. I don't know yet if I do."

He smiled and nodded as if I'd told him we'd take him in with open arms, feed him and his horse, and find him a free room. "Good," he said, and his smile vanished. "You'll live longer if you don't trust everyone. Caution is the wellspring of wisdom, child."

I started to answer him. . . . I don't remember what I was going to say, only that I didn't get the chance to say it. Down the road from us, I heard shouts, a scream, and the clash of metal. "Giraud and Ha!" I shouted, and dug my heels into my horse's flanks, urging her to a flat-out gallop. She balked and slowed down. I dug harder, leaning forward on her withers and clicking my tongue. Her ears went back and she snorted. She started prancing and weaving from side to side. Then the stranger drew his gleaming sword from his scabbard, and without a cry, he and *his* horse launched forward at an incredible pace.

Then, of course, my horse decided it must not be such a bad idea, and she took off in pursuit. Since I wasn't ready, she almost unseated me. She galloped forward with me hanging half out of the saddle, one foot slipped all the way through the stirrup and the other completely out of it, hanging on to the pommel for sweet survival and feeling the cinch slipping as we went. I grabbed a hank of mane and pulled myself upright, and managed with great difficulty to kick my loose foot back into the flapping stirrup—though I couldn't untangle the one that had slipped all the way through. With my weight balanced on one foot and the terrible feeling that my head was about to end up under my horse's hooves at any instant, I raced after the old man.

Ha and Giraud came into view, and I could see they were in desperate trouble. They stood back to back in the center of the road, with three big men attacking them and one sitting on horseback a distance off. The rider held an instrument in his hands and played. It took me a moment to realize that he wore the garb and insignia of a court bard. A full bard.

My first reaction was one of relief. A court bard could sing a calming spellsong, or put the attackers to sleep, or take any of a dozen other useful actions that would eliminate them as a danger. My second reaction was horror, when I realized that the court bard was working with the attackers and not against them.

And the stranger, with sword out, was galloping toward the melee, and I had no idea whether he intended to help us, or whether he was riding to the aid of associates who had been waiting in ambush.

A hard yank to one side got the bit out from between the teeth of my mount, and I slowed her from a headlong gallop to a canter. I sang the "don't notice me" song again, and worked my shortsword out of my belt as I did it. I didn't think my spell would do anything against the bard, but it might be sufficient to confuse the three ruffians who attacked my friends. If I could get close before they noticed me, maybe I could slow them down or stop them, even though I had very little idea what to do with a sword.

The old man charged straight at the bard—so we had an ally. Our numbers were even, if not our odds. An apprentice historian, an apprentice weaver, a dwarf, and an old man were hardly equal opponents for three men who looked like trained fighters and one full bard.

And yet the bard blanched as the old man went at him, and threw his instrument to the ground and reached for his sword. An odd reaction, I thought.

Then I didn't have time to think. I reached the fighters and got in one good stroke, slashing a huge red-headed man across the back of his right shoulder and down the center of his back. He screamed, my horse reared and bolted again, and I was thrown from the saddle. My left shoulder slammed into the ground, and my left arm, and the left side of my head.

I bounced, and slammed down again.

My left boot was still all the way through the stirrup. I hit . . . bounced . . . hit . . . bounced . . . hit. . . .

Rolled onto my stomach, smashing my face into the paving stones of the road.

Skidded.

And lay there, bleeding and in pain, knowing vaguely that my friends needed my help but unable to move.

Darkness descended.

"There . . . she seems to have heard that. . . ."

Voices in the darkness, hands tugging, lifting, hurting.

"Try to give her a little water. . . ."

Drowning, choking, pain.

Coarse, urgent cry—"No! No more water!"

The pain billowing upward, outward, filling everything with white heat, red anguish. . . .

. . . blackness flowing in behind the pain. . . .

"Can you hear me? Isbetta? Can you let me know if you hear me?"

Of course I can, I thought, but I couldn't change thought to action.

"We need for you to wake up," the voice said.

Yes. I knew that. I couldn't remember precisely why it was important, but I had no doubt at all that it *was*. Something big was at stake.

I managed to open my eyes. Blurry faces stared down at me from too close. I wanted them to back away, but they didn't. They moved closer, and I felt hands at my back, sitting me up.

Pain ripped me into a thousand pieces, and nothingness devoured the pieces.

"—thirsty. I'm thirsty. I'm thirsty." Said over and over in a monotonous whisper, until I got so tired of the same two words I wanted to slap the person who said them. I tried to say shut up, and in that way discovered that the voice complaining of thirst was my own.

I opened my eyes. I remembered other times and other attempts, but this time was different. This time I didn't hurt. I didn't hurt at all. I was lying on something soft, beneath a bower of huge chestnut trees, under an early morning sky, and at first I seemed to be alone.

Then I heard voices speaking softly from a little distance off. I sat up and looked around. Through a screen of trees, I saw Giraud talking with Maydellan Ha and the mysterious old man who'd fought beside us. I couldn't hear what they said—only the steady rise and fall of voices speaking with some urgency.

I got to my feet slowly. The last clear memories I had were of falling from the horse during my single attempt at heroism. After that, I only had glimpses of light between patches of darkness, and faint recollections of terrible pain. I'd been hurt. I knew I had, but I wasn't hurt anymore. Even the wound on my shoulder that I'd gotten from the deer had stopped hurting.

My clothes were a mess—cloak torn, shirt shredded at the left shoulder, everything stained with blood.

I pulled back the shoulder of my shirt and twisted around to peek at the skin underneath. A thick, pink scar slashed across the muscle and down toward my chest, and smaller but broader scars showed where I'd been dragged across the pavestones. I slid my fingers up to my head and ran them through my hair; on the left side of my scalp, I found more smooth scar tissue, and a slight indentation in the bone that I was certain had never been there before.

I began to be frightened. How long had I held everyone up? We were supposed to have reached Watchowl Keep in the same day that we left Blackwarren. We were going to ride all day and part of the night if necessary. The whole of the world I knew had depended on us reaching the bards and trying to find a way to undo the spellsong I'd sung, and only haste might save more death and destruction. . . .

And there I lay, on a soft, grassy bed, with my wounds all healed and no more pain, and we weren't at the Watchowl Keep and we hadn't saved anyone.

I rose carefully, expecting stiffness or twinges, or at least weakness from having been ill and unable to move for a long time. Instead, I felt as if I'd done nothing more than spend a restful night asleep. No pain when standing, no pain when moving, no dizziness, weakness, no queasiness. . . .

I joined my friends and the stranger. I noticed immediately that Ha's blackened eyes and battered face had healed, too. I wondered if, after so long, anyone remained to save. "I'm awake and I can travel," I said without preamble. "How many days did we lose? How many weeks?"

Giraud gave me a tired smile. "We only lost the time between nightfall and sunrise. No days, no weeks. Ondan Shanxi is one of the Ko Mystics. He's both a warrior and a healer—his medicine is even of the sort that our friend Ha considers worthwhile, so he didn't get the lecture about nails and boots that you and I got."

Ha gave Giraud a cold look that shut him up. The dwarf turned to me and said, "An ondan of the Ko deserves respect. The Ko are the foremost students and teachers of natural medicine, magic and philosophy in the world. And even I have heard of Ondan Shanxi, who is a renowned practitioner of all three disciplines."

"That you have heard of me," the ondan said, "is perhaps not all to the good. I have never desired fame; only the furtherance of knowledge."

Ha said, "He came down out of the mountains after the Changewinds blew through, to see what had happened and to try to find a way to undo the damage."

The old man laughed softly. "Not entirely true, good Ha. The mountains came down. I merely came out. And I find that you, dear child," he nodded toward me, "are the singer of the spellsong that flattened the world." He smiled at me again with that same calm, kind smile that had so enchanted me the first time I saw it.

I stared down at my feet. "I think I knew better than to sing a bardic spellsong," I said. "But the omens . . . well, I knew I shouldn't, but I was so afraid of the nantatsu—"

"As well you should have been. They're deadly, evil creatures, and best avoided. I happened to cross paths with one outside of Straje that was hunting an evil bard that had tricked it, then destroyed its mountain home. It was muttering of revenge. I never seek out such monsters, but on principle, I kill them when I cross paths with them; they dedicate themselves entirely to the inflicting of pain and terror and death."

I felt my heart drop into my boots. I could see the ondan's revelation was news to Ha and Giraud, too. They had both paled as he mentioned that the monster had been looking for us. "What happened to the nantatsu?" I asked.

"I listened to it until I learned as much as I could from its ramblings. Then I moved ahead of it and presented myself to it as a corpse in the road. It came to me, intending to devour me before going on its way. When it moved within range, I killed it."

I thought of the enormous monster, and studied

the old man in amazement, trying to imagine him killing such a creature. "How?"

He shrugged. "By being where it thought I wasn't, and doing what it thought I wouldn't."

Giraud and I exchanged bewildered looks. Maydellan Ha simply smiled. "Ondan Etsran, yes? The answer to the question, 'How does the single warrior defeat the evil nation?'"

The faintest flash of surprise crossed the ondan's face. "Indeed," he agreed. "You are a gem with many facets, Maydellan Ha."

"Some of those facets require polishing," Ha said. "I wanted very much to study medicine with the Ko, but I knew of no one who knew how to find your temples."

"We often say, 'When the student is ready, the teacher will appear.'"

Neither of them said anything more on the matter, but I had the feeling that between them they had come to some sort of agreement.

"Since you are ready, child, I suggest we resume our travels."

"But you can't undo the spellsong?"

The ondan shook his head. "The spell that you have cast must be uncast. It cannot simply be undone. And your ways aren't my ways—a master of your bardic magic will have to form the uncasting."

So we were going to have to continue to the Watchowl Keep. And only Ondan Shanxi and Maydellan Ha had horses. Mine was gone, Giraud's dead.

"We're not far from Dar Betis," Giraud said. "Maybe we'll be able to replace our horses there."

The ondan shook his head slowly. "I believe we must avoid the towns."

"But how else will we find replacements for our horses?" I asked.

"You're asking the wrong question. Evil coalesces," the old man said softly. "When I feel the pulse of the world, I feel the madness dying away, and the mindful wickedness that has awakened reaching out. It moves into position both before you and behind you, gathering in the places where you have been and where it expects you to go. It searches for you."

He looked directly at me when he said this, and a coldness washed over me like icy rain, and left me shivering. "You mean us, don't you? Not just me."

"I mean you. The evil seeks you."

I didn't want to believe him, but my gut told me he was right. "Why me?"

"Because only the caster of a spell can uncast it, child. Others can turn it, alter it, and try to undo some of the damage that it does, but in all the world only you can truly undo what you have done. If the awakened evil can destroy you, then it gains ascendancy. And that ascendancy, which it seeks always, and which those who follow goodness have always managed to tear away from it, is what it most craves."

"So this evil wants to stop me."

"Don't use soft words for hard truth." The old man studied me. "The evil wants to kill you. If it can reach you, it will."

"Then what are we going to do?" Giraud wanted to know. "If we can't go to the villages to get horses, we're going to lose time—"

The ondan pressed a finger to his lips, and Giraud grew quiet. "She knows," he said. "If she lets her heart speak, it will take her by the safest route."

I had no idea how to listen to my heart. My gut, in its usual fashion, had plenty of worries but no practical advice. With everyone looking at me, I tried to think of what we ought to do, what *I* was supposed to know, and as far as I could tell, I didn't know a damned thing. Something the old man had said came back to me as I was standing there, though, and it made the sort of sense that my head didn't like but that made my gut happy.

"Be where it thinks we aren't," I said. "Do what it thinks we won't."

The ondan studied me, waiting. I had expected praise for reciting his bit of wisdom back at him, and was disappointed when he didn't tell me what a clever girl I was. I wasn't going to get credit for coming up with the words unless I could also come up with a plan that would put them into action. And action was the difficult part. Ondan Shanxi's bright black eyes watched me, and I felt certain that he knew the answer, but that if I didn't figure it out, or gave the wrong one, he would let me lead us to our deaths as a lesson on listening to my heart. My mute, impatient heart.

Giraud's mouth popped open and the ondan raised a single finger, and it closed again. There'd been plenty of times when I wished I could do that. Giraud was never without an opinion. But this time, whatever it might have been, he kept it to himself.

"Where doesn't it expect us to be?" I said, more to myself than to the others. "What doesn't it expect us to do?"

And the answer came to me. I hated it, and knew even so that I had found the solution to the puzzle the ondan had set for me. "We have to go through Watchowl Forest," I said.

Ha erupted. "That's insane!" he shouted. "We have no idea what sort of monsters the Watchowl Forest harbors now. It was deadly before the Changewinds. It won't have gotten better."

Giraud crossed his arms over his chest and glared at me. "No. Not that. Think again, because I'm not going through that forest."

But Ondan Shanxi merely nodded. "Your heart has shown you the path you must take."

Chapter Eleven

We rode pillion into the deepening gloom of the old forest: Ha behind Giraud and me behind the ondan. We rode in with swords in hand. Giraud carried the commonplace book in his pack, and I rode with the lute in its case slung across my shoulders. I was still amazed that it hadn't been destroyed when I fell from the horse; lutes were incredibly delicate instruments, after all. When I mentioned it, though, the ondan gave me an enigmatic frown and said that it would survive worse than a mere fall.

We didn't worry about the lute or the book, however, or meals or anything else. Around us the Watchowl Forest had come to hideous life. The edge of the forest, which had been made up of wide rows of graceful chestnut trees, quickly gave way to taller, narrower trees that crowded closely together. We lost the sunlight beneath tangled, matted branches overhead, their leaves as thick as thatching. The forest began to feel almost airless—no breeze moved against our skins, and breathing felt like sucking air from an inflated sheep's bladder.

The oppressiveness of the atmosphere heightened as we began to see changes the spell had wrought in the forest life. Vines coiled along the branches of trees overhead, uncoiling in silent, deadly loops as we moved near them, so that the forest appeared to be infested with giant, writhing serpents. I could see the animals some of the vines had caught in their coils, hanging from the upper branches like meat in a butcher's shop, while the vines extruded delicate tendrils that pierced the carcasses and sucked the life and the nourishment out of them. A huge clawed deer thrashed above us, caught around the belly and still alive, though already pierced in a hundred places. I will never forget the terror in its eyes.

The deer looked much like the fanged carnivores that had injured me, but this one appeared better adapted to its new life as a predator. Along with the canine teeth and a jaw reshaped with powerful muscles, its hoofed forelegs sported a set of bony, wickedly curved claws, and its eyes sat forward on its head, closer together and high on its narrowed nose. Hunting animals, I've always noticed, have eyes like that. As do humans. Eyes that look at you in pairs.

The ondan said, "Everything here has become predatory. See there?"

He pointed to a fallen, rotted log, where a trio of lush red flowers on thick stalks grew out of the rich earth. Two of them were in full bloom. One looked like a bud ready to open . . . until we moved close enough that I could see it twitching and writhing as vigorously as the vines overhead. "What is it doing?"

"Just an instant ago, it reached out and caught a mouse. I think we would be wisest to stay together at all times, and to assume that everything we see has some secret way of attacking us." He shook his head. "This is a situation that cannot be allowed to continue. When everything is a predator and nothing is prey, everything will die."

Nothing attacked us, though I constantly felt eyes watching me. The vines would loop down towards us, then whip back into the upper branches again as if they were frightened. It seemed like something protected us, for the sounds of animals screaming stopped us in our tracks more then once—the many starving predators caught *something* in that forest.

Finally I asked, "Why do the vines move away from us? Why don't the animals attack?"

"For now, I'm making use of a bit of Ko sorcery," the ondan said. "I've built the *shamadi* temple around us, that travels with us as we move."

"*Shamadi* temple?"

"A construct of the mind, child. A moving house of magic, formed of points and angles and planes that stretch through this world and the Five Listening Worlds and intersect around, beside, above and beneath us."

I wished I knew how to construct a *shamadi* temple. "So we can travel safely through the forest. Nothing will touch us."

"Not so." The ondan shrugged. "At best, my strength is limited. I can hold the temple for a long time before its walls begin to weaken, but they will weaken. Further, I can have some effect against mindless plants, or animals with simple minds. Creatures with more complex minds, however, will be able to find ways in at us. What the mind builds, after all, the mind can tear down."

"So if we run into people . . ."

" . . . You had best be prepared to use your sword."

Birds flapped above our heads. We'd seen crows, of course, and vultures in plenty—they'd had a feast unlike any they'd ever known because of me. These weren't of either sort, though. They were bigger, more ponderous, and though they flew through the canopy above us, they never called out. No cheeps or caws or squawks. I didn't like the feel of them up there, watching. Following. Nothing for us to do, though, but go on.

So we went on.

The undergrowth grew tighter around us, and more vicious. Thorns crowded the narrow trail we followed, and low understory trees leaned toward us as we rode between them, branches grasping like clawed hands. We didn't hesitate to hack off those branches with our swords, but no matter how many we hacked, more moved toward us.

"You see," the ondan said, "already the temple becomes less effective."

I saw.

It was as if we were inside a great house, and outside of it stood hungry children with their noses pressed against the glass—but these weren't looking in wistfully at food on the table. They were looking at us, because we were the food. And, I thought, if I had been standing in Giraud's family's greathouse, panes of leaded glass would have stood between me and the hungry outsiders. Here, nothing but the ondan's "temple" kept disaster at bay.

We pressed on.

"At least," Giraud said, "this route has the advantage of cutting off a great deal of distance."

"It has," Ha said. "And of cutting years off my life, too." He rode with his neck craned, looking up and to the sides and down, up and to the sides and down, his head never resting. "I don't know a dwarf who likes the open sky much—but I know I'd rather have the open sky above my head than these trees. I can see movement up there, but I can't make out what's causing it."

The ondan said nothing.

I shivered and held tighter to the hilt of my sword.

Travel through forest at the best of times is hard going, and through unknown forest, along poorly cleared trails that wind up and down hills and across

rocky streams, it's harder. I tried to keep my sense
of our direction clear in my head, but without the
sun to guide me, I quickly felt lost. I knew from what
Ha told me, and what the ondan confirmed, that the
road to the Watchowl Keep cut straight through the
heart of the Watchowl Forest. If we could keep
ourselves heading mostly south, or even southwest or
southeast, we'd cross it. Proof that the trails we followed had been made by animals, though, instead of
humans, was that none of them followed straight lines
or headed in a specific direction. They looped,
switched back, paralleled themselves, and pointedly
didn't go anywhere. So we were continually leaving
one trail and whacking our way through writhing,
hissing underbrush until we found another—more
often than not, as we worked our way deeper into
the forest, we found ourselves on foot, one leading
each horse, one following behind to keep anything
deadly from moving too close.

"Clearing ahead," Ha said.

"Does it look like the road?" I called. I was third
in line, leading the ondan's magnificent black horse,
while the ondan brought up the rear.

"No." Ha cleared his throat. "Maybe. It's hard to tell
from here, but I think we've found someone's house.

No one found this news cheering. My own expe-
riences with houses since the Changewinds blew
through convinced me that I'd rather be in the
woods—but there it was. As we got closer, I could
see the thatching of the roof, and the wattle-and-daub
packed in between the timber framing. It looked like
an ordinary house. The only *ordinary* house I'd seen
since the disaster had belonged to the dying bard in
Blackwarren, and it had remained ordinary because
he'd managed to keep the Changewinds from touching
it. Or him.

Maybe this is another such house, I thought. I
found myself hoping.

We stepped out of the forest into the clearing, carefully because we had to assume that someone was watching through the upper windows with bow drawn and arrow nocked. But we did step out. Somewhere around the house, which did not sit beside the road, there would certainly be a path that led to it. And after we discussed the matter, we decided that we might have a chance to acquire a couple of additional horses, if any had been present and had survived, and if the people of the house hadn't.

We approached through a garden that showed early signs of neglect. A few weeds grew among the neat rows. Several staked plants had toppled and been trampled, with no effort to set them right. The plants hadn't been watered. I could see nothing that told me something was terribly wrong with the place, but nothing reassuring me that it was right, either.

"Barn will be around the other side," Ha said.

The ondan said, "Perhaps we ought to take the time to find out if anyone still lives here."

We skirted around to the front of the house. From there, we could see a broad path, the two-tracked sort that would have been made by a wide cart. It already showed heavy overgrowth by the forest's predatory plants—I thought traveling along it looked more dangerous than the going right through the woods had been, since the trees in the woods took up space where the deadly vines and creepers and thorns couldn't grow. The path gave them plenty of room.

Nothing encroached into the cleared circle, though.

"I'll just knock on the door," Ha said, and stood on the broad stone stoop and knocked.

The door swung open. Ha looked back at us. "Wasn't completely closed," he said.

"Don't go in alone," Giraud said, handing the reins of their horse to me.

"Wait," the ondan said. "I'll accompany you."

"Not without me you won't," I said. I had no intention of standing in the clearing alone, holding the horses. I tied both of them to the hitching post and followed the others.

They moved into the room and stopped. I heard them gasp. But I couldn't see past them until I pushed Giraud (the only pushable one of the three) out of the way.

I wished I hadn't.

That sickening sweet-rotten odor that bypasses all logic to go straight to the gut hit me as I got fully into the house. Two bodies lay on the floor, decomposed and swelling. Vines coiled out of their gaping mouths—thick, smooth, fleshy vines black as tar, with broad, pale leaves. The plants were as malignantly ugly as anything I'd ever seen, but they were nothing compared to the fruit they already bore.

Attached by their navels to ropy tendrils of vines were half a dozen human-looking . . . what shall I call them? Gourds? Mannequins? Offspring, perhaps. Those closest to the bases of their respective plants were nearest to being ripe, and I had the feeling that when they ripened completely, they would resemble in every way the humans from which their parent plants sprouted.

The male plant—it couldn't have been a male plant, of course, or it wouldn't have borne fruit, but it was the one upon which the man-fruits grew—had three offspring that were recognizable. The first was full-sized, gray-haired, brown-skinned, with a skinny body. The hands, feet, and face were still blobby and unfinished—fingers and toes were stubs, the eyelids looked like they were fused together, and some sort of filmy membrane covered both the nostrils and the half-opened mouth. The second had the unfinished look I'd only seen before when I helped Maura dar Kastokan wrap the body of her newborn baby for burial. It hadn't lived more than a few minutes, poor thing, and had been small enough to fit in the palm of her hand.

The third was a brownish blob with stubby protrusions that would become arms and legs and head. Two flowers just beyond that had already set fruit. Two more were open, and flies buzzed around them.

The story was the same with the woman-plant, though I guessed the development of the woman-fruit was at least a few hours behind that of the man-fruit. None of the women looked so near completion.

"That's obscene," Ha said.

Giraud walked outside and threw up on the stoop.

The ondan alone of all of us moved closer. "How does it seed?" he asked.

For a moment, I couldn't understand his curiosity. More than anything else, I wanted to be away from the clearing and on the road to the keep. Then, however, I realized his curiosity had a purpose beyond mere gruesome curiosity. Something had killed the man and the woman who had lived here. Something had planted the seeds of those two vines in their mouths. That something was presumably still around.

The fruits of plants carried the seed. The fruit of this plant looked human and acted human. So now we faced not only people who were mad, and people who wanted to kill us . . . but people who weren't even people.

"Get away from there," Ha said.

The ondan didn't seem to hear him.

I looked more closely. As I watched, the fingers on the ripest of the man-fruits stretched and puckered, and little fingernails appeared on them. The toes developed, too. And then the eyes opened. Blank eyes, pale blue and as empty as the space between the Abyss and the knife-edged rock that lined its floor.

"Get back!" I shouted, but still the ondan didn't respond.

The man-fruit's arm began to slide toward the old

man, bonelessly, horribly, and Ha reached forward and grabbed him and pulled him back. I leaped forward and swung my sword down, striking the base of the plant just above the head of the dead man. I swung again and again, hearing as I did the thin keening wail of the nearest of the man-fruits.

I became aware that someone stood next to me, dispatching the woman-fruit plant. Giraud. He looked pale but grimly determined, and he handled his sword with an efficiency and a finesse that I would have suspected was beyond him. My historian friend bore marks of becoming a warrior after all.

When we finished with the vines, he and I hacked apart the vine-offspring, too. Pulp flew; no matter how real they looked on the outside, their insides held no bones or organs that I could discern. They seemed to be made up of nothing but bands of fibrous flesh running in all directions around a dense core of bright reddish material that looked and felt to me like wood.

Ha stopped us. "Leave them," he said. "If we've found these, there will be hundreds or thousands of others we won't find. The only way we can get rid of them all—if we even can—is to make it to the keep."

Giraud, sweating, said, "These won't go walking around." I was almost certain I saw tears in his eyes, but I couldn't understand why.

When we got outside, I asked him.

"You don't have anyone," he said, "and you haven't for a long time. So you wouldn't think of this, I guess. But me—I had brothers and a father. What if when the bitch-queen killed them, she had their bodies out where these plants could seed into them? What if I saw my da walking down the road toward me, or either of my brothers? What if, Isbetta? How would I know whether to hug them because they were still alive, or kill them because they weren't?"

I gripped his shoulders and stared into his pale

face. "You would know because your real brothers and father are dead. Anything you see that looks like them has to be something evil."

He shook his head and glared down at me. "*I* never saw them dead. I don't know for sure that they didn't find some way to escape at the last minute. And my heart will tell me there's always a chance, no matter what my mind says." He closed his eyes and took a slow, deep breath. "You know there's always a chance, Izza."

I did know. Some perverse part of me whispered in the back of my mind even then that my father might still be alive somewhere. That what I had heard from Birdie had been false. That my dreams of being reunited with him weren't hopeless.

Hope. I clung to the threadbare dreams it spun for me, never letting myself admit that I was lying to myself. I was lying to myself about so much. Telling myself that I would be able to undo the damage I'd done. That the world would go back to being a familiar place. That everything I had ever cared about might somehow be restored. I could see the stupidity of my hopes, but I couldn't release any of them, even as I watched the fabric they were made of tearing and shredding before my eyes.

Giraud stared into my eyes and nodded. "There," he said. "You do see."

I nodded slowly. "Yes. I do."

We found the barn locked, the horses within it frantic. They hadn't been fed or watered since their people died—I didn't know how long that had been, but it was long enough that the buckets hung on pegs in their stalls were empty and bone-dry and not a wisp of hay remained in any of the hayracks.

Again, and oddly, they were untouched by the Changewinds that had reshaped everything else in the world. They were just horses—four broad-chested, sturdy-legged plow beasts with backs wide enough to dance on. And when we'd watered them and given them something to eat, they became sweet, docile creatures.

The old couple had no saddles for their horses. They'd owned a heavy wagon, certainly a produce wagon of some variety, and a lighter one that would only do for transportation. Both were in good shape, and had we been planning to travel toward civilization instead of further away from it, we would have taken one or the other.

But while we hoped we would soon reach the road that led to the Watchowl Keep, we would be going further into land where people didn't live, and where horrors reigned unchallenged. With horses, we would have some mobility. Tied to a cart of any sort, we would be trapped by the road we wished to travel.

So Giraud and I tied the plow horses in two strings, and he rode the first one, and I took the second. Once we were away from the farm, I wasn't sure how we were going to get back on the backs of our fine steeds; we wouldn't have the mounting block in the barn to climb on, and neither of us was likely to consider climbing a tree as an option.

We met the ondan and Ha coming out of the house. They carried supplies.

"We want to reach the keep by late today, but we might not," Ha said, looking way up at the two of us. "Might as well take some food along in case we need it." Then he grinned. "Yah. And now the two of you get a feel for what it's like for me, don't you?"

It took me an instant to realize he was talking about his height. I grinned at him. "Or we could trade. You could ride mine and I could ride yours. Then you'd get an idea what it feels like to be me."

He arched an eyebrow and smiled. Then his eyes shifted, and the smile died. His hand moved to the hilt of his sword, and he unsheathed the weapon. The ondan, too, gripped his weapon. "Move," Ha said under his breath. "Fast."

I turned in time to see people walking toward us through the forest. They were naked, all of them, and they moved unbothered by the needle-tipped plants, the coiled vines, the biting flowers. Their expressionless faces studied us, and their oddly fluid movements brought them toward us at a slow-looking walk that nonetheless covered more ground than it should have, and faster.

Five or six of them were repetitions of a little girl, several more were identical copies of a young man who could have been her brother. I turned my horse toward the two-track path we hoped would take us to the road, and urged the giant horse into a run. It broke into a heavy-footed, graceless gallop, as frightened by the approaching monsters as I was.

Behind me, I heard Giraud shout, and the sickening sound of a sword slashing through something soft and wet and heavy. And the same high-pitched scream I'd heard in the house when we killed the vines tore through the air again. Hooves pounded the ground behind me. Above me, the coils of vines began to drop. We were going to get killed before we even made it to the road—we were never going to make it to the keep. I hacked through vines with my sword while the horse tried to run through the clearest parts of the path; I swung and stabbed and slashed keeping them away from the horse I rode, the horse I led, and myself, while vine sap covered my hands and face and clothes, numbing my skin.

I longed for the protection of the ondan's magical temple, but he was fighting his own battles and couldn't give shields to anyone. I heard his shouts behind me, along with those of Ha and Giraud. I knew I wouldn't get any help until we reached the main road—maybe I wouldn't get any there, either.

But getting there was the only goal I could think of that might make my situation easier. So I dug my heels into my horse's sides and leaned forward along his withers, tightening my thighs as I did. The horse, a good animal, pushed himself harder.

We galloped around a curve in the road, straight into a trap the human-looking vine-monsters had set. They'd dragged logs across the road, blocking the passage, and now they stood along either side in front of their barricade, waiting, holding sharpened sticks in their hands. I felt the coldness of their blank, unblinking eyes as they stared at me.

Hands grappled for my legs as we rode by, trying to pull me from the horse's back. I slashed through them with the blade, and felt the fingers go limp as the acid plant juice spattered all over me. I swung at faces and heads, and gripped my beast's mane with my left hand so that I wouldn't lose my seat. My wrist ached from swinging that sword, from the bone-jarring impact of cutting my way through obstacles. The muscles of my arm and shoulder and back burned. The sword felt like it weighed twice as much as a man; worse, when I lifted it and swung it, it seemed to fight against me.

Neither my mount nor I had time to make any adjustments in our course, and even if we'd had the time, we still didn't have the space. The horse tucked his forelegs under him like a prize jumper and lifted his massive body over the lowest part of the barricade. I heard a rear hoof drag a little as he came over, and felt the shock as he missed his stride, but he was steadier than I would have imagined. He faltered for two steps, then regained his footing, and I was finally able to regain my own balance. I lost the horse on the lead-line. She had balked at the fallen trees and broken free, taking her halter and most of the rope with her. I heard her fighting behind me. I didn't look back.

More rumbling hooves followed in my wake, and I prayed that all of my companions would get safely away from the waiting monsters. I couldn't do any more than I already was to make that happen, though. The vines were still dropping at me, the tree branches reaching out, the flowers still snapping and biting.

Sweat blurred with tears, burned my eyes and scored my cheeks—blinded me. Something lashed across my face before I could get out of the way, and the right side of my mouth and my cheek went numb. I felt like that side of my face had fallen off. My breath came hard. I hurt everywhere that wasn't numb, but I kept swinging. I had to keep swinging or I would die. More vines, and more vines; claw-handed trees scrabbling for my eyes; movement at the edges of my vision that I knew I didn't want to see, didn't dare see. Overhead, the birds, big and heavy and silent, flapping along, going in the same direction that I was. The horse blowing and snorting as he ran, tossing his head, while lather darkened the hair on his sloping shoulders and his sweat soaked through my leather breeches and made my seat precarious. He was as tired as I was, and as scared.

The scents of horse-sweat and my own terror and crushed and bleeding vines and moist, soft earth; the shouts and keening screams behind me and the wind rustling through the leaves overhead and the whispered flap, flap of the birds above and the muted thudding of my mount's hooves on the rutted, overgrown road; the feel of my pain and the cool air we stirred up as we galloped and the steady, heavy rhythm of warm, wide horse beneath me; the blacks and greens of the dark forest striped with blades of light that cut through from the sky to the ground like daggers, and hellish, writhing movement of the forest all around me; the taste of my blood and my sweat on my tongue—all those details blurred together and numbed me and made me mute and stole rational thought, and I became a sword arm welded to a torso attached to a horse, moving, moving, moving because if I failed to move, I would die.

Then, without my realizing when it happened or how, I reached up to swing at a vine and no vine was there. I slashed to my right to cut away the grasping talons of a twisted branch, and my sword met with no such branch. I dared a look upward, and saw a strip of blue over my head. I looked to my sides and found that nothing green grew right beside me, and the trees closest to me in every direction were chestnuts, broad-trunked, gracefully branched, unmoving and untouched by anything that did move. Except for the birds. Those—massive gray creatures with heads the size of cantaloupes and gleaming yellow eyes—sat in the branches and watched.

Let them watch, I thought. If I had a bow and sufficient arrows to do the job, I would have shot them. But I didn't. Let them sit in their trees and stare, then.

I looked down at the ground and saw broad, black paving stones beneath my horse's hooves. The road. I'd reached it. I slowed the horse to a walk, then turned him back to face the way we'd come. And I waited. A moment later, Giraud burst from between the trees, and Ha and Ondan Shanxi thundered out behind him. They were bloody, sweat-soaked, and pale, and their horses blew and shuddered and stared around them with white-rimmed eyes. But they'd survived. Like me. More trouble certainly lay ahead of us, but we'd beaten the Watchowl Forest.

Chapter Twelve

We killed another dozen of the plant-people just before we reached Galarialle, and heard movement in the trees all around us as we skirted the forest town. Unlike the other inhabited places we'd passed, though, we didn't see corpses everywhere, or even bones, which I guess after that much time, we could have expected. Galarialle lay silent and still, devoid of any signs that it had ever been inhabited.

Once we got past it, we began to travel faster again. Several facts motivated us. The first was the pressure of our mission. The second was our fear of spending a night in the middle of the Watchowl Forest, even on the road. The third was the uncanny, inescapable certainty that we were being watched. With time to recreate his spell, the ondan rebuilt his traveling temple around us. I modified the "don't notice me" song to include all four of us, and changed it to a four-beat rhythm with some judicious reworking of the tune so that I could sing it while we trotted.

The road stayed good.

The birds that had been following us went away.

And at last, as twilight leached the light from the sky, we rounded a final curve and discovered ourselves at the Burrinee River, and saw, glaring down at us from the far side of the river and from the top of an imposing cliff, the Watchowl Keep. Our relief at reaching our destination was short-lived . . . in fact, it lasted precisely as long as it took for the four of us to realize that the central portion of the bridge that crossed the river was a drawbridge, and to discover that the drawbridge was raised. From the other side. The bards of the Watchowl Keep were at home, but they weren't welcoming visitors.

We all stood on the bridge watching the water race by beneath us. At the point where the Burrinee passed the keep, it was wide, deep, and fast. Though I knew it was neither as high nor as deadly as it would have been in early spring, when runoff from the mountains would have swollen it to flood stage, still I couldn't avoid looking at the inky swirls and dimples that marred its surface and thinking about the snags and deadfalls that lay beneath, waiting to catch the careless swimmer and trap him until he drowned.

No one said anything for a long time. Then Ha cleared his throat. "I don't suppose we could just shout at someone up there and ask him to let down the bridge."

Another long silence followed that comment. Giraud broke it to say, "Figure if anybody there is still alive, it's because of this bridge, don't you think?"

"They have very good defenses," the ondan noted after another little while. "See how the far side of the bridge is built with pins and held up by chains attached to the cliff?"

We all looked into the deepening gloom, then nodded.

"They can pull those pins. If anyone got past the raised drawbridge without their welcome, they could just start winding in the chains. The pins that hold the structure together would come out, and the bridge would fall apart, and the wood that held it together would go into the water with whoever was on top of it at the time." He sighed. "It's a very good design for a bridge," he added.

"They've probably got sharpened stakes or something underneath, too, in case they have to pull the pins," Ha said. "That's what I'd do, anyway."

"Yes." The ondan nodded. "We must certainly assume they've done that."

We stood there a little longer, watching the water rushing by all around us, and I said, "Maybe we could just camp on the bridge tonight. I'm sure tomorrow we'll think of some way across."

"If we were attacked while we slept out here, we would have no place to run. We'd have the water to our sides and back, and the attackers in front of us. They would have all the advantages," Giraud said.

Both the ondan and Ha looked at him with approval. "Quite right," Ha said. "Good thinking."

Giraud said, "That's what happened to the warriors in the Battle of Fremish. It's a hard story to forget."

"Then where will we sleep?" I asked. "The road wasn't too bad during the day, but I bet it gets worse at night." As if to prove me right, behind us and some ways off, something screeched. I shivered.

"We'll figure something out," Giraud said.

We turned and started back to the riverbank. Behind us something enormous groaned. My heart leapt straight into my throat and my knees knocked together. I spun, yanking at my sword. The ondan and Ha were faster, while Giraud cleared his blade at the same time I did. The horses stomped and whinnied. In the darkness, I couldn't figure out what it was that threatened us . . . and then I realized the raised part of the bridge was growing larger—first wider, then wider and shorter. And then I realize that it was doing the groaning; its wood creaked and protested as it moved closer to us. Someone inside had decided to let us cross.

The bridge settled into place, and after a moment's hesitation, all four of us led our horses onto it. We didn't know yet whether we were moving away from danger, or simply toward another form of it, but I know in my mind I'd decided that any odds of doing something in our favor were better if we crossed the bridge than if we stayed where we were.

The drawbridge lifted again behind us, almost as soon as the last horse had stepped off of the plank. No one and nothing was going to follow us across; I found myself letting my breath out slowly. It almost felt, once we were across the bridge and on the far bank, that we'd reached a place where sanity still existed.

"I almost wonder if the Changewinds came here?" I said.

Giraud rested a hand on my shoulder. "I feel it, too. Like there's a wall around this place that nothing evil can pass."

The ondan chuckled. "That's because there is."

All three of us peered at him through the dark, trying to get a good look at his expression. I said, "Are you serious?"

"Indeed. A rather clever sort of wall exists around this place—I couldn't see it until we stepped through it, and even now, I cannot begin to guess how it's been created. Nonetheless, it exists."

"Then we're finally safe."

Ha snorted. "Safety is an illusion. If anything, we're finally in a place where the dangers are more likely to be known."

Right in my ear, a voice murmured, "Well said. Quite well said."

I glanced at the ondan. "Did you say that?"

"No."

"Ha, you didn't say that?"

Ha said, "I didn't."

"And Giraud—"

"Not me."

"Then who?"

The same voice, still right beside me, said, "I'm in the keep. I can hear and see everything you do from up here—I've been watching you for a long time. You're obviously untouched by the madness that has destroyed so many others, but I won't let you come up here until I know *why* you're here."

Giraud and I started in on the story of how we'd come to seek help at the keep. We didn't get any further than describing my singing the spell at the Pillar of the Sun, though, before the voice said, "That's enough. Turn to your left and walk along the cliff until you see a small, green light."

We did.

"Now, one of you touch the light."

Giraud reached out, and for an instant cool green flames enveloped his hand. Then the cliff began to rumble, and a large panel slid back into the rock face. Torchlight illuminated a broad, sand-floored passage that sloped upward and curved to the right, so that even though it was well-lit, we could only see in a little ways. Anything might be waiting for us beyond that curving wall of stone.

"Please step in."

When we hesitated, the voice grew annoyed. "You've come all this way through enormous danger and hardship to talk with us. You're going to have to trust us, now that you've arrived. If you don't, none of us will be able to help you."

Ha sighed and stepped forward first. The ondan followed. Then Giraud. I held back until last—even though my gut told me I was safe and among friends, recent experience left me feeling sure something terrible was going to happen. At last, though, I had to

go forward. The speaker in the keep was right. I'd
come all this way to meet with the bards, to see if
I could undo the damage I'd done. I couldn't turn
back; I couldn't undo the deaths I'd already caused,
but I could prevent more. Maybe.

Maybe.

I followed Giraud up through the corridor, which
climbed steadily in an upward spiral. I heard nothing but the sound of breathing and the soft thudding
of hooves and feet in the sand. I didn't feel like
talking to anyone. Evidently none of the other three
felt much more cheerful than I did. It was, I think,
too easy to recall how narrowly we'd missed death
before.

We reached a doorway, and now heard the disem-
bodied voice again. It said, "Wait, please."

We waited.

"Ondan Shanxi, please step to the wall and rest
your hand against it. The rest of you, stand well back
and wait until the ondan has come through."

"I don't like it," Ha said. "They're splitting us up."

"We are," the voice said. "For our own protection,
and until we can be sure of you. We apologize for
the necessity of this, but you will be reunited shortly."

"I am willing to go first," the ondan said.

He stepped forward and pressed his hand against
the wall. His entire body glowed with the same
unearthly fire that had surrounded Giraud's hand
when he put it in the light. No further doors opened,
though; instead, the ondan simply disappeared.

"Good design," Giraud said softly. "They bring us
all the way up a blind tunnel, and the only way
through to the keep is by magic. If we don't do what
they want, they just leave us in here. We might be
able to get out through the door at the bottom, but
I wouldn't bet on it."

I said, "And these are the people who are supposed
to help us, are they?"

"Look," Ha said, "if they're still safe and sane, their security measures must be worth something. Right?"

"Maydellan Ha. You will please step forward to the wall now and rest your hands against it."

"Both hands?"

"Both hands."

Ha suddenly looked less confident of the good intentions of the keep's denizens.

I looked at him and shrugged. "Go on. If we can't trust them, everything is lost anyway."

The dwarf sauntered forward and rested his hands on the stone. Like the ondan, he vanished.

We waited again, this time longer. I looked nervously at Giraud, and he gave me a quick hug. "It will be all right," he said.

"I know. I'm just scared. What if we've come all this way and they can't do anything?"

"Then at least we know we tried."

Small comfort, looking at the end of the world, to think you tried to stop it. I said nothing of the sort to Giraud.

"Giraud dar Falcannes, step forward and rest your hands against the stone."

He handed me the reins to his horse and took a deep breath. Then he nodded sharply and stepped forward. "See you on the other side," he said. He laughed.

I didn't. "See you on the other side" was what warriors in all the old stories said to each other when they knew they were facing death and expected to be killed at any moment. The old heroes—Blaylock and dar Sturmran and the Fanged One—were all supposed to have said those very words as they bravely stepped forward into the maelstroms of blood and misery that were to be their doom. "I'll see you in the keep," I corrected, and then the green light took him away from me, too.

The horses shifted restlessly. I looked around for some place to tie them, so that when I was called, they wouldn't be left alone to panic and hurt themselves. But the stone walls were smooth. So I dropped the reins on the ground, busied myself with removing all the tack and piling it against the far wall, and let them roam. If the bards in the keep intended to bring them after me, they would certainly know how to retrieve them. And if they didn't, I didn't want the poor horses trapped in the passage with saddles and bridles still on.

"Isbetta dar Danria, please come forward."

I knew what to do. I placed my hands on the stone wall and waited. For just a moment nothing happened. Then I felt a tingling, warm and soft as kitten fur, that brushed all over my body. At the same time, the world turned green—but it wasn't as simple as that. It would be easy to assume that I could still see the passageway and the horses and the tack and our few meager supplies, and that these had all been dyed green by the light. That was what I'd expected. Instead, though, green was the sum total of all I could see. Details and objects dissolved in the featureless emerald light, and the whole of the world ceased to exist except for the single color—and oddly, because green was all there was, after a moment I couldn't see that, either.

Then the pleasant tingling went away. The unpleasant blindness didn't.

I felt hands clasping my wrists, and heard two voices saying, at almost the same time, "Walk, please," and "Don't hurry her, Durral—I don't think she can see us."

"I can't," I said.

I heard one exasperated sigh. "She would come through gate-blind."

"Sometimes it takes a moment for sight to return," the second voice said. The first voice, the one identified as belonging to Durral, had been the voice my three companions and I had heard while we stood out on the riverbank and waited in the corridor. The second voice was younger, female, and with a gentleness to it that made me think she didn't hate me, even if Durral did.

After no time at all, Durral said, "She's had her moment. Can't you see anything yet?" He didn't try to hide his annoyance.

"No. Nothing."

"She's a sensitive," the woman said.

Durral disagreed. "She's lying."

I felt a breeze brush by my face, and had the uncomfortable feeling, when it was far too late to do anything about it, that I had been tested in some way.

"Well, fine, then. She isn't lying," Durral said. "We can lead her blind."

I locked my knees and refused to budge. "What did you do?" I said. I felt helpless, standing there with two people I couldn't see hanging on to me, not knowing whether I stood on the edge of a cliff or in the center of a room, or whether the three of us were alone or on a dais in front of a thousand waiting people who silently watched and judged me.

"We could, but we aren't supposed to and you know it. The rivergate is disorienting enough for the people who come in by it. Don't do anything to unsettle her further." The woman paused, then answered my question. "I just moved something in front of your face, Isbetta; moved it very close to your eyes. If you had been able to see it, you would have blinked."

"Oh." I felt terribly helpless. Frightened. I wondered if I had been blinded forever by my passage through the rivergate. Then, however, I realized that the darkness was beginning to resolve itself into areas that were darker and ones that were not so dark. I blinked, hoping to help the transition along, but blinking did nothing.

Time, however, helped a great deal. "I'm beginning to be able to see something," I said, "though everything is still very dark."

"Wait a moment," the woman said.

I had to wait longer than a moment, but eventually darkness receded and my vision returned.

"Now we need to get her along to Inquiries, Cynta—or do you intend to find something else you can baby her about?" Durral asked. He was short and muscular, broad-shouldered and broad-faced, with dark straight hair pulled back in a heavy braid, and pale, angry eyes.

Cynta had sounded older, so I was surprised to discover that she appeared to be about the same age as me. She was taller, though not tall. Her black hair curled loosely down to her shoulders, and her eyes, as dark as the ondan's, looked at me with a kindness and a compassion that I hadn't seen or felt in years. I could be her friend, I thought. Under different circumstances, if I weren't the one who wrecked the world. I looked away from her—her kindness made me feel even guiltier than I had before.

I looked down at my boots and my filthy leather breeches and asked, "Is that where my friends are?"

I didn't get an answer. Instead, Cynta said, "Durral is right. We need to take you to Inquiries."

Inquiries had sounded ominous when Durral had mentioned it; it didn't sound any better when Cynta repeated the name; and as I stood alone on a polished stone floor looking up at rows of seats filled with men and women whose drawn faces and heavy movements suggested warriors facing one battle too many, I thought it was worse than it sounded. I've heard people say they got butterflies in their stomachs when they were nervous; I had warring falcons. Cynta had shoved me through a heavy, black-painted door with a worried frown and the admonition, "Tell them everything you can." The sound of the door clicking behind me had sounded like a single beat from a death-drum.

They were all bards. Full bards, dressed in the

flowing forest green tunics and pale cream breeches that bards not associated with any court or town affected. They were of all ages, of all shapes and colors, of all heights, of both sexes. They had in common only their clothes and the single expression that stamped each of their faces—an expression of weariness touched with cold appraisal and deep underlying anger. They had suffered, and I was the one who had made them suffer, and they were going to call me to account for my sins. I stood staring back at them, schooling my outward expression to calm as I had done so often when Birdie was in one of her rages. With her, any display of fear, of pain, of weakness, only set her at me harder. I expected no better from these strangers. In fact, I expected worse.

Chapter Thirteen

A few latecomers straggled into Inquiries through a door at the top of the room, just behind the high, distant back row of seats. They filed in and moved down rows and across occupied seats until they reached empty ones scattered seemingly at random. But I noticed that the older bards sat closer to the center, the younger ones further away. Though they wore no outward symbols of rank, then, they still had rank. I kept that in mind.

The heavy door at the top of the amphitheater slammed shut—the second beat of the death-drum. I tried to control my breathing, and I waited. Standing. I had no place to sit and no one around me; the lowest row of seats started well above my head so that everyone looked down on me from far above. I felt very alone, and very small. I still carried the lute in its case, and my small pack on my back. These dragged at my right shoulder and sent little shooting pains down my back and up my neck until I put my burdens on the floor. I slid them in front of my feet. They gave me a little something to stand behind.

The fierce old man who sat front and center above

me stood at last. He said, "We are the bards of Watchowl Keep. You and your friends have come to us seeking help, telling wild tales and saying that you know what set the deadly magical storm winds to blowing. We've watched you since we noticed you and your two companions traveling along the edge of Watchowl Forest. We saw you join up with the ondan. We have seen and heard much that you've done and said. So don't bother telling us any lies." He leaned forward, resting his hands on the low rail that separated us. In a rich, full voice, he said, "Tell us now, from the beginning, how this disaster came to happen."

He sat down, crossed his arms, and glared at me. Around him and behind him, the other bards stared. And waited.

I knew this moment would come. I knew all along that I was going to have to explain to a hostile audience how I had come to destroy the world. I'd hoped for sympathetic listeners, for fewer people, for the opportunity to sit and gather my thoughts, or even that I might be permitted to answer reasonable questions reasonably. Since I wasn't going to get those better circumstances, I had to make the best of the opportunity I had. I had to convince this room full of angry strangers that I intended to make right the wrongs I'd done, and that I would be able to do that only if they helped me.

I said, "My name is—" and my voice cracked. I wished I had a glass of water. I tried again. "My name is Isbetta dar Danria. I'm the—" I could hear my words trembling on the air, as full of fear as mice before a stooping hawk. I drew a deep breath, tried to focus myself as I would have while weaving a complex design or singing a song. "I'm the daughter of Lannee Andras the Liedan and the late King's Bard Haral dar Danria."

I heard little gasps of surprise. There were those

among the audience, I realized, old enough to have been my father's companions and fellow students, and others old enough to have been, perhaps, his teachers. Maybe some of them knew my mother still. According to my father, she'd been a bard. I sensed that I had struck a surprise blow in my own favor, and continued quickly, telling them about Birdie and her plan to sell me, my overheard revelation about the manner of my father's death, and Giraud's and my desperate escape from Blackwarren.

I tried to get a feeling for their mood as I talked, but they were bards, skilled in letting the world see only what they wanted it to see. My father had been the same way. I gathered nothing from their faces; their eyes said they were watching me, their postures indicated that they were listening, but their faces were closed. Maybe they liked me, maybe they hated me, maybe they wanted to see me hanged; their expressions said nothing.

I told them about fleeing into the Stormfather Mountains, about finding the cave that saved our lives and the nantatsu that almost cost us them, about Hearthold Mountain and Maydellan Ha and the book and the songs. Still no response. I could have been talking to a room full of corpses.

I detailed my singing of the song the nantatsu had indicated, and our adventures afterward. I told them what Bard Edder had told me to tell them—about Belangia the Hawkbard and the 'Song of Belangia,' about being instructed to bring the black lute to Watchowl. I passed on Edder's odd remark about it finding its player. And I told them about fleeing and fighting and nearly dying.

Finally, when I couldn't think of anything else to say, I stopped. I stood on the hard, cold stone with my legs aching and my throat sore and my nerves rattled, and I waited. They looked at me, all those bards, and then they began to look at each other. To lean over and whisper to each other. I seemed to no longer exist to them. Once I stopped having a story to tell, I didn't matter at all.

I was too tired by that point to care what they thought about me. I wanted only to find food to eat, water to drink, and a place to lie down. I could do nothing about my first two needs, but my third was simple enough to meet. I knelt on the stone, spread my cloak, placed my pack on top of it and curled up in a little ball with my pack as my pillow and my arms wrapped around the leather-cased black lute. I closed my eyes, and my worries went away.

"Isbetta? You have to wake up now. Isbetta? Isbetta!"

A stranger cajoled me and shook my shoulder. I burrowed deeper beneath heavy blankets, vaguely surprised at how comfortable the floor had become.

"Isbetta, Inquiries is meeting again in half a candlemark, and you have to be there. You'll need to shower and change before they meet, and get something to eat."

I woke up completely at the words "something to eat." I didn't particularly want to shower or change clothes—given the choice between doing that or sleeping for a week, I thought I'd take the sleeping. But food was another matter. I wanted some, and I wanted it soon.

I sat up and rubbed the sleep from my eyes. I was lying in a sun-filled room, in a bed softer and more wondrous than any I'd ever been in, even when I was little and stayed at Court with my father. I wore nothing but my shirt, and felt a moment's panic as I wondered how I had come to be in a strange bed in a strange room, nearly undressed. But after a moment's thought, I realized I recognized the girl who had awakened me. I trusted her.

"Cynta," I said. "How did I get here?"

She laughed. "You fell asleep on the floor of Inquiries, and one of the bards carried you in. I undressed you and covered you up. They decided after all you'd been through to let you sleep." She shook her head slowly, the expression on her face one of bemusement. "I have to tell you, I don't think anyone has ever fallen asleep in Inquiries before. I've heard mention of it from every bard I've passed this morning."

She was kind to me. I tried considering her kindness in light of the impression I'd gotten while speaking to the bards, that I was something despicable—that I was nothing but a problem with which they all needed to deal—and keeping in mind that I knew what I'd done, and how many people I'd murdered, and how desperate a situation I'd thrown my world into. I couldn't make all the pieces fit. So I nodded and said nothing.

Cynta gave me an encouraging smile. "Come on get up. If you'll get in the shower, I'll call down to the kitchen and tell Cook to send your food up now. It will be here by the time you're out and dressed."

I thought about that. The shower didn't present much of a problem, but getting dressed did. I'd cut up my only other shirt for bandages, and both of my sets of breeches and tunics were filthy. I said as much.

"We have clothes in stock for students," she said. "I can have a set brought up for you."

She directed me into the bathroom. I recognized the plumbing as the sort we'd had when I was a child, and didn't have to ask for directions—one humiliation spared me, anyway. After I showered, I found folded clothes waiting for me on the towel shelf. I pulled it on—fresh underwear and a uniform that was a variation on the one that the bards wore, consisting as it did of pale green shirt, a quilted white tunic, a narrow white cloth belt, and black leather breeches. I found worn spots on the clothing, and places where both the shirt and the tunic had been carefully mended. I found that while I slept, someone had cleaned my boots for me.

Being clean and wearing clean clothes felt wonderful. I toweled off my hair and braided it to get it out of my way, then headed out to rejoin Cynta.

She sat in one of the two chairs at the small table next to the room's single window. "I got something for me, too. Figured I might as well eat with you so that we can talk."

She wanted to talk with me. That, I thought, probably meant bad news. I didn't want her to jolly me along, though, discussing the weather or food or my childhood and youth. I settled myself in front of the place she'd sat for me, and before I even took a bite, got right to the point. "So what have they decided to do to me?"

Her eyebrows twitched, and she tried to hide a smile, but failed. "Do to you? We aren't going to do anything to you."

"Right." The smell of the food—fresh fruit and a slab of broiled mutton as thick as my thumb, some sort of boiled, sugared grain, and slivers of hard cheese sliced across waybread—got to be too much for me. I hadn't had anything *good* to eat since the nantatsu fed me. I dug in. If it was going to be my last breakfast, at least it would be a delicious one.

"I'm telling the truth. No one is going to do anything to you, Isbetta. We compared your story with the ones your friends told, and none of us can see where you could have done anything differently. Everyone regrets the terrible outcome, but . . ." She sighed and took a bite of her cheese on waybread, chewed thoughtfully, and frowned. "I have to tell you, if everything that happened to you had happened to me, I don't know that I would have even made it out of the house. Weren't you scared?"

I nodded. I was surprised she was trying to see

events from my point of view. I definitely had not expected anyone to do that. "I was."

"Having someone trying to sell you . . . and finding out the same person had murdered your father . . ." She shook her head again and took a large bite of her mutton. "And then to escape and be captured by a monster, do what you were told to do, and find out later that the nantatsu had been coming after you again anyway . . ." She looked up at me and smiled. "You're very brave. We—the bards, that is—spent most of the night talking about this. We aren't certain that we can teach you how to undo the 'Song of Belangia,' but we think we can. And we're going to do everything we can to help you."

After we ate, she leaned up to a metal tube sticking out of the wall—one that I hadn't noticed before—and said, "Cook, please send someone to the number three guest quarters to pick up the dishes." Then she pointed to the lute case. "Bring that. We'll need it."

We obviously weren't going to waste any time. I took the lute and followed her through a maze of passageways, down a central spiral staircase so long I began to wonder how anyone had ever managed to lug me all the way up to that tower bedroom without waking me, and at last into a bright, airy room full of books, instruments, and in the center, a long wooden trestle table and perhaps twenty straight-backed wooden chairs. Maydellan Ha already occupied one of them, Giraud another, and Ondan Shanxi a third. The dislikable Durral was there, and the bearded old man who had asked me the night before to tell the bards what had happened. Up close, I realized that he was built like a bull, and I could see much more clearly the ferocity of his eyes and the hardness of the set of his mouth. Three other bards, these somewhere between Cynta's age and the old man's, also waited.

Everyone turned to look at us when we came through the doors, and I felt as awkward as I had the night before, standing in Inquiries. I felt my face growing hot, and looked down at my feet, hoping that no one would notice.

"Isbetta dar Danria," a man's voice said. I looked up, and one man smiled at me. Not the old one, or Durral, but a tall, lean one with sun-browned skin and straw-pale hair. "I'm Remeys. I was a friend of your father's while he was alive . . . and I knew your mother. You look very like her."

I felt a surge of hope. "You know my mother?" But he hadn't said "know." He'd said "knew." And even as the words burst from my mouth, I realized I shouldn't have said anything. The expression on his face confirmed that. He paled and I saw a flash of pain in his expression. I didn't even need to hear him say the words to know that she was dead.

"She was . . . very dear to me," he said.

"Later," the old bard said. "Later, damnall. We have things to accomplish. And the first is to find the owner of the lute. It has found its way home to us after all these years—the fact that it has chosen now to do so is not coincidence."

I carried the lute case to the old bard and handed it to him—and felt an overwhelming wash of regret as I did so. Though I had no claim to it, I felt as if I was giving away a part of myself.

Odd the reactions people have when they've been through stress, I thought.

The old bard lifted the lute out, every bard in the room gasped.

I hadn't taken time to look closely at the instrument while I carried it. I'd seen it once when Giraud and I had taken it up from under Bard Edder's floorboards—but that had been in very poor light. Then I'd carried it and I'd done my best to protect it, but part of doing my best, as far as I could see, meant keeping the lute safely encased. So aside from that one quick look I got when we took it, and the second when we checked to make sure it hadn't been damaged when I fell off the horse—also in poor light, I might add—that's all I'd done with it. I admit, seeing it in the warm light of the conservatory, it took my breath away, too.

It had the typical shape of a lute—round back, short, wide neck, sharply back-turned head. It had an unusual number of singled and doubled courses—unlike the lutes I was most used to seeing, the first two strings on this were singles but the other six courses were doubled. Its oddness went beyond that, however. Every bit of it was purest flawless black, from the inlaid semiprecious stones around the rosette to the beautifully carved pegs, to the metal frets, to the gut strings. I couldn't think why Bard Edder would have taken the trouble to dye the strings black, but I had to admit the final effect was stunning.

The old bard stared at it. He ran his fingers over the instrument like a blind man studying a particularly interesting carving. He closed his eyes, shivered, and opened them again. He looked at me. "Did you play it?"

"It wasn't mine to play," I told him. "Bard Edder told me to bring it, so I brought it." I sensed more in his question than idle curiosity, though, so I added, "We didn't exactly have time for songs around the campfire, anyway. We spent most of the trip fighting our way through one problem or another. If you follow my meaning."

He nodded. Then he sat on a tall stool, rested his left leg on the top rail, propped lute on leg, and began to tune.

I'm an admirer of a well-played lute. Giraud has a bit of talent with one, especially if you don't mind listening to sappy love songs about the wistful maid who died of a broken heart when her true love sailed out to sea. I'm fonder of the bawdy ballads and the adventure songs, and of course of the dances, but Giraud has a pleasant voice, and had a very nice lute, and I was willing to listen to him sing of broken hearts and twining vines. He taught me to play it when we had time, and I found that I could pick out the tunes I liked fairly well. I inherited my father's ear for music, and evidently some of his facility with instruments as well. Though I can't say that I was brilliant on lute, I knew how one was supposed to sound.

The bard finished his tuning, and played a few experimental notes on his new instrument. They sounded *off* to me, and I thought maybe he had the tuning wrong. Everyone else waited, patiently, as if what he was doing were as important as figuring out how to undo the 'Song of Belangia.' I kept my mouth shut and waited to see why.

Then he quit plucking around at it and dove into a song I recognized—"Sinking of the *Raiders' Pride*." It's usually a good, lively song, full of drama and tension, and with a nice bit at the end where, just when you think all is lost for the heroes, they find a way to attack one more time and take down the *Raiders' Pride* before their own ship founders and they have to row home in dories. He didn't sing the words, but the tune is as unmistakable as a best friend's face—even under the circumstances, I couldn't mistake it. And the circumstances were odd—deeply odd. As I said, I like lute music and I liked the song the old bard played, but listening to that rendition of it, my skin started to crawl. In the back of my mind, I could see images of destruction, men fighting each other on the tossing decks of ships, blood spreading across the scrubbed planks, bodies flung overboard to sink into the depths of a stormy sea. I'd never felt the horror before in the tale of the *Raiders' Pride*. I'd never heard the men screaming;

I'd never seen them dying, I'd never thought of the terrible waste of life, of the *tragedy* of that battle. I couldn't see the heroes anymore in the song—I could only see the cannons pounding both ships to ruin, and the sons of distant mothers dying horribly a long, long way from home.

Not even the rousing ending could wipe away the pain I felt. He brought the song to a close and I found myself sniffling, with a few stray tears running down my cheeks. Nor was I alone. All of us, from oldest bard to youngest, and both dwarf and *human*, stood crying. All of us, that is, but the old bard.

He stared down at the black lute and said, "I can't play it."

The bard Remeys said, "No. We should have felt a surge of joy at the end, where the heroes win the day. But I felt nothing of that. I felt only horror, at the deaths and the pain and the loss."

"Me, too," Cynta said.

"And me," another bard agreed. The rest nodded.

The old bard turned to the ondan. "How about you?"

"Only the same effects everyone else seems to have felt. *Seen*, rather. I wasn't so much listening to you play as watching a battle at sea. I found it most disturbing."

The bard looked at the rest of us to see if anyone had something other to offer, then frowned. "Disturbing doesn't seem to be a strong enough word. The music this lute made sent shivers down my spine, and holding it now is making my skin crawl."

"I can see that it has been strongly spelled," Ondan Shanxi said softly.

Everyone turned to look at him.

"I noticed it when I picked up Isbetta after her fall from her horse. I lifted the instrument to get it out of the way, and even through the case, I could feel the power of the spells the builder had placed on it. It has a personality, I believe. Maybe you could even say it has thoughts of its own—thoughts about what it should do and who should play it."

"You picked it up?" Remeys asked.

"Only briefly, to move it to our campsite. I found the merely lifting the case so unpleasant I was delighted to put it down again."

The old bard said, "That's precisely how I feel." He stood and laid the lute back in its case.

Remeys said, "Perhaps it means to come with me. Considering . . ."

The old bard's face brightened. "How foolish of me. I never considered that—I only thought of it seeking me out."

Remeys picked it up—and a look of horror twisted his face and froze it.

He put the lute down so quickly I could almost say he threw it, and backed away. "No. Not me that it wants. And I can't imagine anyone who would pick it up with it doing that."

The old bard sighed. "Perhaps it isn't the tool we need to reverse the 'Song of Belangia.' We've held that note before us as if it were sacred—we've been waiting for the black lute to return because we were sure she left us the key. But perhaps the note was meaningless. Or intended for another time, another disaster."

A younger bard recited:

> "The mighty bard
> Who wields the black lute
> Who at the gate stands
> Who carries a flute
> With ties of blood
> Unbinds the spell
> Breaks the world free
> From its magical hell."

The old bard shrugged. "I remember the note. The

puzzle of it has always been the flute with the ties of blood. No one has ever known what that meant."

Cynta looked at the old bard. "Bard Troman, she was dying when she wrote it. You cannot judge it the way you would judge her usual work. And anyway, this wouldn't be the first time that someone has looked at the vision spun out in a crystal globe and seen something that could be taken two ways, only one of which was obvious at the time."

"Then we should have every bard here try to play the lute?" the old man asked. He glanced in Cynta's direction and sighed. "And when none of the bards can bring themselves to touch the instrument, do we admit that Lannee erred in the casting of the spells, and that the black lute will be useless to us?"

The ondan cleared his throat. "I don't know why the spelled lute is so important to your plans," he said, "but I think, regarding its player, that you may be overlooking the obvious."

Bard Troman looked at him. "What an interesting observation. I'd like to think I'd passed the point of overlooking the obvious in my rash youth, but perhaps I'm mistaken. If you see a solution, please share it with us, ondan." He didn't have the reverence in his voice that I was used to hearing when people spoke to the ondan. In fact, to me he sounded slightly sarcastic.

If Ondan Shanxi heard the sarcasm, he gave no sign of it. He said, "I'd note, Bard Troman, that Isbetta has carried the lute without the first complaint of distress or discomfort since she took it from the dead bard's house."

Bard Troman nodded. "True. But she isn't a bard, so that's meaningless. The black lute is a bardic instrument built for bardic use."

The ondan nodded. "You are certainly correct when you assert that it has been built for bardic use. From the spells woven into its making, it appears to have been built as a weapon. A powerful one, in fact—

one built to take a bard's magic, shape it, amplify it, and target it."

Troman paled and said nothing.

The ondan smiled a grim, tight-lipped little smile. "Ko magic, good bard, focuses on seeing reality, on acknowledging details as they are and not as we wish them to be, or as we remember them, or as others see them. I am, within my ondanary, best of all at seeing." His smile went away. "It was my special talent that brought me through the dangers I've faced and led me to these two children and the dwarf. Isbetta, untrained though she is, has the bardic gift in abundance. Giraud has certain gifts that will be useful wherever he goes, though I suspect for him to survive to use them, he will either have to find a place like this, whose inhabitants are outside of the reaches of the government of Terosalle, or else leave Terosalle entirely."

"And the dwarf? You with your clear sight have discovered this band of heroes," Troman said. He had begun marking with a pen on a pad of wood-pulp parchment, but he wasn't writing. Instead, he was drawing: little knives and spears and roped twisted into nooses. I thought it clear that no matter who had championed us and our cause and permitted our entry into the keep, it hadn't been Troman—and whoever it was had done it contrary to Troman's opinions and wishes. The old bard said, "Surely, you have heroic claims for your dwarf, too."

"None that need concern you. Our only reason for seeking out your people is to get training for Isbetta, so that she can unsing the 'Song of Belangia.' And I would suggest that the black lute found its way into her keeping because she is the one with whom it has chosen to work." The ondan sounded so reasonable and so kind that he made Bard Troman look almost foolish by comparison. I noticed the way his own people looked at him when the ondan finished speaking.

The other bards murmured to each other. Troman flushed. "The black lute is an instrument. A fine one, but nothing more than spelled bits of wood and bone and gut. It chooses nothing."

The ondan shrugged and folded his hands on his lap. "I see life as it is, not as I wish it to be. You have been working since the disaster happened, trying to find a way to reverse the damage because you wish to claim that your bards rescued everyone who was scarred by the 'Song of Belangia'—by this spell your own people let loose through carelessness. But you know as truly as I that your bards can do nothing to reverse the spell save teach the girl what she needs to know to go back to the mountain. She will need the power the lute can give her to succeed, and you would rather deny her that than give up the political edge you think you can gain from having your people named as the heroes—"

"You dare to imply," the old bard interrupted, "that I would put political gain ahead of the good of my world? I should have you thrown out for that."

"I *state*," the ondan said, "that you want the best for your people, and have lost sight of the fact that sometimes they may not be able to achieve what is best for them on their own."

I sat listening to this, feeling a bit sick to my stomach. I hated fighting, and I especially hated fighting that centered around me. I wished I could be anywhere else until they worked out their differences, but that wasn't to be.

The bard said, "You make great claims for the girl. You say she has bardic potential, when in fact she probably did nothing more than loose a resonance spell laid upon the Pillar of the Sun by some ancient wizard. But I will not have it said that I put my own political ambitions ahead of the welfare of the rest of the world. I have never acted solely on self-interest before, and I'm not doing it now."

"Then test the girl."

"Test her how? She has no training. She can't sing any of the lays, or any of the spellsongs."

"One of her spellsongs got her past my notice until her horse stumbled and she lost her rhythm."

"I heard nothing of this. You're saying that she has demonstrated magical ability away from Hearthold Mountain and the Pillar of the Sun?"

"Yes," the ondan said. "Not much, and it has been uneven, but yes."

"Then you won't object if I test her now."

"Without preparation? Without any training? That's hardly fair."

"You claim she's a potential hero. I say if she had any ability at all, someone would have sent her to a bardic school long ago. As old as she is now, she will have to have an enormous amount of latent ability for us to train her. So fair or not, let's see what she can do."

"Then let her play the black lute," the ondan said.

The old bard's mouth dropped open. "You jest."

"Either I'm right and she can use it, or I'm wrong and this is hopeless anyway."

They glared at each other from across the table, two old men as different as old men can be, both fierce, both unbending, and both determined to be right at all costs. I wished I could run away. I said, "I didn't mean to cause this trouble. I only brought the lute—"

Bard Troman waved me to silence.

Ondan Shanxi glared at me with a look that told me I would have been better to keep my mouth shut.

Both men stared at each other again.

Finally the bard said, "Very well. Have her play the black lute."

Chapter Fourteen

In such a way, I found myself facing my second hostile audience in two days—for after the ondan insulted their highest master and called into question his integrity, any compassion that might have been in their eyes died. They hoped to see me fail. Even Cynta's expression had chilled. Their hope for my failure was as clear on their faces as it would have been had they sat cursing me aloud.

Remeys handed me the lute, and pointed to the high stool. "Sit there and brace it on your leg so you don't break it." His tone added his opinion that I was an idiot child; he didn't need to put that into words for me to get the message.

"I know how to play," I told him. I caressed the warm wood of the black lute, feeling comfort just in touching it. No one else liked it? That wasn't my problem. I . . . loved it. When I touched it, I could feel the wood singing beneath my fingers. It seemed happy to be with me. I could almost hear its voice as I held it, even though I had yet to touch the strings. I was sure, hugging it against my chest, that it wanted to be with me, which may sound silly when talking about a box of wood and string, but it was the way I felt. I glared up at Remeys and, in the coldest voice I could manage, said, "What I don't understand is what my playing will prove."

Troman spoke for him. "It will prove nothing, and nothing is all it needs to prove for us to send you back the way you came."

I wasn't sure what he meant by saying that. Well, the second part, that he intended to send me back where I came from . . . that part I got well enough. But the first bit, about proving nothing and nothing needing to be proven, sounded like bad poetry to me—the sort where the poet has put so much work into his fine words that he forgets to make them mean something. I decided I'd do myself a favor to play a song I knew well, rather than one that I thought would impress my listeners. I couldn't bring myself to start into one of my favorites, though. I couldn't imagine any of that cold group being amused by my version of "Mistress Moirna's Breeches" or "Laddies in the Bath" or "What the Donkey Said to the Cock." I liked the reels too, but bards sang as well as played, and the reels were just instrumental. They way I had it figured, the bards would let me play one song, or a part of one song, and probably as small a part as they could get away with. I didn't think they cared much about fairness. However, I had to believe that what I was doing mattered. We'd come so far, and their willingness to help us depended on me proving myself to them even if I didn't know what they were looking for.

So that left the sort of music Giraud preferred—wistful ballads. Of those, the one I did best and minded least was "Lady of the Glass Lake." It's sad, of course; it's the story of a handsome young man who, while walking by a lake on a foggy morning, meets a beautiful girl. He falls in love with her at once, and the two of them seek each other out by the banks of the lake every morning, until at last he wants to be introduced to her parents so that he can ask for her hand in marriage. She runs away from him weeping, and he pursues; she says that he must never meet her parents and he insists. The young idiots in these songs always insist, of course, and the pitiful young women always eventually give in.

In any case, like her kin of other weepy songs, she finally tells him that she will take him to meet her parents, but that he must carry a token that she give him and must not let it out of his hand until he once again stands on the shores of the lake beside her. She then hands him this token, a single greenish coin, and leads him down into the waters of the glassy lake. He follows, marveling at the beauty of the underwater world and the magic that lets him breathe there without drowning. I wouldn't have followed on a bet, not if a thousand gold coins hung in the balance. But young idiots always do the ridiculous.

Anyway he goes down under the water, and he meets her parents, who are magical lake people, beautiful beyond words and enchanting. They treat him to a great feast, and tell him how much they care for him, and how delighted they are that he loves their daughter. But after the feast, the girl's mother and father insist on standing one to either side of him and taking his hands in theirs, welcoming him into the family, and as the girl's mother takes his hands, she dislodges the green coin from his fingers and it drops to the floor of their underwater castle. Immediately the castle fills with water, the young man drowns, and the girl, of course, dies not long after of a broken heart. The parents bury them together in the deep heart of the lake, which, in deference to the young lovers, is forever after still as glass, no matter the weather above.

The story itself is silly enough, but the melody is lovely, and the lute part is poignant. Plus, I could do the fingerings, including some fierce stretches and the trills and hammer-ons and pull-offs that add to the difficulty and make the piece more impressive. It was still a common folk piece, but I thought it was a good one.

But besides being good, it was also the most difficult bit of music that I knew except for the reels, and I couldn't watch my audience's reaction to it. I had to concentrate on getting all the words right, plus playing the music on an unfamiliar lute with an extra course and a flatter, wider neck. The lute at least sounded good to me when I played it, and I threw myself heart and soul into singing the song and making myself feel the tragedy of it. And I didn't even miss that hellish bit of fingering in the bridge from the first position and the first string to a barred eighth position with most of the notes played clear across the neck on the sixth and seventh courses and back to the third position and the first, second, and fourth strings. That bit always gave me trouble, and when I was past it, I let out a mental breath and relaxed a little.

I was so lost in what I was doing that I forgot to think about anyone listening to me. I was singing for myself, telling myself that sad story all over again, and this time believing it. When I reached the end, I felt almost reluctant to stop playing, and at the same time I felt drained.

I looked up.

Every person in the room wept, save only for me. A few knelt on the floor, sobbing into their hands. The old bard had his head on the table, and his shoulders heaved as he cried. Giraud curled on his chair with his knees up against his chest, his face hidden in his hands. I could see him shaking. Tears streamed down the ondan's face, and he tried to catch his breath, and that, I thought, was astonishing.

I waited for my audience to get itself under control.

And I waited.

And I waited some more.

Some of them quit crying alone and started leaning on each other, weeping like the blasted bereaved.

I realized that the situation was out of control—that, as I had done in Maydellan Ha's cave, I'd once again started something fiercer and madder than I was capable of finishing.

"Stop it," I said, and when they didn't listen, I shouted, "STOP IT!" I might as well have tried to stop a flood by my word alone. I stared at the lute. It might not have worked for Troman, and it might not have worked for Remeys, and it might not work for any of the other bards, but it had damn well worked for me. And if it had worked for me once, it would work for me again. What I needed, I thought, was something cheerful. Something to make everyone laugh.

I thought better of that, though. I could just see them standing around laughing as helplessly as they were weeping right then. Trading the flood for the drought, I thought, and decided that I would have to play one of the reels. A cheerful one. No words, just music. No story to manipulate the emotions, and nothing that would linger after I finished playing. I considered only an instant, then jumped into "The Wellsbro Beggar's Reel." I tapped a foot to keep my beat and focused on keeping the melody right to the front of the music. I didn't let myself slip into the endless variations—just skipped up and down the neck with a syncopated four-beat tune that, sure enough, started drying up the tears. I saw other feet beside my own begin to tap, and then people who were sitting stood, ready to dance. I watched them, waiting for the last of the weepers to dry up. The second the last of the sobs died away, I stopped the song in mid-phrase. The few bards who'd been dancing broke off as if they'd been puppets who'd had their strings cut. Faces cleared, and eyes turned in my direction.

Remeys stared at me, no longer glaring; still, I couldn't guess at the meaning of the look I saw in his eyes.

Bard Troman glanced from me to the window to the ondan to Remeys, then settled on watching me. His eyes were red, his furrowed cheeks were tear-stained, and his mouth took on a thin-lipped line that I didn't like at all.

With all eyes on me, I felt like fidgeting, or turning to look away, or staring down at the lute, but I didn't. I met the master's eyes.

At last he nodded, and while I saw nothing of satisfaction in the gesture, I could make out nothing of anger, either. He said, "They were remiss. You should have been trained long ago."

I wanted to ask him who had been remiss; I assumed he meant my foster-mother and my guild-master, but I couldn't be sure. I waited.

"Edder should have spotted you, or Dans dar Pell should have."

I must have looked as surprised as I felt, for he nodded. "Dar Pell was one of ours. In towns where bards disappear and are never heard from again, we make sure we have sources of information other than the ones the villagers will know about."

But dar Pell, I thought. He'd been a bogger, out in the day cutting peat bricks, then through the town after his day's work was done checking to see who needed more peat for their fires and who, not so incidentally, I realized, had a good bit of gossip or a bit of news to share with him. He'd been well liked, but a less musical man I'd never met.

And he certainly must have thought the same of me. I only saw him when he came by Birdie's, and when I was home with Birdie, any song that might

have been in my heart during the day had gone to
its hiding place for the night.

So even though he had to have known that I was
a bard's daughter, he must have believed that I was
one who'd inherited no talent for music, and he must
have believed, like everyone else, that I'd been well
treated to find a place to live and someone willing
to stand behind me for a guild education.

The old master straightened the front of his tunic—
a gesture at odds with his ferocious demeanor—and
said, "You have your father's way with a song, and
can think on your feet as well. That reel was a clever
touch. Broke the spell you cast with the first song
and didn't bind us all up in a second spell. Good
thinking on your part."

I swallowed. "Thank you."

"You don't need to thank me. You earned your
welcome to Watchowl Keep several times over. You
. . . and your friends." He seemed unhappy about
that; nor could I blame him. Neither Giraud nor Ha
had done anything to deserve censure, but the ondan,
in trying to champion me, had been rude. Had I been
Bard Troman, I would not have been happy about
extending him welcome, either.

The more I thought about it, the more I wondered
why the ondan had been so rude. Perhaps he and
the master had known each other before. Perhaps
they shared an unpleasant history. Or perhaps they
knew each other by reputation, and didn't like what
they knew. I considered that possibility and thought
it likely. It said nothing negative about either of them;
even I could see that the disciplines and practices of
the bards were very different from those of the Ko.
Ondan Shanxi told me the Ko renounced the world,
all material possessions, all worldly and physical rela-
tionships, and all the affairs of men, secluded themselves in far-off places, and devoted their lives to the
gathering of knowledge without ever intending to use

it for practical purposes. The bards, on the other hand, intended to affect the world around them, and trained for most of their lives to learn to control the magic that would let them influence the actions of others. They renounced nothing; did not deprive themselves of good food and good drink, or of monetary gain, of wealth and titles and family, or of the amusements offered by the opposite sex, or, if they preferred, their own. They went out into the world and tried to change the part of it that they lived in for the better.

Those two philosophies seemed to me to have very little room for common ground, and I thought the two masters of their own philosophies might have little liking for each other's ways. So when the master of the bards dismissed me, telling me that Cynta would be by later to tell me what would be expected of me, I regretted leaving. Everyone else had settled in around the table with the air of people who expect to be up all day, and perhaps all night as well.

When Cynta tapped on my door, I was grateful beyond all words. Twilight had already descended, and night was not far behind. I'd wearied of the four walls of my room, wearied of leaning out the window and staring down at the river, wearied of plucking half-heartedly at the old lute someone had seen fit to leave in my room for me to practice on. I'd talked once into the tube in the wall, discussing with the cook my requirements for a late afternoon meal. I'd paced. I'd fretted. I was ready for news.

Cynta, thank Neithas, came ready to supply it.

"I can't believe they hate each other so much," she said, settling into one of the two chairs by the window.

"The master and the ondan?"

"You saw it too, then?"

I nodded.

"They never raised their voices with each other.

In fact, they were terribly polite." Cynta opened the basket she'd brought in with her and began setting out food: cheeses and three different varieties of hard salami and a bit of smoked pork, a bowl of berries, some honey, a bowl of lovely golden-brown crackers, a little pot of cream whipped into a froth and sugared, some milk, a bottle of wine.

As my eyes got wider and wider at the feast she spread before us, she began to laugh.

"I told Cook I would starve—that I hadn't had any breakfast and that you hadn't either."

"But Cook knows we had," I said. "He gave *me* supper, too. Rice and broth and black bread."

"I waited until the day cook left and the night cook took over the kitchen before I went in," she said, and grinned at me. "Night cook must think none of us eat during the day—he provides food for the bards who stand night watch and for the late-arriving travelers and all, and for those of us who tell him we'll simply starve if we don't get a bit of something."

She started slicing salami. I did the same; after all, rice and broth and black bread is filling for the stomach, but leaves the soul wanting more.

I said, "But you were telling me about the ondan and Bard Troman."

Around a mouthful of salami, she said, "Terribly polite. The way you would expect of two tomcats in an alley, when both are pretty sure the other is big enough or mean enough to take him. If you know what I mean." She sawed of a huge hunk of cheese and popped that into her mouth.

"Surely. I wondered what was going on between them when they were glaring at each other earlier."

"It might become a problem, but it isn't yet. After all, the ondan has turned you over to the master for teaching."

I almost missed what she'd said—almost, but not quite. I quit spooning cream onto the berries I'd taken for myself, and put down the spoon. I ran what she'd said through my mind again, and said, "He *what*?"

She nodded, not seeming to notice my change of mood. "He said he brought you here so the master could teach you."

I frowned then. "But that isn't true. Giraud and Maydellan Ha and I were already on our way here when he joined up with us." I stared out the window, but I wasn't seeing anything out there. I was too busy thinking. "He has no right to assume responsibility for me. Nor any right to tell someone else he's turning me over to him for training. I'm on my own; I have no family or foster-family or guildmaster anymore, and I alone am responsible for decisions made regarding who I study with and what I'll do."

"But . . ." Cynta looked at me. "You didn't ask him to bring you here? You didn't make some agreement wherein he took responsibility for you?"

"No. He helped us along the way—" I paused, wanting to be sure I said what I was thinking and didn't say it wrong. "—and I'm grateful for his help. I might have died after the fall from the horse, had he not used his skill as a healer. But while I'm beholden to him on a personal level, he owes all of us, too. We fought together, and I don't think any of us would have arrived here had we been traveling alone." I whacked a piece of white cheese off of the block and stabbed it with my knife. "I didn't swear loyalty to him, or tell him I wanted him to provide for me."

"Maybe he just thought—"

I cut her off. "I don't care what he thought. I'll be happy to study with Bard Troman, but I'll do it because he and I agree about it. Not because the ondan has given permission."

"But the permission has already been given."

"It means nothing. He had no right to give it."

Cynta looked at the feast spread in front of us, her

expression mournful. "Oh, gods. Then we're going to have to talk to the master. And probably tonight. You'll have to tell him what you told me."

"Fine."

"Do you suppose you and I could finish eating this, first? I don't often get such delicacies from Cook, and if the master comes up here and sees them, he'll take them away."

I nodded and we began eating faster. I wasn't hungry—my anger saw to that as much as my earlier meal. But like Cynta, I had rarely in my life had such good food. I didn't see any reason to let it go to waste.

Bard Troman was not amused. He glowered at me, and I had the feeling he thought I was trying to trick him in some way, or at the very least to waste his time.

"If you only intend to agree with what he agreed to, then we need not discuss this," he said.

"And how am I to know if I care to make the same agreements, or something different? He didn't discuss this with me, and I don't know what he agreed to." I crossed my arms over my chest and tried not to be intimidated by his workroom, which held more instruments of more types than I had ever seen, and books in shelves from floor to ceiling all around the walls, and sheets of music spread like snowdrifts in all the room's corners, and in the center of what appeared to me to be controlled havoc, his desk. The room would have been intimidating on its own. Containing the master, though, and putting him behind that desk, which deserved to be declared a county, or at least a borough, the room seemed to me to be the place where my life would at any moment end.

I was, in a word, terrified. But I was determined, too. I wouldn't allow anyone to have more say-so in my life than I had. Not ever again.

And finally Bard Troman saw my point, and I told him the details of how Ondan Shanxi had joined us, and after I finished, he told me the details of my apprenticeship with the bards as it had been set out by him and the ondan.

I was to have been a beginning apprentice, owing my seven years service once again. I was to have had obligations of duty and work to the Watchowl Keep for five years after that. During the time that I was apprenticed, I was to have had apprentice pay, and never mind the fact that apprentice pay is intended for children, not adults. I was to have only the same rights as any other apprentice—children's rights.

I looked at the master and said, "This goes. Every bit of it."

"This is the standard contract of apprenticeship."

"I know it is. But I'm not the standard apprentice, and I won't be treated as if I am."

"You need us. You have no guild. And if you want to take training with us—"

I cut him off. "Just stop it. This isn't about what I need. This is about what you need. If you want me to risk my life to go back to Hearthold Mountain to sing the undoing of the 'Song of Belangia,' you'll face the fact that I'm not twelve years old. I won't sign away the next seven years of my life to be a virtually unpaid groveling worm. We work out an accelerated apprenticeship with merit testing for the work I do, full junior bard's pay beginning with the successful undoing of the Song of Belangia, and no obligations of duty and work when I attain full bardship."

"That's ridiculous."

"You think so, do you? Do you think it's fair that I already earned journeyman status as a weaver, but had that stolen away by my foster-mother and my guildmaster because they wanted to sell me as a slave? Do you think it's fair that I never received any pay as an apprentice, because my foster-mother and my guildmaster were in collusion, and my money went to line their pockets? Do you think it's fair that I spent all those years in the care of my father's killers because you and the rest of his colleagues didn't bother to come looking for me when he disappeared? As if I didn't matter?" I glared at him. I was so angry I shook, and I felt that I would either cry or scream in the next instant. Instead of doing either, I forced my voice to go very soft, and I said, "I've already paid my dues and more, bardmaster. I won't pay them again. You *need* me. I am the only person in the world who can undo all the trouble, and I won't do it under terms of indenture or slavery. I'll do it only as your free equal right from the start." I leaned forward and put both palms flat on the edge of his desk, and said, "When you can meet me on my terms, we'll talk."

He blinked at me. "I see."

"I hope you do."

"I think you could at least consider reduced pay while you're learning, and at least several years of obligation to the keep following your . . ." He interpreted the look I gave him correctly, for his next words were, "I suppose I do see. Those demands weren't your opening negotiations, were they? Those were your terms?"

"Those were my terms."

"And if we refuse to meet you on your terms?"

I smiled at him. Not a friendly smile, I'm afraid. A rather nasty smile, the sort you might give to the neighborhood bully who has beaten you up for years, when you meet him alone and you are finally are carrying your staff and he has his arms full and has just bent over to pick up a package he dropped. "Then I will pack my belongings and leave, and you can find someone else who is capable of setting the world aright."

He nodded. "Yes. You are both your father's and

your mother's daughter, and combine the worst, apparently, of both of them." He sighed. "Then your terms you shall have." He pulled pen and ink and parchment out of a drawer in the desk, and began to write.

Chapter Fifteen

When we'd signed the papers, and after I watched the master bard burn the other ones, I swore him to secrecy, as I had with Cynta. "Don't tell the ondan we changed the apprenticeship agreement. Let him think the version he signed still stands."

The old man sighed heavily. "If you've always been this much trouble, I can see where your foster-mother wanted to sell you."

He didn't say it unkindly, however, and I realized that he had been joking, even if the joke wasn't as funny to me as it was to him. I laughed politely and said, "I have a reason."

"Then let me hear it."

"I want to know why the ondan signed me into apprenticeship. I want to know what he was thinking, and why he thought he could do that without me protesting—and if he knows we've changed the agreement, he might feel that he has to hide something."

"You don't trust him."

"Bardmaster," I said quietly, "I don't trust you. I don't trust anyone but Giraud, and Giraud I trust provisionally. As long as he continues to act the way I expect him to act—"

"—like a young idiot—"

"—I'll listen to him without questioning every word of advice he offers. No one else gets that courtesy. No one."

"As humans, we have to learn to trust each other," he protested.

"As someone who got burned more than once, I say you earn trust, and until you earn it, you don't get it."

I could see from the look on his face that he was regretting ever letting me into the keep, whether I was the answer to everyone's prayers or not. I didn't care, though. I didn't see any reason to lie to the man about what I thought of him and the rest of the world. Maybe it was tactless, but I'd surely earned the right to my opinions.

"Then you have no more reason to distrust the ondan than you have to distrust me."

I watched him, trying to decide if he was ready for any more honesty. I guessed he might not be, but I decided to risk telling him what I thought anyway. "Maybe I do. My gut says he's a good man, but his actions in apprenticing me to you don't make sense to me. I don't dare trust what I don't understand." I settled myself in to the chair opposite his desk and closed my eyes. "I imagine there's a simple explanation," I said, as much to comfort myself as to reassure the master.

He said, "I'm sure there is, Isbetta. But until we find it, I'll keep our arrangement a secret between the two of us."

We knew we were racing against an implacable enemy: time itself. Those forces that both Ondan Shanxi and Bard Troman insisted on naming Evil, with an emphasis in their voices that made it more personal than just the opposite of good, gathered and grew stronger with every day that escaped us. I heard whispered rumors that anarchy had spread as far as the capital, that some of the bards who went out to spy didn't come back—and not because they were killed, but because the evil or the madness overtook them.

The havoc didn't seem to be dying down. Outside the walls of the keep, it still ruled. And inside the keep, the bards who maintained the warding spells to protect us grew weary and frayed, and their tempers got shorter and more combustible.

Cynta came off of spellcasting duty to teach me finger exercises, voice, focus, and visualization, spell-shaping and spell theory, improvisation . . . I had to master an unending stream of knowledge in a finite time. She and I kept out of everyone else's way. The spell-casters didn't want to see me, because I was the reason they had to spellcast. The historians and theorists didn't want to see me either; the book I'd brought back was one of the Three Lost Keys, all of which had been missing for so long they'd begun to believe they didn't exist. But if the book I'd come back with, the Red Key, was lost, then the other two Key books might still be sitting around somewhere, too, waiting to cause trouble.

She and I sat together all day every day for a full week, and I learned more about music in those seven days than I'd learned in the whole of my previous life. After that week, she passed me on to several of the bards who specialized in various forms of fighting. In three days, they took me through a rudimentary course in the blocking of mental suggestions and forces of attackers and practice in spellcasting while under duress.

I hated every minute of those three days, because my training consisted of playing set pieces on the practice lute I'd been given while the bards pelted me with beans and small stones, and then fruit, and then larger stones, and finally spells. My task was to play and sing through my allotted pieces without losing my place, while still building and maintaining a protective barrier that would keep out their projectiles.

Three days, and during those three days, I played my fingers raw and sang my throat to hoarseness, and suffered agony in my back and my knees. And sometimes my head and shoulders, too, when the projectiles got through. Meanwhile, I had to keep my voice steady and play correctly. On the fourth day, they changed the focus, so that I also had to concentrate on song dynamics—on putting emotion and belief into the songs I sang.

The bards kept me away from magical songs. We discovered early on that anything with the potential to alter behavior when sung resulted in the bards having to shield themselves against my spells. I didn't mean to cast spells, but according to Bard Armayra, I had years of magical potential built up inside of me that had been waiting for an outlet. When I began to train, she said I became like a dam that was forever threatening to burst. According to her, she and the rest of the bards were going to have to find a way of lowering my magical level—but not, she added, until after I'd sung the reversal of the "Song of Belangia."

While I struggled with my crash course in bardic magic, and the spell-casters labored to keep the madness outside from slipping inside, the scholarly bards, plus Giraud and Maydellan Ha, closeted themselves with every book they could find. According to Giraud, they worked their way from the history of magic to the theory and on to practical applications, one book at a time, dissecting the spell I'd cast and trying to understand why something that was outwardly so simple had exploded with such complex results.

Giraud said they had plenty of theories—and all

of them were ugly. He said the one he thought was most likely to be true was that long before he and I arrived on the mountain, a wizard had done some sort of spell on the Pillar of the Sun, and that his spell had waited for another spell to activate it. That spell would have had disastrous results no matter what the next spell to be cast from the pillar had been. My spell had simply been the worst of all possible spells to follow.

I considered that. Considered the fact that much of the evil that had happened might have been set in motion long before I arrived at the mountain. Perhaps even long before I was born. I might not have been the single cause of the destruction of everything I loved.

I wasn't ready yet to absolve myself of all guilt, but I did begin sleeping better.

Or maybe that was just due to exhaustion.

Ten days of living, eating, sleeping, breathing bardic magic. Ten days, and I thought I was casting spells in my sleep. I still had not done anything with the black lute, nor had I cast any spells except for warding spells while I sang songs, but I was gaining control of my voice and my breathing, learning to use my belly and not my throat, and feeling pleased with myself because I was making progress. I could visualize solid three-dimensional images and rotate them to any angle in my mind's eye. My fingers ached, but they moved faster and hit the strings I wanted them to hit. And neither stones nor spells got through my barrier.

I woke in darkness from dreams of self-satisfaction and success, and instantly realized something was wrong. My pleasant little room seemed too close and somehow watchful; the darkness, which I had never minded, felt like a stifling blanket. The little shields I kept around my bed to wake me in case of danger

yielded to the stronger, more aggressive shields Cynta
had taught me to weave. I spun them almost without
thinking. The endless drills came my assistance and
they locked in place around me, close and tight and
hard. I had my eyes open, but only barely—I tried to
keep my breathing regular and deep, as if I were
asleep, but I knew the pattern had broken when I
woke. Breathing always changes from sleep to waking,
and if someone is listening for the change, no amount
of artful acting afterwards can undo the damage that
first uncontrolled instant of wakefulness has caused.

I tried to hear breathing, for more than anything
I felt certain someone stood in my room, studying
me. Someone. Something. Some *thing*. Intelligent,
wary, malicious. Intent on hurting me.

I rested my hand on the dagger that stayed always
beneath my pillow when I slept, and tried to get a
fix on the direction of the person or thing that
observed me. I couldn't. The sense of danger, the
miasma of barely controlled rage and hatred, came
from everywhere in the room at once, filling it like
cloying smoke.

This invader knew I was awake. I felt his amuse-
ment along with his hatred, and I got scared. I
grabbed the dagger and dove from the bed to the
floor, hoping that my sudden action would prod
something from the intruder that would give away his
location. All I wanted was a target, a place to throw
my weapon.

I didn't get it.

Instead, the door to my room flew open and Cynta,
burst in, breathing hard.

"What?" she shouted.

The feeling in the room didn't fade like the scent
of smoke, or flow away like water down a gutter.
It shattered like a pot full of water being thrown
to a stone floor, throwing shards of insane fury
everywhere.

I wasn't the only one who felt it. Cynta crouched and pulled her hands over her head and her shields flew up so quickly they glowed. She cried out—the sort of softly muffled cry someone makes when she's been punched in the gut but doesn't want anyone around to know. Something got through before the shield went up, I realized.

The effects of the silent explosion lingered, then died away, and I finally felt secure enough to say, "Cynta, why did you yell 'what?' when you ran in here?"

"I heard you scream," she said.

"You couldn't hear anything from my room. Your room is down a floor from mine."

"I know that . . . but I heard you scream," she insisted.

"I didn't scream."

She'd unfolded; she began walking around the perimeter of my room very slowly, moving through the darkness with precision and an air of direction. "We'll talk about this later."

The character of her movements and the tension in her voice forestalled any further protests from me. I waited, watching her, hoping the first bell of morning would soon ring so that I would have an excuse for getting up. I didn't want to go back to bed or face the idea of trying to sleep again.

She moved near the bed. Then away from it. Then back again. "Something scarred your shields," she told me.

"It might have. I felt something in here—I think that feeling was what woke me up, or maybe a light disturbance of my sleep shields—but I couldn't see anything."

She turned away from the bed and walked to the table by the window. "Nothing should have been able to get in from outside." She leaned one palm on the center of my little table to balance herself, and with the index finger of her other hand traced a line along the sill of my window. I heard the soft intake of her breath. "And nothing did. The spells we put around the keep are still intact."

"So that means—" I started to say, but she cut me off.

"It's early, but you and I might as well get going. I'm to work with you today. We'll be doing some final work in shielding and some preliminary work in spellcasting. The scholars have almost constructed the song you're to sing to reverse the 'Song of Belangia.'" She gave me a hard look, one that said, *Don't argue; don't ask questions; just come on.*

I said, "I don't think I could have gotten back to sleep anyway. After . . ." I chose my next words carefully " . . . nightmares, I've never been able to sleep well."

She smiled at me and nodded. I'd gotten her hint.

"Just let me get dressed and get my lute and I'll be on my way. To the . . . practice room?"

"I'll wait," she said. "We can stop by the kitchen and pick up something from Cook before we go to work."

I pulled my apprentice garb on, shoved my feet into my boots, and grabbed up my lute. Cynta pointed to the dagger lying on my bed and I slipped it into my belt. That interchange passed without either of us speaking a word. I knew she thought someone could hear us—there was no other reason for her to act the way she was. But I couldn't imagine who might want to listen in to our conversation—neither of us knew anything that would qualify as important gossip or vital secrets. Neither of us would be able to give away essential information to a spying enemy, because we weren't the ones who had such information.

But she evidently thought something we had said or might say was of interest to the unseen listener. I tried to imagine what.

I was ready to leave. She said, "Breakfast, then," and led me out into the hallway. She stopped to lock the door and took the time to spell-ward it carefully. I tried to watch what she did, and listened to the eerie little tune she hummed under her breath while she touched the keypad. At some point I was going to have to learn how to do the spell-warding myself. Not yet, though. Not until the business that occupied all of us was done.

She led me through the curving hallway and down the stairs. At first I thought we were going to the kitchen, as she'd said. Then I realized she'd taken another path through the building altogether and that we were going someplace I'd never seen.

She hummed as she walked—not absent-minded humming, but a bit of spellcasting the purpose of which I couldn't begin to guess. I could almost see the shape of the spell she surrounded us with, but I couldn't unravel the threads to decide what it did. I felt like I was looking at the work of a much more advanced weaver, trying to figure out how she'd created the complex patterns I was admiring, and finding that I didn't even have the knowledge to ask intelligent questions. I hated feeling ignorant, and I hated feeling helpless, and I especially hated feeling inept.

I supposed I would get used to it, however.

She stopped in the hall, still humming, and rested her hands against the stone wall in front of us. It slid back, and she stepped through. I followed, though warily.

When the stone slid into place behind us, she turned.

"We should be able to talk safely here," she said.

We'd stepped into a bubble in the center of what appeared to be solid rock. Light suffused the room, but not from any discernible source. Neither windows nor the visible lines of doors marred the smooth curves of the stone that arched over our heads and rolled away from us at the sides to curve at last beneath our feet. I tried to imagine carving a form of such perfection, and couldn't. I tried to understand the mechanism of the door that ceased to exist when we stepped through its barriers. My mind could not comprehend that, either. Finally I satisfied myself with the miracles present, and let my curiosity about them go. Other, more immediate mysteries awaited my attention.

"Fine," I said. "So what happened in my room, and what did you find at the window that made you so scared?"

Cynta's face was pinched with an anxiety so acute it looked like pain. She sat cautiously on the floor, settling herself down like an old woman disguised in young woman's flesh, like she expected her bones to break if she moved to fast or too hard. "The spell came from someone inside the keep."

I nodded and waited.

"I don't know who." She shook her head. "I *should* know. There are ways to tell who has cast a spell," she said. "It isn't easy, and not everyone can do it. Even the best of bards sometimes can't do it. But magic is nothing but the energy of the person who uses it, wrapped in a package of music or words that holds within it the caster's intent." Deep, slow breath. "If you know people—if you let yourself get to know them, and if you care about them . . . I mean deeply care . . . you can begin to recognize their spells from the feel of the magic."

I waited. Cynta wasn't always direct to her point, but from what I'd seen, she arrived there sooner or later, and I'd discovered that if I would just be patient, I would learn more than just the single fact I had expected to comprise the answer to my question.

"I . . . that's one of the things I'm good at," she continued. She was sitting cross-legged, arms and hands still clenched and tight, back straight and stiff as an old pine. "And its something I always do. That's . . . how I knew something was wrong with you. I didn't precisely hear a scream . . . but . . ." slow shaking of her head, biting of the lower lip " . . . your shields aren't like anyone else's, and something made your shield scream . . . and I felt it."

"So you didn't have to hear me with your ears?"

"Right."

"But what does that—"

Her hand came up. "I couldn't feel the magic in your room until I stepped in and disrupted it. When the spell that was in there shattered, that was the first I realized you weren't alone in the room. But when it shattered and parts of the rebounding energy hit me, something familiar hit me, too, and I didn't know why."

She looked up at me.

"You figured out what had happened when you touched the window."

"I confirmed something that I didn't want to believe.

"I told you that purpose is wrapped up in the spell, and that I can make out purpose as well as—some-times—the identity of the caster?"

"Yes."

"Whoever watched you—and the one who watched you was careful to disguise the making of his spell, so I don't know who it was—watched to figure out how you are connected to the black lute. And more importantly, to determine how to break the bond between you and her. There were a number of furious bards when she chose you. One of them means you harm, I think."

My head spun. "What are you talking about? Who chose me?"

"The lute."

Now I was lost. I'd thought Cynta would tell me

who had been spying on me. I expected to hear from her some tale of discovered treachery at the hand of one she'd considered her friend. None of *this* made any sense to me at all. The lute was a *she*? It was supposed to bond? It had chosen me, and not someone else, and this left people angry? I sat down opposite her and said, "We'll never get anywhere if I just ask you questions. I don't know what questions to ask. So tell me."

"No one would have told you anything about that lute before because it was such a . . . grim story . . . and you're still an outsider . . ." She sighed. "Well, I know most of the tale. I don't know if anyone knows all of it."

Chapter Sixteen

Cynta sat up straighter and shifted around, trying to find a comfortable position. "I wasn't here for all of it, but at least I've heard the tale. Go back about ten years. There was a bard here named Lannee. Perhaps you heard her mentioned when the master was discussing the making of the lute."

I nodded. "I wondered at the time if she might be my mother."

Cynta winced. "I hope not. Probably not. It is a common enough name in these parts—we have two bards here now who share the name. In any case, *this* Bard Lannee taught time-sight songs, and did a great deal of research and writing, and apparently quite a bit more than that. If you listen to the rumors, she had affairs with most of the male bards here and a not inconsiderable number of the female ones."

I interrupted. An instant into her story, Cynta had already lost me. "What are bardic time-sight songs?"

"Songspells that open windows into the future. I thought you'd know that."

"I've spent my last seven years learning to weave."

"Right. Sorry. But as I was saying, apparently

Lannee spent as much of her time on sex as she did on magic. That's important. She was brilliant, and beautiful, and enormously respected for her theoretical work in time-sight, and for her applied spellcraft, too. She was *not* respected for the manner in which she managed her personal life. Her endless stream of indiscreet romances kept relations between other bards in an uproar, and led to a couple of rifts between colleagues that still exist today." Cynta sighed.

"And it didn't end well. About a week before everything fell apart, she had some sort of argument—several people heard the shouting from outside her room; and everyone knew that one of her affairs had gotten ugly, though even today no one knows who she fought with or what they fought about. After that fight, though, she started working all the time; she said she'd seen something in time-sight that scared her, and she needed to pin it down. She broke off her romances with everyone and disappeared into her quarters, only showing up from time to time for meals. She quit giving her classes, she quit presenting research, and she didn't talk to anyone about what she saw coming."

Cynta brushed her curls away from her face and shook her head. "At last, when she didn't come down to meals for two or three days in a row, someone checked with the cook and discovered nothing had been sent up to her for that same length of time. So several of the masters went to her room, just to check on her. They hated to disturb her; apparently her work habits were such that slight noises and disruptions could throw her off for hours. But they got up their nerve and knocked on her door. And when no one answered, they knocked harder.

"At last, they battered their way through the door. What they found was very strange. She was dead, but by the time they reached the point where they were willing to break down her door, they were almost certain they would find her dead. Nothing about her death was normal, though. Her body hung from the ceiling, her ankles tied to a beam. A big block of black wood beneath lay her; no one knew the type of wood it was, or where the block had come from. Her body was bloodless, but no blood was found anywhere in the room; her wrists had been slit—the knife still lay on the block of wood beneath her.

"At first, everyone was certain that she had been murdered; further, they thought whoever had fought with her that night before she changed so much had murdered her.

"But her room seemed to have been locked by her own hand from the inside; there were no signs that anyone else had breached the wards that lay around it. And the knife that had slit her wrists was her own."

"How awful."

Cynta said, "It gets worse. Everyone began to suspect everyone else. Lannee had never been prone to depression, to strange moods, to self-destructive behavior. Her only real character flaw was promiscuity. The rifts between the various bards who had loved her—and they were many—grew deeper and uglier. Actual fights broke out, and several prominent bards left the keep and never returned.

"Only after more than a month, after Lannee's body had been buried and her room cleaned out and all her belongings moved to storage so that another master could take her rooms, did one of the archivists—well, you know him. Remeys. The one who said he knew both of your parents. Anyway, he finally got around to cataloguing the contents of her commonplace book. We all keep them, you know," she added in a thoughtful aside. "We keep notes on what we're working on, on whether what we do fails or succeeds, on personal problems, and whatever else happens. That way, if anything happens to one of us, our colleagues will be able to reconstruct our research and our work won't be lost."

I nodded. I'd been far too close to a bard's commonplace book. "And Remeys found something in her commonplace book?" I guessed.

Cynta's expression went bleak. "Her suicide note."

"Suicide?"

"She had witnessed a time-sight event that suggested a deadly eruption of magic was building, and she had been doing research to figure out how that eruption could be stemmed or averted. Her notes said the bard was already born who would stem the evil, but that the weapon this bard would need was not yet in existence. The weapon was to be a soul-lute. You have heard of such instruments?"

"No."

"Bards have always considered them evil. Not only lutes can have souls—any instrument can. They are instruments made by sacrificing a human being, and binding the soul to the instrument or the materials that will be used to make the instrument before it can escape to return to the Summerlands."

Suddenly I knew where this horrible story was going. "The block of wood . . ." I said.

Cynta nodded. "She poured her blood and her soul into that wood—sacrificing herself voluntarily to create the materials to make this incredible instrument."

I'd held that lute. Played it. "The black lute."

"Her notes said that once the wood was readied, it should be given to Bard Edder to be turned into a lute. She said the instrument would then find its way to the bard who would play it."

"And everyone assumed that bard would be someone from the keep."

"Right." Cynta gave me an approving look, evidently pleased I could figure out some of the simpler points on my own. "Her sacrifice of her own soul, offered freely by her own hand, she said, would create a lute that would not turn to evil; she could not ask for anyone else to fulfill the conditions that would save the world from the fate she foresaw."

"And things didn't turn out the way anyone guessed they would."

"No. We all thought Bard Troman would be the one to play it. He had loved her longer than any of the others, I think. Or perhaps Remeys. He was one of her lovers, and ardent; he almost died of grief after her death. There were others we thought she might have chosen. But no one else had her way with time-sight, or does even to this day. And she didn't write down what she saw coming . . . she just left that poem in her commonplace book, and that was more of a puzzle than a help. Perhaps she thought writing down her visions would seal them into fact. Maybe she thought the future she saw might be averted. But I don't think so . . . otherwise, why would she have killed herself? Izza, everyone wondered for years what she saw coming that was so terrible she killed herself to fend it off. And if the madness that devours the world now is what she saw, then every guess any of us made was wrong."

I thought about that lute, black as moonless night, more beautiful than any instrument I had ever seen . . . and haunted by the soul of a suicide. A suicide that shared both my mother's name and profession. I shuddered, wondering if I would ever be able to pick the instrument up again. "What can this lute do that another lute can't?"

"I don't know," Cynta said. "I don't think anyone knows. The creation of soul-instruments is forbidden, and such instruments as are found are destroyed in such a way that the souls bound to them are freed to move on. Not the black lute, of course, because Lannee gave her life to recreate herself as the weapon that would fight off the future she saw. But all we have are rumors of what such instruments can do.

There was a flute once that made listeners dance until they died of exhaustion. A war drum that was so terrible that when it beat, enemies of the drum's army died of terror . . . but the drum supposedly terrorized the soldiers in its own army, too, so that only a few could be induced to fight, and they had to have wax stoppered into their ears before they would march before the drum. A guitar . . ." She shrugged. "Different stories, different magics, but all of them frightening . . . and the fact is, none of those stories can give you any idea what to expect from Lannee's lute."

I thought about that for a moment. "I'll tell you now—if I had known the lute was haunted by a soul, I never would have touched it, not even to bring it here. That kind of magic terrifies me. But what does the lute have to do with the bard who watched me in my room?"

Cynta cleared her throat. "This is ugly—and I'm not sure that I know for certain. I can only tell you what I felt from that spell. But this is what I think. The lute chose you. She picked you out above all the bards who were presented to her. And she won't choose anyone else as long as you're alive."

I stared at her. "But if I'm dead . . ."

Cynta nodded slowly. "If you're dead, the lute will certainly choose someone. What she created herself to do she has not yet done. And I'm betting that whoever was watching you thinks he can influence her choice."

"Then I'm in danger even here."

"A bard wants the black lute. And so I think he means to see you dead."

I've had better news.

For the final two days of my emergency training, I worked only with the master. We sat together in the top of a heavily shielded tower, with shields around me and shields around him. And I played the reversal of the "Song of Belangia" that the bards had worked out. I played nothing else. First he sang it for me, so that I could learn it. Then I sang it back to him. Then I added the lute part. He shouted at me when I forgot words or missed my fingerings, screamed imprecations at the gods when I made mistakes, and from time to time, for no apparent reason, threw things at me.

After two days, when I had done the song hundreds of times without error, he finally deemed me ready to go back to the Pillar of the Sun.

We walked down out of the tower, and everyone stared at me. "We're ready," he said to the first bard we met in the halls.

He walked with me to a workroom. A number of bards waited for us, including Caylan and the bard Remeys. Giraud and Maydellan Ha and Caylan and the ondan were already there, as well. I hadn't seen any of them but Caylan since my training started; and not even Caylan those last two days. What I'd been through must have shown on my face, for Giraud held me tightly when I walked over to join him, and looked at me with worried eyes. "No one told me you'd been sick," he said.

"I haven't," I told him. But I was exhausted, and the most pleasant thing I could think of at that moment was curling up in my bed and sleeping one day for every day that I had studied. "I've only been working hard."

Remeys smiled at me, and said, "Once we're through this, you won't find life so onerous. New apprentices have simple duties, if dull ones."

I must have let my surprise show on my face, for the bard raised an eyebrow and said, "Your ondan was telling me that you would join us as an apprentice once this matter at the Pillar of the Sun was concluded. I assumed you . . . knew."

I hoped my expression hadn't told anyone too

much, for I felt the ondan watching me closely. I answered, "Yes. Caylan told me he had arranged this several days ago. I simply didn't think anyone else would know."

He nodded. "Of course."

Though I looked at him, I also watched the ondan out of the corner of one eye. Shanxi looked visibly relieved by my response. So Bard Troman hadn't betrayed our agreement.

The master raised a hand. The rest of us fell silent. "All of you have been chosen, or have chosen on your own, to travel to Hearthold Mountain for the uncasting of the "Song of Belangia." You know you face danger—perhaps death. I'm giving each of you a chance right now to change your minds. To stay behind."

"I'm going," Giraud said.

The rest of the people in the room all concurred. "Then we won't wait any longer. Isbetta is ready, I am ready, the rest of you were told to be ready."

I stared at him. "I thought I'd at least get a night to sleep before we took to the road. We'll have so much fighting to do on the way to the mountain . . ." I shut up. All the bards were staring at me as if I'd lost my mind.

"You didn't think we were going to travel overland, did you?" Caylan asked.

"What other way are we to go?"

"Remeys will open a Gate for us."

I had no idea what she meant by that. Everyone else, though, nodded as if what she said had made perfect sense.

Bard Troman took pity on my ignorance. "You've never seen a Gate, Izza; it was still a lost magic in your father's day. It is a rare one even now. Remeys has spent years studying the ancient manuscripts and daybooks, and a few years ago, he discovered a songspell that opens a door between places. He'll sing the songspell and the air will part for us, and we'll step across to the mountain. It will be the work of an instant, and will be, perhaps, the only safe part of our journey."

Remeys smiled and nodded once.

Another of the bards came into the room, lugging a lute case. "I came as quick as I heard," she said, putting the case on the floor as if it were full of spiders. "I brought it. Please don't ever make me carry it again."

Bard Troman turned to me. "The black lute. You'll have to carry it, I'm afraid. It has taken even more of a disliking to all of us since you began your training. None of us cares to touch it now."

I nodded and walked over, lifted the case, swung the strap onto my shoulder. I felt the stares at my back as I did, and I thought about what Cynta had told me of the lute—that someone wanted it enough to kill me for it. Even through the case, I could feel the soft, welcoming hum the lute gave off. I wondered that I had not been able to feel it before. Had I felt it, and just ignored it because I couldn't explain it?

I turned and looked into the faces of those who waited for me. I hoped to see something evil in one of them; I hoped to be able to catch a shiftiness of eye, cold and callous smile, something that would tell me which one of them meant me harm. But all the faces of all those who would accompany me on the trip to the Pillar of the Sun were guileless. Trouble waited for me, but Maydellan Ha and Giraud would stand by me. And Cynta. If only they knew to look for trouble. Cynta knew.

I told the master, "I'd like to talk with my friends for just a moment before we go." He frowned at me, and I gave him the same hard look I had when I was hammering out my terms of apprenticeship with him. His frown grew darker; I could tell even then that he was growing tired of me. But if I died before I had the chance to sing the reversal of the "Song of Belangia," he'd have worse problems than thinking me impertinent. So I stood my ground, and he shrugged, disgusted, and I pulled Ha and Giraud out into the hall. I made sure no one was looking. Then I hummed a shield into place, as Cynta had taught me, surrounding all three of us. I fixed it with my mind, and when I was sure it would hold, I said, "One of the people going with us wants to kill me and take the lute. I don't know which one, but you are going to have to watch with me."

Giraud looked surprised, but Ha didn't. "There are intrigues going on here that I can only guess at," he said. "Some of them have been in motion for a long time, girl. So we'll watch out for you. But you watch your back, too. Whenever you think an attack won't come, that's when it will hit you."

We didn't say anything else. I hugged both of them in turn; we'd been through a lot together, and we weren't done yet. And I was terrified that we wouldn't all live to see how the story turned out.

Remeys had a beautiful voice. He stood at one corner of the room and sang the spellsong that opened the gate. The words, in an ancient tongue, meant nothing to me, but they obviously meant something to the bard, for as he sang, a curtain of light opened in the air beside him, and everyone who waited for this "gate," which looked nothing like any gate I'd ever seen, began to step through.

I went last, as I'd been instructed, with only Remeys after me. I stepped through, feeling my heart pounding and my gut twisting—and for nothing. One instant I was in the stone chamber of the keep, the next I stood in the basin of what had once been Hearthold Mountain, next to the Pillar of the Sun. The pillar stood as it had stood when we left it, both weeks and lifetimes ago—unchanged. It shimmered in the sunlight, reflecting rainbows into the grass. The bards and my friends stood around the outside of the basin, facing outward, weapons drawn. Remeys came through the gate behind me, and as he did, it shimmered out of existence. He smiled at me and briefly rested a hand on my shoulder.

"You'll do wonderfully," he said. "You're even stronger than your mother was."

I looked at him, debated asking him what I really wanted to know, and decided I might as well. "You said you knew my mother. And Cynta said you were in love with a bard named Lannee. And I was just wondering if the two were the same."

His smile died, replaced by a bleakness so all-encompassing I thought it would swallow me. Remeys nodded, momentarily without words. He just looked at me, pity and sorrow and pain in his eyes, until at last I stared down at my feet. His soft voice made me look at him again. "You didn't know?"

"No."

"Then you didn't realize until just now that your mother was . . . dead?"

It was my turn to discover that no words would come to me. I just shook my head.

"You know about the lute, too, then." This as a statement, not a question.

I nodded.

"I'm sorry. I'm sorry I couldn't give you better news; I'm sorry you found out now."

I felt the lute thrumming at my back, and became aware of a sense of urgency that emanated from it. I pulled away from Remeys. "I have to sing," I said, and wondered even as I said it if I would be able to hold the lute, or sing, knowing what I knew. That my mother, who had left me and my father when I was very young, had killed herself to become the spirit of that lute.

Then I lifted my chin. I would do what I had to do.

I removed the lute from its case and tuned her. She sang beneath my fingers, and I heard inside my head a voice that had never been there before. *Caution, my daughter. We have far yet to go, and the danger for you has only just begun.*

But what I've just said is not entirely true. I heard the lute speaking to me, and that is was she said— but I heard no words. I only felt them. And my gut told me that the lute spoke the truth—that bad things were coming, and that we had begun to run out of time. "I'm ready," I said, though I'd never felt less ready to begin anything in my life.

"Then start," Bard Troman said. "We'll guard you."

The master and I had discussed how I was to sing the unspelling song. I knelt on the grass in front of the Pillar of the Sun, and rested the lute on my thighs. I'd told him how many times I'd sung the first song; he thought I might have to sing this second as many, or even more. So I tried to get comfortable. I became aware that Maydellan Ha and Giraud had moved back from the perimeter of the circle, so that they flanked me. Remeys held up a hand and I waited before starting the song.

He walked back to Ha. "We're going to need you to stand out with us, to fight if we're attacked."

Ha shook his head. "We're the last line of defense."

"But we'll be stronger with you in the circle with us."

Ha looked grim. "Nevertheless, we're standing here to protect Izza. We won't move from her side until the song has been sung.

Remeys sighed. "I understand, I suppose. She's your friend. I just think we could protect her better if we were all together."

With a shrug, Ha said, "You're entitled to your opinion. But we aren't under the orders of the bards, and we'll do as we please."

Once Remeys had rejoined the circle, I looked around again to see if there were going to be any other interruptions. When I could see that there weren't, I took a deep breath, plucked the first notes of the unspelling song, and began to sing.

> "Unbreak, unweave, unspell,
>   Remove, return, repair;
>   To pristine state unwind
>   The spells I've woven here . . ."

I could hear faint voices behind me now. I kept singing, kept my eyes on the Pillar of the Sun, and my breath focused and my shields up. And I hoped that the voices I heard, which echoed up from a distance, didn't spell trouble for my friends. I couldn't focus on them. I couldn't help them. In fact, until the song was sung and the world had returned to the state it was in before the singing of the "Song of Belangin," I couldn't do anything more to help myself than focus some part of my attention on maintaining my shields.

Chapter Seventeen

I sang and played, and as it had before, my voice seemed to resonate with the Pillar of the Sun. It echoed through the basin, filling it. While I sang, I prayed that the scholars—and especially Bard Troman—had done their work well in crafting the spell, for I was completely at their mercy in singing. If they'd made mistakes, I would be the first to bear the brunt of them. I prayed that my friends would be safe, and that my future colleagues would survive, too. I prayed to Neithas, because I did not know the goddess of the bards, and I had no arrangements with her—and because I knew weaving more than singing, I prayed that my words would weave a strong spell, that their fabric would form a pattern that would set the world aright and protect those I loved.

And my mother sang with me. I could feel her—and I could feel her love for me in every note I played. I don't know why she left me and my father, but I sensed then that she did not do it because she didn't care about us; that in fact her caring had set her on a path that would one day protect me. That leaving had been the hardest thing she'd ever done.

The pain of who she had been and how she had conducted herself left me as I sang. I can't say that I understood her. But I knew at last that she'd loved me more than words could express, and that in that moment, while the two of us were together and joined in something that mattered, not just to us but to the world, she was happy once more—she felt that she was fulfilling her life's purpose. And in those moments, I came to love her again, too.

Singing with her, I lost my fear. Joy filled me, and the music took me outside of myself, as it had never done before and has only done a few times since. But if I was lost in the joy of the moment, I was alone. I stared at the pillar and sang and kept my focus on what I was doing, but in the back of my mind, I could hear shouting, and then fighting. I was aware of the moment when Giraud lunged forward from my side, and aware that he did not resume his place there. I knew when Maydellan Ha shouted in anger. I heard the clash of metal, thuds and screams, the sounds of fear and pain and anguish. I could not feel them as I sang—my magic and the magic of the lute erased my normal feelings for that brief time. I felt as if I'd drunk a potion that had set me outside of the world's pain, knowing that when the potion wore off I would feel it twice as fiercely.

Above me, the sky began to darken. Then I felt wind against my skin. Nothing touched me, though I kept expecting that someone would run me through with a sword at any moment; my shields were up and as tight as I could make them, but I still had a hard time believing that a wall I created with my mind and will would be enough to spare my life if a warrior wanted to slaughter me.

Finally, I felt my mother's spirit pull away from mine. I stopped singing, and stood with my shields still hard around me. And I looked at how the world had changed while I sang.

The basin had become a killing field. Dead dwarves lay scattered across what was, once again, rocky ground. The mountains had returned, and the peak of Hearthold Mountain towered over me, wreathed in black clouds. Living dwarves tended the dwarvish wounded, and, I realized after a moment, to the wounded and dying bards as well. I looked for people I knew. Cynta wasn't among the dead . . . but she wasn't among the wounded, or among those healing them, either. And Bard Troman was missing, too. I saw the ondan, though; he worked side by side with the dwarvish healers. And Remeys, with his head bandaged and one hand wrapped in bloody cloth, cleaned up the body of a young woman that I'd never had the chance to get to know. I feared most for Giraud—and could not find him. I began to go from body to body, expecting the worst. Then I realized that the huddle of dwarves nearest the passageway that led down into the mountain surrounded not another dwarf, but my oldest and dearest friend. I let the lute hang on its strap over my shoulder instead of putting it in its case, and ran to his side.

He lay on the rocky ground, pale and ash-gray, while three dwarves tried to stop his bleeding, and one of the bards whom I didn't know struggled with a healing spell that wasn't working well. Someone had hacked off Giraud's left hand just above the wrist. His left ear hung in tatters at the side of his face, though it was still barely attached. He'd lost a lot of blood, and though his eyes were open, he didn't respond to anyone or make any sounds. I would have thought he was dead, but his chest rose up and down in deep, uneven gasps.

The dark sky let loose with a torrent of rain just as Maydellan Ha finished what he was doing and came over to join the bardic healer and his fellow dwarves. "He's in shock," he said to them. "The magic will only do so much, and not fast enough. We need to move him into the caves and get him warm, and get some fluids into him. Then get his feet higher than his head and cover him with someone's cloak. Have you stopped the bleeding?"

One of the other dwarves nodded. "We're holding it now, but we need to be able to sew him soon."

"Fine. If you can't sew, then cauterize. I'll check on him in a few minutes. I still have other people I have to look after."

"Maydellan—" I started to say, but he cut me off with the curt wave of a hand.

"Later. I'm busy now."

He went to the next body on the ground, and I stood in the center of the basin feeling useless. Everyone else either lay on the ground in pools of blood or knelt beside them, trying to save their lives. I had no healing songs to sing. I knew none of the unmagical skills that Maydellan Ha so valued. One of my friends lay dying and I could do nothing for him, nor could I do anything for the others who'd bled in the battle that took place while I sang.

A hand settled lightly on my shoulder. "He'll be fine," Remeys said.

I jumped and turned to look up at him. He smiled down at me—tall, handsome, distinguished, even with the bloody strips of rag wrapped around his head.

"What happened?"

"While you were singing, and while the madness was still upon them, the dwarves attacked us. We thought that might happen—we'd discussed the possibility, and believed we were adequately prepared. But we dared not use bardic magic to fight them, for fear our spells would interfere with yours and somehow alter it. We fought them hand to hand, then—the ondan saved more of us than anyone else but you."

"Me?"

"I wish you could have seen. As your spell took hold, the madness washed out of them. One by one they disengaged from the fighting, backed away, and put down their weapons. But more attacked than we had anticipated, and we'd already taken heavy losses when that happened."

"So the spell worked? The madness is over?"

Remeys shrugged. "I would think so, but we won't know for sure until we go down into the villages and see what has become of the people who are there. As soon as our survivors are fit to travel, we need to head to the nearest village."

The nearest village was Blackwarren. I didn't want to go back there. "You should be able to tell from here, shouldn't you? The dwarves here are fine, aren't they?"

"They're too close. The spell might have only a local effect, and we have to know whether it has traveled and undone the evil in the outlying regions. But you don't need to worry. If the spell went out as it should have, we'll be traveling behind a spreading wave of normalcy all the way back to the keep. If we have to modify the spell, you'll have to come back here to sing again."

I closed my eyes and took a deep, steadying breath. My gut was screaming at me—that something was wrong, that I was in terrible danger, that I needed to get to safety. My gut, as usual, had no specific suggestions to offer about what the danger was or where I should go who how I should get there. I opened my eyes again and asked Remeys, "Where are Cynta and Bard Troman? I haven't seen them."

Remeys's expression went bleak. "I think I know, but I am afraid to say it, for fear that it might be true. Perhaps they have some good, logical explanation for their disappearance. If not, though, then we're in danger."

My gut twisted tighter. "The Black Heron," I whispered. "Bard Troman must have been the Black Heron." And I'd been his fool—telling him about my suspicions regarding the ondan, and working with him alone to get the spell just right. He had been the main designer of the spell I'd just sung; the spell that was supposed to have undone all the wrong the first spell had worked. That was to have set the world right. "Oh, Neithas, what have I done?"

"What have we *all* done?" Remeys said. "Isbetta, you can't take the blame for this. We all believed that the one bard we could trust no matter what was Troman."

"Where could he have gone, though?"

"I don't know," Remeys admitted. "Though he stands to gain a great deal if he acts quickly, and if he can elude us."

"How?"

"Imagine that he claims he is the one who unsang the 'Song of Belangia.' Imagine that he says he undid all the evil that was done; if he goes to the new queen and tells her this, how can she refrain from making him Queen's Bard? And if he becomes Queen's Bard, what part of our lives will he not eventually control?"

"But he can't say he unsang the 'Song of Belangia,'" I said. "I'm the one who did that—and I'm alive, and I have the lute."

He nodded. "A point I guarantee you the Black Heron has not overlooked. Your job is to make sure that you stay alive until we get you to the queen."

I swallowed hard and nodded. "Well, then, sing us a doorway to the queen's court, and we'll get there before Bard Troman and tell her the truth about what happened."

Remeys shook his head. "I can't. At least not until we know for sure that the spell did what it was supposed to. Remember, Troman created that spell almost by himself, then trained you to sing it—we think we know what it was supposed to do, but we could be wrong. We have to be sure before we go marching into the queen's chambers and say we fixed everything and . . . well . . ." He looked at me and sighed. "You see what I mean."

I nodded.

"But you're right that we need to travel fast. If he didn't create a song gate right away, but did what we're doing, we'll still have a chance to get to the queen first."

"Let me tell Maydellan Ha what's happening so that he can tell Giraud when he wakes up . . ." Remeys was shaking his head at me. "What? Why not?"

"He's busy, and we need to go now."

He was right, of course. I wiped the rain out of my eyes and said, "Let's go."

Remeys waved to the ondan, who trotted over. "We're going to Blackwarren, and then on to Greffon. We need someone else to go with us, to vouch for us."

The ondan looked back at the dwarves who were dragging the last of the wounded and dead into the tunnels. When he looked back at us, his lips thinned and his brows lowered. "Yes. Someone needs to tell the queen what has happened here today. For us to be betrayed by . . ." He glanced at me. "She knows the truth?"

"She knows about Troman and his little helper Cynta."

"Good."

I felt queasy standing next to the ondan while we waited for Remeys to create a gate for us. I still couldn't understand why he'd apprenticed me to the master bard. After that, I didn't trust him anymore, even though I knew I ought to. He'd probably had some logical reason for what he'd done—perhaps he'd even suspected that Bard Troman was our enemy. Ondan Shanxi, I reminded myself, was the one saving the lives of the wounded while Troman fled for the capital and the queen to try to further his own ambition. Ondan Shanxi stood and fought beside me in some bad spots.

When I had the chance, I would ask him why he'd chosen to speak for me with the master bard instead of letting me speak for myself.

Meanwhile . . .

I clutched the black lute close and set up a light shield around myself—one that I could strengthen in an instant if the danger I sensed became apparent. I don't know why I did, other than that I was heading back to a place I'd left in a hurry, and with reason, and the lute was the only real weapon I had.

We'll go in quickly, I thought. We'll see that everything is fine, or else that it isn't, and either way, when we've seen what we need, we'll leave. I won't have to run into anyone I know . . . if anyone is even left. We'll go on to Greffon, and I'll never have to go near Blackwarren again.

Then the gate opened, and Ondan Shanxi stepped through it into shimmering nonexistence, and I followed, black lute pressed tight to my chest. And Bard Romuya stepped in behind me.

We stepped out almost simultaneously into the Blackwarren I remembered, onto the very street where I'd lived. Thatch-roofed wattle-and-daub houses leaned in toward me; the mud street under my feet sucked at my boots; the bog stink filled the air. No more stone houses, no more glass windows. Blackwarren lay quiet, though—far to quiet for an afternoon. Women should have filled the street, carrying laundry or wicker reeds or chickens; children should have run between the houses; old men should have sat against the walls smoking and telling lies. But I saw no one, and heard no one. I smelled the sweet, sharp odor of peat burning, but only thinly; before, the air had always been thick with it. A few people had survived the nightmare, then. But which few?

I began to hum softly, strengthening my shields. I admit the place scared me too, and that I wished I were elsewhere. "It looks normal," I said. "So let's go."

Remeys was at my right side, and the ondan at my left. "Not yet," Remeys said. "We haven't seen anyone."

I muttered, "It's better if we don't," but Remeys moved closer to me while the ondan walked toward Birdie's house. "Not there," I whispered after him, but he didn't hear me. He knocked on Birdie's door.

"We're with you," Remeys said. "Don't worry so much."

I hummed and focused more intently. Shield up, I'm safe and grounded, nothing can touch me, nothing can hurt me. Over and over—and my shield pushed Remeys's hand away.

"Calm down," he told me. "Drop the shield. We're not going to let anything happen to you."

Birdie poked her head out the door. She had a new scar on one cheek, and she looked thinner, but she'd survived the madness. I shouldn't have been surprised. She would have been one of the hunters, not one of the hunted. Her eyes narrowed as she looked at the ondan, and she said, "What do you want?"

I knew she held a nail-tipped club behind her. I wanted to shout out to the ondan that he was in danger, but I didn't. I felt something . . . a faint voice in my head that said "Be still." I kept humming, and touched the fingers of my left hand to the strings of the lute, and resting my right hand over the rosette. Waiting.

Birdie stared at the ondan, also waiting. I shivered. The aura of evil hung around her like a storm cloud.

"Birdreece dar Kinla," the ondan said.

"Get your damned shields down," Remeys whispered. "You're going to blow this."

And my gut screamed *trouble!* The ondan knew Birdie's name. He hadn't stopped at her house by accident. He probably hadn't met me on the road by accident. I glanced at Remeys, found his face twisted by fury, realized he had his guitar in hand

and was beginning to sing at me. I sang my shields harder.

The ondan, oblivious to me, said to Birdie, "Once a black heron gave you the egg of a white heron, and told you to destroy it."

Birdie's face went white as death.

The ondan glanced back at me, saw what I was doing, didn't look at all perturbed. He turned back to Birdie. "You see the egg before you now, grown to a creature who has nearly ruined what was once a perfect plan."

Birdie shifted behind the door, and the terror in her eyes deepened into something approaching madness.

"You knew what would happen to you if ever you crossed the Black Heron," the ondan said, and beside me Remeys sang at me, and I felt the pressure of his rage even through the shield I sang. I felt the compulsion to silence, to surrender. I fought it.

Birdie shrieked, "You can't blame me I was going to kill her got away from me the others wanted money for her!" all in one breath, and the ondan raised his hand, and murmured something, and Birdie burst out of her house with the club already arcing over her head, and light shot from the ondan's fingertips at the same moment that the spiked head of the club buried itself in the ondan's skull.

He didn't fall, but Birdie did. I was hoping . . . praying . . . that he would topple to the ground, leaving me to deal with just Remeys, but he lifted the club out of his skull, and I watched, sickened, as the crushed place closed itself up. He turned to me and smiled. "The other two are dead already—I stepped through a gate Remeys made for me a few days ago to be sure. And you can stop that odious singing now. I need to talk to you."

I kept playing. The pressure of Remeys's magic against my shields almost buckled my knees, but I pretended that he wasn't pitching anything worse at me than rocks and fruit. I had nothing with which to beat them—no songs I could sing to attack or destroy. The best I could manage was a holding action; I could keep my shields up and keep the two of them away from me (*maybe*, the doubtful voice at the back of my mind whispered) until someone came to help me, but that would at last be futile. Because I could only sing for so long before exhaustion slowed me, and help wasn't coming.

"Exactly," the ondan said. "Help isn't coming. So stop your singing and drop your shields. I own you, girl. Have owned your life since your father tried to ruin my plans years ago."

He could read my thoughts, I realized. He'd been responsible for my father's death, and indirectly for my mother's as well. He was the Black Heron.

The ondan shook his head. "Not precisely. Remeys and I together are the Black Heron. He worked inside the keep, I worked outside. Together we intend to rule Terosalle, and someday all the world. You, however, by surviving, and putting yourself in the way of our work, and by adding your own inflections to the 'Song of Belangia,' spoiled what would have been a perfect little two-part spell to throw everyone in these parts into slavery to us. That little element of hope and idealism you put in softened the part you sang, and your damnable resonance with the Pillar of the Sun sent it out much further than it was ever intended to go. Now that the damage has been undone, we're going to have to recast the damned thing ourselves. And for that, Remeys is going to need your lute."

I kept singing, and my shields kept holding . . . but Remeys was a strong bard with experience I couldn't begin to imagine, and he was determined to break through my defenses. I was equally determined that he wasn't going to get through. They weren't going to touch the lute.

"We will, though," Ondan Shanxi said. "We'll have it, and you will be our hostage so that it will agree to work for us. As long as the lute does what we say, you won't be hurt."

They were lying. Once they had what they wanted, I'd be dead or as good as dead. I couldn't understand why they would want to destroy the world—they'd seen the pain their spell had caused before.

"It's not about destruction," the ondan said, and at the same instant I felt a sharp stab of fire in my side. A weak spot in my shield had allowed some of whatever Remeys aimed at me to get through. "It's about unimaginable riches. We will hold the world at our feet. We will command everything. Everyone. No one will keep anything back from us. We will be gods in Terosalle—we will take whatever we desire." He smiled at me, his eyes narrowing. "And what we most desire right now . . . is the lute. You have no weapons to use against us. We will get what we want. But if you fight us much longer, you won't enjoy what happens to you when we get it."

Remeys changed his song, and the ondan raised his finger, and his smile grew bigger. I couldn't hold off both of them at once.

And then, from nowhere, I recalled a song my mother used to sing to me when I was tiny, before she'd left my father and me to do whatever it was she'd had to do. She'd sung that lullaby to me every night while she sat by my bed. My idea was stupid . . . but I remembered Ha and Giraud and the lovesong, and all the bards in Bard Troman's study when I sang "Raider's Pride."

Stupid idea, but . . .

I kept my shields up, and started to sing.

"Sleep, child, sleep,
    Trust that morn will come,
    Rest your head and close your eyes

And wait for the new dawn,
Still, child, still,
For I am near your side,
Hush and rest your sleepy head
And sleep the whole long night."

I had no weapons. No spells to kill or maim. All
I had was that lullaby, that one gift from my mother.
I sang it, and she sang it with me, and we sang it
again and again, ringing the notes clearly on strings,
echoing them back from lute to voice, from voice to
lute, adding depth and strength born of our passion,
and of my memories, and of love, which is the stron-
gest magic of all. Together, we bound the song to the
ondan, and to Remeys.

"Sleep, child, sleep,
Trust that morn will come . . . "

Their eyes closed. Remeys stopped singing. The
ondan's hand lowered.

"Rest your head and close your eyes
And wait for the new dawn."

They dropped to the ground, softly. Snored. I kept
singing, taking no chances. I spun the song around
them tighter, and then I added a new last verse.

"Sleep, monsters, sleep,
Sleep for a thousand years.
When you wake forget your hate
Give no more cause for tears."

It wasn't good poetry, but it seemed to work as a
spell. They curled on the ground, not moving at all.
When I stopped singing, they didn't budge. When I
tied their hands and feet, they didn't twitch. When

I found a couple of horses and managed, with much difficulty and swearing, to drag them up an incline and onto the horses' backs, and when I tied their hands and feet under the horses' bellies so they wouldn't fall off, they kept snoring. Gentle snores, with no threat in them.

They didn't wake when I walked them back up into the mountains, which were mountains once again. They didn't wake when the dwarves untied them and locked them away in a cell built into Hearthold Mountain to keep them.

They do not wake today.

Chapter Eighteen

I discovered when I got back to Hearthold Mountain that Bard Troman was dead—that he'd been stabbed in the back and shoved over the lip of the basin, and that his body had been discovered at the same time that the dwarves had discovered Cynta's. Her body bore signs of having fought—the dwarves thought she'd seen either the ondan or Remeys kill the master, and had tried to save him.

I wept for the master, and for Cynta, who had been a friend, and who would have been a friend throughout my life, I think, if she had lived.

Giraud healed slowly, but he healed. He met a bard in the keep when we returned to Watchowl, and eventually he married her. He is the keep's historian now, and still a dear friend. He gave up his family name and title, and became Giraud dar Ven, which of course means Giraud the Writer. As such, he is safe from Varelle dar Kothia Surdosti. For all she knows, all the dar Falcannes are dead.

Maydellan Ha is completing his medical studies now with the Ko. He will, I am sure, be a fine doctor. He is ever gruff and surly, but there is a kindness about him that I dearly love. We remain friends, and I hope we always shall.

And what about me? I could have taken several different paths. With the black lute, I was one of the most powerful bards in the country, and I could have easily become Queen's Bard after freeing my people from the "Song of Belangia."

Or I could have, I'm sure, worked my way into the position of Master Bard of Watchowl Keep.

But either of those paths would have been a betrayal of my mother. She had given her life to ward off the evil that she saw coming . . . and though she hadn't always been there for me when I needed her, she was there when I needed her most. I couldn't use the sacrifice she'd made to further my own position. She needed to be released from the lute it had served its purpose, but its purpose was past. I wouldn't let her hang in limbo, soulbound to a box of wood and string, when she needed to return to the Wheel, to rest and some day find a new life for herself. A happier one, I hoped.

So I went out one moonlit night with Maydellan Ha and Giraud, and the three of us built a fire out of aged ash. When the fire leapt high and the coals at its base burned white hot, I hugged what was left of my mother and told her good-bye, and felt her thanks for my releasing her. Then I gently laid the black lute in the fire and watched until it burned to ashes.

I took the third path, the path I had earned on my own. I went back into the keep and continued my training as a bard. I'm a bard now. Not a powerful one, not a famous one. But I've found what I love, and I live it daily. And I'll have a song to sing for the rest of my life.